BENTLEY

Bentley—Vested Interest #1 by Melanie Moreland
Copyright © 2018 Moreland Books Inc.
Registration # 1145110
All rights reserved
ISBN: 978-1-988610-03-0

Edited by
D. Beck, E.S. Carter

Cover design by
Melissa Ringuette, Monark Design Services

Interior Design & Formatting by
Christine Borgford, Type A Formatting

This book is a work of fiction. The characters, events, and places portrayed in this book are products of the author's imagination and are either fictitious or are used fictitiously. Any similarity to real persons, living or dead, is purely coincidental and not intended by the author.

BENTLEY

MELANIE MORELAND

DEDICATION

Family is not only blood.
Friends become our family through love.
To my friends, old and new, I dedicate this book to you.
Phyllis, Patti, Sharon,
Laura, Edwina, Karen,
Trina, Deb, Jackey.
Hugs and love.

To my Matthew
My world is complete because of you.

CHAPTER 1

BENTLEY

I STEPPED OUTSIDE and inhaled a lungful of air. After the past four days of steamy, oppressive heat, the rain that soaked the ground and broke the humidity had been a welcome relief. In the early morning hours, it was cool and fresh.

"Your paper, sir," Andrew, my houseman, said.

I nodded and took my copy of *The Globe and Mail*, looking down the street, pleased to see my car approaching. As usual, Frank was on time, a fraction early, actually—the same as me.

The car rolled up to the curb, and the rear passenger door opened. Aiden Callaghan, my head of security and right hand, eased his massive form out of the seat, and waved his arm with a flourish.

"Your ride, Eminence."

Ignoring his tone and usual jibe, I slid into the back seat, snapping on the seat belt. I unfolded the paper, the newsprint still crisp and unblemished. Often, if Aiden grabbed the paper before I did, it was creased and smeared, the edges dark with coffee stains or sticky from whatever donut he was shoving in his mouth at the time. The man was an endless pit, it seemed.

"Mr. Tomlin's office, sir?"

"Yes, Frank."

I began to study the financial section, when Aiden's finger bent over the top of the paper.

"Not even a good morning, asshole? Thanks for being here so early? Nothing?"

I rolled my eyes and snapped the paper back into place. "That's what I pay you for."

There was silence.

With a low groan, I folded the paper. "Good morning."

He leaned back with a grin, resting his arm along the top of the leather seat. "Morning, sunshine."

"Don't push it."

"Can I ask why we're heading to a meeting at the crack of dawn? You own the company you know. You could schedule meetings for times not typically seen only by night owls and prostitutes."

I bit back my smile at his dig. "I have a full day."

"I think you like to piss off Greg and get him into the office extra early."

I glanced out the window. It *was* early. There was next to no traffic, which for Toronto, was unusual. I preferred early morning meetings. I rarely slept past five, and I liked to start my day not long after I woke.

I lifted one shoulder in a dismissive action, then grinned. "For your information, Aiden, I'm certain night owls and prostitutes have long since headed to bed. Besides, I did tell you I didn't need you to be there this morning."

He shook his head. "Nope. I told you, we aren't taking any chances."

With a sigh, I brushed a small piece of lint from my pants. "They were idle threats. Nothing has come of them. You're being overly cautious."

He bent forward, all traces of levity gone. "Whoever it was, threatened your life, Bent. I don't take that as idle. They mentioned the deal you're determined to finish, so they know something about you. Until it's done, I'm sticking like glue." He sat back. "Plus, it gives me a chance to piss off the big shot lawyer, too." His grin returned, wide and wicked.

Aiden and Greg seemed to have a love/hate relationship. Aiden respected Greg, yet there seemed to be a constant push and pull between them.

I'd met Aiden when we were at university. When I opened my business, I brought him and another friend of ours, Maddox, on board. They'd been with me ever since.

Greg became my lawyer six years ago. He was an odd man, his personality dry and cool, but brilliant. He was what I needed in a lawyer. Emotionless, in control, and always wanting to win.

My phone beeped as we arrived at our destination. I glanced at the screen with a grimace.

"Greg is running late. His car wouldn't start. He'll be about forty-five minutes."

"Great. Breakfast then? The place over on Queen?"

I peered out the window. "I'm not overly hungry. You go. Take Frank and get breakfast. I'll grab coffee in the shop over there."

"Bent," he warned, "not alone."

"Aiden, no one is around. No one knew my schedule but you, Greg, and me. You can watch me walk in, and be back in forty-five."

"I don't like it."

I held up my hand. "I want a coffee and some time to read the paper. Go." I grabbed my newspaper and flung open the door. "I know lots of self-defense moves—you trained me yourself. If someone comes at me with a coffee cup, I can take them."

I slammed the door behind me, and strode across the street, not giving him a chance to argue. I was certain he'd go grab something and sit around the corner watching, but that was up to him. I was in a public place, and highly doubted I was in danger. He was being his typical, overprotective self. I wanted to be alone and gather my thoughts. And coffee was on the agenda.

IT WASN'T ONE of the chain shops, but it was packed. I could smell the baked goods and rich scent of coffee in the air. People were everywhere, coming and going. All the tables were full, but I could see a few were getting ready to leave. I stood in line, tapping my foot impatiently, waiting my turn. I got my coffee in a takeaway cup, and added a cranberry-lemon scone to my order that looked tempting. After paying, I turned and scanned the room, scowling at the lack of an empty table. I walked farther into the store and rounded the corner, spying a vacant chair against the wall. At least I could sit and wait for a table.

I strode toward the corner, cursing when my foot caught on something, sending me lurching to the left. Luckily, I kept hold of my coffee cup, but some of the contents spurted through the opening and landed on the table tucked behind the wall. My paper fell out from under my arm, and my cell phone skittered across the worn linoleum tiles.

"Oh, shit," a horrified voice exclaimed. "I'm so sorry!"

Without looking, I slammed my cup on the table, then grabbed my paper and phone off the floor. I booted at the shabby rucksack that had tripped me, knocking it out of the way. It was small and old, the edges worn and ragged, the brown color faded in spots.

"Hey, no need to kick my stuff!"

I lifted my head, meeting the angry gaze of the owner of the rucksack. A girl glared back at me, her dark brown eyes challenging.

My gaze flew around the table where she was sitting. All alone at a table for four, she took up the entire area. Books, an old laptop, coffee, an empty plate, a second, larger rucksack, and her jacket were flung around.

"You don't have enough room? You have to use the floor space, too?"

Her cheeks colored, but she didn't back down. "It fell off the chair."

I snagged the handles, dropping it on the empty chair beside her. "You should have picked it up off the floor."

"Are you hurt?"

"No."

"Then stop being such an ass."

I blinked at her. "You can't call me an ass."

"I think I just did."

"You don't even know me!"

"So, once I get to know you, I can call you an ass?"

My lips quirked.

"I mean, dude, I said I was sorry, and you're the one who slopped coffee on my papers," she responded in a snarky tone, dabbing at the drops of coffee with a napkin. "What else do you want from me?"

Dude?

It took me a moment to find my voice. "The least you could do is to allow me to sit since you're the only one with any room at their table."

She pursed her lips and shrugged. "Knock yourself out. I'm working, so don't bother me."

"I have no intention of *bothering* you. I require a place to sit. That is all."

She waved her hand and bent over her notepad. Sitting, I shook out my paper, folding it into a neat quarter to read an article that caught my eye. I wiped at the damp corner where my coffee had dripped and tried not to glare at the girl who made it happen.

Despite my best intentions, my gaze drifted back to her. She gnawed at the end of her pen as she read her scribbles. Long, curly, honey-gold hair tumbled over her shoulders, and she reached up to toss the long strands back, the movement catching my eye. Her face was oval, her skin creamy. She had high cheekbones, and her mouth was full and rosy. I noticed several glints in her ears, and I caught the flash of color by the back of one lobe. It appeared to be some sort of tattoo. She glanced up, her rich chocolate gaze meeting my stare.

"Want to take a picture?" She winked. "It lasts longer."

I felt a strange heat creep up my neck, and I cleared my throat. "I was wondering how it was you managed to take up the biggest table in a shop that is so busy at this time of the day, is all."

Her grin was broad and mischievous. Those chocolate orbs shone with mirth.

"Special privileges."

I relaxed against the chair back, taking a bite of my scone, closing my eyes briefly in appreciation. It was still warm, thick, dense, and buttery. I swallowed and met her stare. "Oh? How do you rate special privileges?"

She pointed at the scone. "By making those."

Her words surprised me, and I smiled in delight. "You made these? My compliments to the chef. They're great—really delicious."

"Well, the ass has manners."

"May I remind you it was your rucksack that caused me to trip in the first place?"

"I realize."

I chuckled. "And still *I'm* the ass?"

She shrugged and looked back at her notebook. "I call them as I see them."

I wiped my fingers and took a sip of my coffee. "You bake scones here every day?"

"Every morning before I go to school."

"School?"

She indicated her books. "Yes."

"Isn't it early for classes to be back? It's only August."

"I'm taking extra courses over the summer."

"What are you taking?"

Raising her head, she tapped her pen against her chin, staring at me. Too late, I realized I was talking and interrupting her.

"I apologize. I didn't mean to interfere with your studies."

"Are you always so formal?"

"I beg your pardon?"

"Like that. Your speech."

"I suppose I am."

She glanced around, tugging her sweater tighter. I noticed it was thick and heavy—an odd garment for summer. I felt compelled to ask.

"Do you always wear such thick sweaters in the summer?"

She sighed and shook her head. With a grin, she stuck out her hand.

I looked between it, and her face. Her hand was small, the fingers delicate. There were silver rings on two of her fingers, and a heavy Celtic band on her thumb.

"I'm not going to keep chatting with a complete stranger, even if he's cute and likes my scones. I'm Emmy."

She thought I was cute?

"What happened to me being an ass?"

"Oh, I still think you are, but you have a great smile when you relax. So, let's try this again." She raised her hand higher. "Hi, stranger, sitting at my table. I'm Emmy."

I clasped her hand in mine, shaking it. Her skin was soft, her palm cold. "Pleased to meet you, Emmy."

She leaned forward, still holding my hand, her voice quiet. "This is the part where you tell me your name." She winked. "Unless you prefer me to continue to call you *ass*."

I started to laugh. She was droll.

"Bentley."

"Bentley?"

"Bentley Ridge."

Her eyes dropped as she withdrew her hand, running her fingers over the table.

"Bentley Ridge?"

"Yes."

"Your name is *Bentley Ridge*."

"We've established that, Emmy. Yes."

"Did your parents not like you or something?"

"Excuse me?"

"It sounds like a swanky subdivision. Come live at Bentley Ridge Estates where the living is easy!"

I gaped at her.

She slapped her hand over her mouth, her dark eyes large in her face. "I shouldn't have said that." She bent close again. "But seriously, has no one ever said it to you?"

"No!" I snapped. I was sure people had thought it, but no one ever stated it out loud. "They haven't."

"I'm sorry. I spoke without thinking."

I picked up my coffee. "I'll find another place to sit. You can go back to studying."

Her hand shot out, grabbing my arm. I looked down at her fingers against the navy fabric of my suit—pale, small, and frail.

"No, please, I was teasing. I do that when I'm nervous—make jokes and say things without thinking. I'm sorry."

I huffed and sat back down, unsure why I did so. She grimaced anxiously and plucked at the sleeve of her sweater.

"I have a condition," she announced.

"I'm sorry?"

"I get cold easily. I have really poor circulation. So, when you're hot, I'm comfortable. When you're cold, I'm freezing. That's why I wear a sweater in the summer, and it's why I'm sitting at this table. It's sort of tucked away and the air conditioning doesn't work well back here, so it's not as popular." She grinned, and a deep dimple appeared on her left cheek. "In the winter, it's reversed, and it's so hot here no one wants this table, but it's perfect for me."

I realized she was trying to make up for her teasing by sharing something personal, and my annoyance lessened. "Is it serious?" I asked, somehow curious. "Your condition."

"No, it's something I've dealt with since I was a child. It's like a temperature malfunction; more annoying than anything." She shrugged. "People think I'm overdramatic, but it's a simple fact of life for me." She went back to her work.

I sipped my coffee and finished my scone. It truly was delicious.

I studied my table companion again while she had her attention on her laptop screen. She was frowning, tapping her chewed pen on her chin, mouthing the words she read. Her brow furrowed and she pulled her sweater tighter. I wondered if there was a way to make her more comfortable. Startled, I shook my head at the strange thoughts. She looked my way, and our gazes locked. The sunlight streaming through the window caught her eyes. The light was bright enough I could see small flecks of gold around her pupils, like bursts of sunshine. Her expression was no longer challenging, but gentle. The need to share something with her filled my thoughts, and I leaned closer.

"My father was Winston Bentley Ridge the second. I'm the third. I hate the name Winston, so I use Bentley. I know it's pretentious"—I shrugged—"but I'm told often enough I am as well, so it fits."

She smiled at me. A huge smile that showed off her straight, white teeth.

"So, a *pretentious* ass then?"

I gave up trying not to laugh. She was honest to a fault. "You got me."

"Rich too, I suppose."

"Rolling in it."

"Yep, I figured. All rich, pretentious assholes come to Al's Coffee Shop for the scones."

"Of course. They're amazing. I heard it at the club."

I found it odd I was sitting there, joking with a random girl about my life—and, enjoying it. Possibly, it was because she didn't believe a word I said, even though some of it was true.

"Where's your bodyguard?" She lifted her eyebrows dramatically. "Is he waiting for your signal to pounce? Take me out for my insolent behavior?"

"No, you're safe. He's having breakfast down the street. He'll be along shortly. If I change my mind, though, you'd best run."

"Are you serious?" Her mouth was agape.

"About having a bodyguard? Yes."

"Wow. I've never met anyone with a bodyguard before today."

"It's not a big deal."

She snorted. "Yeah, we all have one. Mine must be having his nails done right now. He likes them short, so they look good when he holds his gun."

Once again, I chuckled.

She glanced at her watch. "Oh *shit*. I'm late!"

I watched, amused, as she slammed her laptop shut, gathered up her papers, and shoved it all into the larger rucksack haphazardly, yanking on the zipper to get it closed. It took everything in me not to tell her if she organized things better, her possessions would last longer and be in better shape. The rucksack was falling apart—both of them were. I wondered why she carried so many items that she needed two rucksacks. I reminded myself it was none of my business. Seeing my car pull up outside, I stood.

"I'll see you out."

She waved her hand in front of her face. "Oh Lord, such manners."

Smirking, I indicated she should go ahead of me. At the door, I reached around her, letting her out first.

Outside, Aiden stood by the car, his arms folded over his mammoth chest.

"Whoa. Is that him?"

"It is."

"Well, you're safe, I believe."

"I think I'm good."

She turned, and her hair lifted in the breeze, the color vivid in the sun, a mixture of blonde and brown that swirled around her face. I had the strangest urge to lift my hand and tuck the loose strands behind her ear. Instead, I cleared my throat and stepped back.

"Thank you for allowing me to share your table, Emmy. Have a good day."

A look of disappointment crossed her face, then she nodded.

"You too, Rigid. I am sorry about tripping you. Try to use your smile a little more, okay?"

"*Ridge*. It's Bentley Ridge."

She ignored me. "Can I tell you something, Rigid? My name isn't Emmy."

"It's not?"

She leaned up on tiptoes, close to my ear, her small hand resting on my forearm. "No. It's Winifred."

"*Winifred?*"

"Yep. Winifred Windfall. That means, really, I'm Freddy Money. So, Bentley Ridge isn't that bad."

I could feel the amusement growing in my chest once more. I felt the brush of her lips against my cheek.

"Have a good day."

She spun on her heel and walked away, peeking over her shoulder with a wave.

I watched her until she disappeared around the corner, my grin fading as she did.

CHAPTER 2

BENTLEY

"WHO WAS THAT?"

I glanced over at Aiden with a shrug. "Some girl I spoke with in the coffee shop."

"You spoke with *some* girl?"

"We had a conversation, yes."

"She's hot. You get her number?"

I rolled my eyes. "She's a university student. I highly doubt she's interested in spending time with a thirty-two-year-old man."

He looked concerned. "She looked older than the normal student. What's her name?"

"Emmy . . . I think."

"You think?"

I waved my hand. "Inside joke."

He narrowed his eyes. "Did you approach her or did she approach you?"

"For fuck sake, Aiden, don't start. She isn't someone out to get me. I was looking for a place to sit, and there was an empty chair at her table. I sat there. We chatted. No big deal."

I turned, checked for traffic, and hurried across the street, hoping Greg had finally made it into his office. Aiden was right beside me, mumbling.

"It's not like you to *chat* with someone, that's all. Or say, 'inside joke.' Never mind the fact I saw her kiss your cheek. You don't let people get close."

He was right on all his facts; I couldn't argue. I rarely went out of my way to talk to a stranger, even pretty ones. I never got close to people because I liked my personal space. But I didn't want to talk about it. I pulled open the door and strode to the elevator, pushing the button.

"Give it a rest, dude."

He gaped at me. "Did you just call me 'dude'?"

I hid my amusement.

He crossed his arms, the material of his shirt stretching across his shoulders. "What's going on with you, Bent?"

I ignored him, scrolling through my phone.

"I wish you'd gotten her name. I could vet her; make sure she's on the up and up."

I huffed in annoyance. "It was a chat in a coffee shop. It was two people sitting at a table, being polite. I'll probably never see her again, so there is no need to *vet* her. You are driving me crazy with this shit!"

"It's my job."

"To protect me or drive me crazy?"

He grinned. "Both."

With a heavy sigh, I walked past him and into Greg's office. It was too early for his assistant to be at her desk, and since his door was open, I went in, unannounced. He was at his desk, two coffee cups already empty. I swore he lived on the stuff. He stood, reaching to shake my hand. He was tall and heavy-set, with a thick neck and chest, a head of wiry, brown hair brushed high off his forehead, and brown eyes. His face was long with heavy jowls, his expression impassive. He looked older than his years. He never gave anything away, which made him a great lawyer.

"Greg."

"Bentley. Sorry about the delay. Faulty battery, it seems. I had it replaced last week, and the one they put in was defective."

"I assume they will be replacing it."

"Oh, yes. And then some."

Knowing Greg, "and then some," meant a lot of free mechanical work for his car. He was a master of manipulating situations to go in his favor. His negotiation skills were infamous.

We got down to business, going through some new deals I was structuring. He made notes, offered suggestions and opinions. Aiden was silent, but I knew he was absorbing the entire conversation. He had a knack for remembering details. I pushed the last of the paperwork Greg's way. "I don't like the wording in these two documents. It's too vague."

"I thought so, as well. I'll get it changed."

He pushed another file my way. "I took the liberty of changing some wording in this one. The non-compete wasn't detailed enough."

I scanned the document and signed it. "Good catch."

"It's my job," he stated dryly. "You should know by now I have high standards."

"And rates. Your bills rival every other expense in my company."

"You get what you pay for. I'm sure you agree I'm worth it."

Before I could respond, Greg's assistant arrived, bringing him in another black coffee and a plate of dry, whole-wheat toast. She brought me in a mug of coffee and a bottle of water for Aiden. She had been with Greg since he opened his business. He still addressed her as Mrs. Johnson. I did, as well. Greg didn't believe in treating employees as anything other than that. Employees. He didn't particularly approve of my less structured way of dealing with my staff, and he disapproved of working with "friends."

I took a long sip of the hot brew, leaning back in my chair.

"What's the word on the Lancaster deal?"

Greg swallowed the last of his toast and drained his coffee. "Dead end."

"How is that possible?"

He shook his head. "Whoever bought those two parcels of land doesn't want to be known, Bentley. There are so many numbered corporations; I can't track down who really owns them. I'm not even sure if they're the same person. The red tape is endless."

I stood, pacing the room. "I still don't know how they bought them right out from under me."

He shrugged. "It was a closed bid. They bid higher."

"I overbid. I was certain I'd get them. You were, also."

"I thought you would. They obviously wanted them, and you were outbid."

I fisted my hands, flexing my fingers, tightening them, trying to relax. "But why? I own all the land between them. They're small pieces. It hardly seems worth the effort."

"And they're standing in the way of you building your vision. I think they'll come to you with an offer soon enough. I assume they'll be looking for a lot of cash."

"Right. The parcel of land I want is still going up for sale in September? The large one?"

"Yes. Bids are due mid-month. The decision will be announced in October."

"I want it."

"I'm aware."

"Once I have that piece, I can build, even if they don't sell."

"Not to the same specs."

"Close enough. Once I start, they'll sell."

"Unless you're outbid."

"Don't let that happen, Greg."

"Again, it's a closed bid, Bentley. I'll put in the offer you want, but I have no control over the other bids."

Shoving my hands into my pockets, I stared out the window as I rolled the small beads hidden in the folds of the material. The action always calmed me.

I had bought some land a few years prior, with a vague idea in mind. As it grew and developed, I realized I needed to purchase more of the area. Slowly, I accrued additional land in the neighborhood. Then, it was as if I became cursed. I got into a bidding war for a large piece, which went up for sale last year, and it cost me way more than I wanted. When the two parcels of land that sandwiched the middle piece became available, I overbid, determined to get them so I could move ahead with my dream of revamping the neighborhood. Upscale homes, expensive boutiques, restaurants, and clubs. Furious didn't describe my state of mind when I lost the parcels of land to an unknown entity, and all efforts to reach out and purchase them had proven fruitless. Greg was like a dog with a bone, but even he and all his resources couldn't find the identity of the purchaser. It was frustrating.

"Any other threats?" Greg inquired to Aiden.

"A couple. Very few people know of Bent's plans for the area, but they seem to be fully aware."

"A leak, perhaps? Computer hacking?"

"We've checked and double-checked. We've added security, changed passwords, encryption, and protocols. We have even cut back on the number of people with access to information. It's down to a handful."

"Is it worth it, Bentley? Is this project that important? You usually walk away when a deal isn't working and move onto something new."

I spun around, facing him. "I've been working on this for a long time. I want to see it through."

"Someone is threatening your life."

I waved my hand. "It's not the first time. It's a couple of anonymous, vague notes."

"And pictures of you that mysteriously appear."

I had to admit those were troublesome, but I shrugged. "They want me to back off. They see what I do—the huge potential in a once overlooked area of the city. If I step back, they'll move in and do exactly what I am going to do, making themselves a fortune."

"There are other projects. Other ways to make money."

"I'm not letting some coward hide behind miles of paperwork and numbered companies, and scare me off. No one is going to kill me over a land deal."

"Stranger things have been known to happen," Aiden interjected. "You're not taking this seriously enough."

"And you're taking it way too seriously. We've dealt with this in the past."

"I don't like it. This situation feels different."

Greg reclined in his chair, contemplative. "I agree with Aiden, it does."

I looked between them. "Well, I never thought I would see the day the two of you agreed on something."

"Think about it, Bentley. I heard of some other parcels of land coming up for sale. Take on a different project."

I shook my head, stubborn and defiant. I hated manipulation, especially by a faceless enemy.

Greg shrugged. "Okay, fine. I'll keep digging."

"Good."

I shook his hand. "Keep me posted."

My day was a busy one, and I went from meeting to meeting, finally ending up back in my office late in the afternoon.

It was strange how every time my mind was free, memories of the morning filtered through. The sound of Emmy's voice. The way her eyes flashed with wit. The dimple that appeared when she smiled in a certain way. For some reason, I wanted her to smile at me. I wanted to hear her laugh. I even liked the gentle way she teased me about my life. In the short time I had sat with her, she made me feel . . . lighter. As crazy as it seemed, I wanted the chance to see her again.

My phone rang, and I picked it up.

"Ridge."

"It's Greg. I have those documents redone. I'll have them sent over tomorrow, and you can sign them. I'll have the courier wait, and he can bring them back to me."

"Great." I paused, as an inane idea formed. "Wait, I'll come to you, and sign them there."

He sounded surprised. "Are you sure?"

"I'll be over same time as this morning."

"Do you have other meetings this end of town?"

"Yes. See you tomorrow."

I hung up, and turned my chair around, studying the bustling city outside my office window. I didn't have a meeting. I had no business in that area of the city tomorrow or the rest of the week.

Except . . . I fancied a scone.

Perhaps, if I were lucky, a smile from the girl who made it.

CHAPTER 3

BENTLEY

THE NEXT MORNING, I was inexplicably nervous. I picked out my favorite suit—dark gray with pinstripes—and added a brilliant blue tie. I studied my face in the mirror. I certainly wasn't model material, but I'd been told I was handsome. My hair was thick, a sandy brown in color, curly and unruly. I had to use product to keep it in place. I only allowed a slight wave at the top where it was a touch longer. I was tall, and because of the workouts I did with Aiden, my shoulders broad and my waist narrow. My eyes were a bright blue—something I inherited from my mother, and my brains from my intelligent father. My personality came from my upbringing. Quiet. Staid. Always able to control my emotions.

Boring, Aiden would tell me.

I withheld my plans from Aiden today. I knew he'd be pissed, but I'd deal with him later. I slipped into the car, holding my paper. Frank raised one eyebrow in a silent question.

"Mr. Tomlin's office."

"Mr. Callaghan?"

"He won't be joining us."

His lips thinned, but he didn't say anything. The drive was silent, as I read my paper undisturbed. When we arrived, I stepped out. "I'll call you when I'm ready. It will be about an hour."

He drove off, and I crossed the street. I tugged down my shirtsleeves, feeling edgy. I didn't know if she'd be there. Perhaps she wouldn't want to speak with me again. I had been rather short with her. I thought how much I liked the soft press of her lips on my cheek, and the way her voice sounded in my ear. I straightened my shoulders. I was being ridiculous. Chances were, I would get a coffee and a scone, and head to Greg's office.

But if I was being truthful, I hoped she would be at her table.

I pulled open the door and joined the line. It was as busy as yesterday. This time, I got a larger coffee, and was pleased to see a pile of scones. Cinnamon raisin today. After adding one to my order and paying, I went directly to the back, making sure there was no rucksack waiting to trip me. She was at her table, head bent over as she scribbled away. Her hair was in a thick braid hanging down her back, and today, I could clearly see the tattoo behind her ear. A bass and treble clef twisted to form a heart, the black and red ink vivid against the creamy white of her skin. Glinting in the light was a row of earrings that went right from the lobe to the top.

She tilted her head, her voice dry. "Did you want a picture?"

"Good morning, Emmy. Or should I call you Freddy?"

She chuckled. "Whichever you prefer."

I slid into the empty chair across from her. "Not much into selfies, I confess."

She snorted. "That's when you take your own picture, Rigid."

"Ah. Then taking yours would be?"

"Stalking," she deadpanned, making me chuckle. "You need to learn the lingo if you're gonna hang with the cool kids."

I broke the scone in half, taking a bite and savoring it. She certainly could make delicious scones.

"Is that what you are, Emmy? One of the cool kids?"

A pained look passed over her face, and for a moment, she looked sad. Her smile reappeared, and she shook her head. "Nope. Never have been."

"How long ago, exactly, were you a kid?" I asked, trying to appear nonchalant.

"I'm twenty-five. How old are you?" Her eyes widened mischievously, and she leaned forward, her voice almost a whisper. "Are you like, *ancient*? Thirty?"

"Thirty-two, actually."

She laid a hand on her heart. "My God, one foot in the grave. No wonder you act so oddly."

Oddly? My lips curled in amusement as I repeated her word in my head.

"If you mean polite and respectful, then yes. Ancient is a good word."

"I mean you need to loosen up a little. Act your age."

I scowled as I sipped my coffee. I thought I was acting my age. I didn't know anything different.

I studied her. It was warmer today, but she was dressed in a man's pale blue shirt that was miles too big on her and wrapped in a cropped navy sweater with loose sleeves. I had noticed her leggings when I sat down, and the old sneakers on her feet. The sleeves of her shirt hung down past her wrists, leaving the ends of her fingers showing. She was almost huddled in her chair; her shoulders bowed in as if warding off the cool air. Without thinking, I stood, pulled off my jacket, crossed to her side of the table, and slid it around her shoulders. When I retook my seat, she was staring at me, her hands clutching the lapels of my jacket.

"Why did you do that?"

"You looked cold. I thought it might help."

"Thank you."

I inclined my head with a teasing grin. "Men of an older

generation know how to treat a lady."

I noticed the way she burrowed into my jacket. The odd thought of wanting to wrap her in my arms and help her get warm drifted through my head. It bothered me to see her chilly.

"You're only seven years older than I am. Hardly a different generation. It's nothing really."

I ignored her remark. I had a feeling the vast differences between us were more than simply age. "May I buy you another coffee?"

"No, thank you. I've had two."

I held up my bag. "Scone? I assure you, they are delectable."

"Such a charmer, but no."

"Where did you learn to bake scones?"

"My grandmother. She was Scottish and loved her scones. She made them all the time when I was young. I had her recipe book, and I practiced until I got it right. I started adding different ingredients to them to make them interesting. One day, I needed help to persuade Al about an idea, so I made them. They were a hit, and Al and I came to an agreement."

I wondered what sort of help she required as I wiped my fingers on my napkin. "Smart man."

She chuckled, the sound low and soft. "I'm glad you like them."

I sipped my coffee. "They are the only sweet thing I have allowed myself in a long time."

She made a face. "Oh. One of those."

"I'm sorry?"

She sighed, leaning back in her chair. "Rigid is a good name for you, isn't it? I bet you live your life planned to the letter. Your diet is perfect, you have a workout regime, you get your suits made by the same tailor, and your hair cut the exact same way by the same barber. You know what suit you'll wear with what specific tie. Everything organized and in line."

"Nothing wrong with being organized."

"Nope. If it works for you, then great."

"Not your style?" I asked, curious.

She fiddled with the edge of her dog-eared notebook. "No. I'm lucky to be on time for my classes. I'm sometimes grateful to find clean clothes because I forget to go to the laundromat. I rarely plan my day, because I like to see what happens during the course of it and go with the flow. I tend to get caught up in the moment, and it leads to me being late for things. I get into a lot of trouble at times, but I handle it." She grinned. "I bet you're punctual, aren't you? For everything."

She had me there. "Yes, I like being on time. What about school?"

She smiled, tracing the edge of one of her books. "I make school a priority. I love learning and my courses, so I do show up for those on time."

"So you *can* be structured, you simply don't choose to be."

"I suppose." She wrinkled her nose at me. "Can you be spontaneous?"

"Of course I can."

"Name the last spontaneous thing you did."

I sat back with a smirk. "I dumped my bodyguard and came here, hoping to have coffee with you."

"So, he doesn't know you're here?"

"Nope."

She indicated to the right with a jerk of her head. "I wouldn't be certain of that statement."

I turned and looked in the direction she had glanced. Aiden sat at a table near the front, glaring at me. I twisted back, slouching.

"*Shit.*"

"Are you in trouble?"

"It would appear that way."

She lowered her voice, becoming almost breathy. "And you did it to come see me?"

"Yes."

"Why?"

I shrugged, unable to explain my strange behavior. "I have no idea. I liked talking to you yesterday."

"I wasn't very nice."

"I liked your directness. You made me laugh. Very little makes me laugh."

Her breath hitched. "That's so sad."

Before I could respond, her eyes grew large. "Uh-oh. He's coming over."

Aiden appeared at the table, crossing his arms. It always seemed to double his size, making his already tremendous bulk seem enormous.

Emmy looked up at him with a bright expression. "Hey, Mr. Bodyguard!"

He glared at her, then at me. However, she refused to be ignored and tugged on his sleeve.

"Hey, Tree Trunk. We're talking, and frankly, you're interrupting. Maybe you could, I don't know, go back to your table?" She smiled at him, broad and mischievous. "I could give you my driver's license, and you could run a background check on me. Make sure I'm not a danger to your boss or anything. It would help pass the time for you."

I tried to hide my amusement at her brashness. Aiden narrowed his eyes and looked shocked when she thrust out her hand. "I can't believe I have to do this, two days in a row. Hi, I'm Emmy."

For an instant, I was certain he would refuse to react. Then he loosened his shoulders and accepted her gesture, engulfing her small hand within his. "Hey, Emmy. Sorry to interrupt. I need one moment with Bentley, and I'll be out of your hair."

She gazed up at him. "Wow. You have *incredible* eyes."

He was taken back. "Ah, thanks."

"Are you going to give him shit?"

"Um . . . yeah."

"Okay, then." She waved her hand. "Have at."

He winked at her. "For a little thing, you got balls."

"Big cojones," she informed him.

He chuckled. "Good to know."

He turned to me, his humor disappearing. He leaned forward, his hand resting on the table, and his voice low. "We are going to talk about this later. But for now, I've sent Frank back to the office, and I will be over there"—he pointed to the table at the front—"and will go with you to Greg's. Next, we'll do whatever else you need to do and head to the office. Then we are going to have a chat, am I clear?"

I knew when to push Aiden and when not to. I nodded. "Clear."

He straightened. "Good. Nice to meet you, Emmy. Your scones are wicked, too. Bent raved about them yesterday."

"Thanks."

He held out his hand. "I'll take your driver's license, though."

"No!" I snarled. "Leave her alone, Aiden."

"She offered."

"She was teasing you. Leave."

Emmy scribbled something on a piece of paper, handing it to Aiden. "Will that suffice?"

He shoved it into his pocket and nodded. "For now."

He sauntered away, sitting back at his table.

"What did you give him?"

"My name, address, and date of birth. He can work for the rest."

"You didn't have to do that, Emmy," I assured her, pushing aside the memories of his remarks yesterday about vetting her.

"It's fine. He takes his job seriously."

I cleared my throat. "Sorry about that."

"He cares about you."

"Yeah, he is a good friend, and I'd be lost without him."

"Yet, you came here alone?"

"I wanted to see you, and I thought he might make you uncomfortable."

I wasn't sure how to tell her the actual truth. I wanted to spend a little time with her, alone, as me. Bentley, the man. Not the person who needed protection. Just me.

"It's fine, Rigid. I'm good with it."

I met her gaze, her eyes bright in the light. They were warm, intelligent, gentle, and so dark they looked like the richest espresso you would sip in the early morning hours; the kind that brought you to life.

Strangely, that was how I felt when I sat across from her. I made yet another spontaneous decision.

"I'm going to take you out."

"I'm sorry?"

"On a date. Friday evening."

"And, what may I ask would this date consist of?"

"Well, the usual, I suppose. Dinner. Drinks. That sort of thing."

She laughed softly, shaking her head, the light catching the blonde glints of her hair woven into the thick braid. "I see. Like a *date*, date."

"Yes. Eight o'clock."

"No."

"Pardon me?"

"I said no."

"Why?" I scowled. "I thought you said the age difference was fine."

"It has nothing to do with the age difference," she stated patiently.

"Aiden won't intrude."

"That doesn't bother me either."

"What then?"

"If you want to ask me out on a date, I suggest you do so."

"I thought I had?"

"No, actually, you informed me you were going to take me out. You never, in fact, *asked* me."

I blinked at her, unsure how to respond, and cleared my throat. "I beg your pardon." I leaned across the table, all teasing gone. "Would you accompany me to dinner on Friday?"

She pursed her lips. "I'm not sure I can."

"Do you have plans?"

"No."

"Are you married? Seeing someone?"

"No."

"You don't like me? You find me repugnant?"

Her lips twitched. "Far from it."

I ran my hand through my hair in frustration. I was certain I'd never worked as hard for a date. "Then what could possibly stop you from going out with me?"

Her bravado fell away, and for the first time, I saw a glimpse of her vulnerability. She looked uncertain, her fingers clutching at the lapels of my jacket, twisting the material nervously. She crouched forward, her voice soft.

"I don't think I have anything I could wear that would be appropriate."

"I'm sorry?"

"Look at you, Bentley. Your suit probably cost more than my rent for an entire year. I don't have a dress suitable to go out with you." She hesitated, casting her gaze downward. "I wouldn't want to embarrass you."

An emotion I had never experienced swept through my chest. Tenderness dripped into my heart at her pained confession. I liked hearing her say my name, though.

"Emmy."

Her eyes remained locked on the table, her color high.

"Look at me, please."

She met my gaze, and I hated the look of uncertainty I could see there.

"Understand something. I don't care what you wear. You can wear exactly what you have on now, and I would be proud to be seen with you. That being said, I am open to going somewhere less *fancy* than I'm used to. I know a couple of small places I like because the food is good, and the atmosphere friendly. I won't even wear one of my suits. How about that? A casual dinner out." I sucked in a deep breath. "Would you have dinner with me Friday, Emmy?"

She beamed, her eyes glowing. "Yes, I would love to."

"Excellent." I handed her my phone. "Perhaps I could have your number to call and arrange it with you?"

"No more morning visits?"

I shook my head as she added herself to my contacts, then took my information, so she had my number. "I wish, but no. I have early morning meetings scheduled the rest of the week. I will have to survive without your company or scones for the next couple mornings."

She stood, handing me back my phone, and slipped my jacket from her shoulders. I slid it on, trying not to notice the fact it now smelled like her. Soft, summery, light. I smiled at her and moved closer. "Just so we are clear? You look lovely—although, I'm wondering who the shirt belongs to."

She glanced down, fingering the worn cotton. "I have no idea," she quipped. "They come and go at my place, leaving their clothes all the time."

My eyebrows shot up, and she giggled. "Relax, Rigid. I got it at Goodwill. I have a tie I usually wear with it, but I couldn't find it. I wore it anyway, even though it doesn't feel complete."

"Laundry day?" I guessed.

She nodded. "Tonight, I hope."

She allowed me to carry her rucksacks to the front. Again, I wondered why she carried two of them. She disappeared behind the counter for a minute, and I waited patiently for her to join me outside. Aiden was leaning on his car, watching us intently, and I turned, blocking his view. I handed her the heavy bags. "May I offer you a lift to school?"

"No, I like to walk." She held up a small bag. "I got you a couple of extra scones to see you through the mornings before your meetings. If you warm them in the microwave, they'll be good."

I took the bag, touched. "Thank you. I will enjoy them."

We stood regarding each other. Unable to help myself, I ran the back of my hand down her cheek. "I hope the rest of your week goes well."

"I'm sure it will. I have something to look forward to now."

She stepped back and began to turn away.

"Wait!"

She spun around. "Yes?"

I shoved the small bag containing the scones into her hands, and loosened my tie, yanking it over my head. Before she could react, I tugged it down her neck, lifted her heavy braid, and slipped it under the collar. I slid the knot up loosely. I wanted to give her something, and my tie was the only thing I could think of at the moment.

"Because, you know, the outfit isn't complete without a tie," I offered with a grin. I felt an odd thrill at the sight of my tie resting on her neck, the brilliant blue blazing against her shirt.

She glanced down, her grin bright. "It does. Especially *this* tie." She leaned up on her toes, kissing my cheek. "Thank you," she breathed out, and pushed the bag back into my hands. She stepped back, her face aglow.

"Have a good day, Rigid."

I had no idea what that girl was doing to me, or how she made me feel lighter, happier than I had in a long time.

Still, she did.

I raised my hand in a wave.

"You too, *Freddy*."

CHAPTER 4

BENTLEY

AIDEN DIDN'T SAY a word as we crossed the street. I knew he was behind me, but I didn't acknowledge him. He was silent in the elevator, and aside from a nod to Greg, remained that way as I went through the documents, making sure the wording was what I wanted. I signed and handed them back to Greg.

"I want to meet next week about my bid."

"I assumed as much. Wednesday?"

I glanced through my schedule, and before I replied, added Emmy to Friday. Simply seeing the words on my phone made me happy.

"Something funny?"

I glanced up. "No. I needed to add something before I forget." As if I could possibly forget. "Wednesday is good."

He tapped away at his computer. "Okay. See you next week. I'll come to the office?"

"No, I'll come here."

He regarded me curiously. "That's twice you've come to me. What's going on with you? We usually meet in your office."

I shrugged. "Trying to be accommodating."

He threw back his head, laughing loud. "Good one. Now, really. What's going on?"

Ignoring him, I stood, and smoothed down my jacket, remembering the way Emmy's hands had held the lapels. "I'll see you next week."

His amusement followed me out of the office. Aiden rose, following me to the elevator, still not speaking.

"Just spit it out," I snapped.

"Oh, feeling a little testy you're being ignored? Imagine that."

I started to speak, and he held up his hand. "We'll talk when we get to the office."

"You're being—"

He pushed forward, glaring down at me. I was tall, standing at 6'3", but Aiden had a good four inches on me. He was tense and angry, and I was certain he had expanded. His chest seemed larger; his bulging arms gigantic.

"I *said* the office."

I nodded, not wanting to make him angrier. When we got to the car, I busied myself on my phone. Unable to resist, I texted Emmy.

> *Have a good day, Emmy. Looking forward to seeing you on Friday evening. When you have a moment, please send me your home address.*

She responded instantly.

> *So formal, even in texts. You already have my address. I live above the coffee shop. Apt C. Use the back stairs to come up. I look forward to seeing you, as well, Mr. R.*

She lived above the coffee shop?

I thought about the building that housed the coffee shop, and apparently, her home. It was two-storied, old, the brick crumbling in places. Located close enough to the school she could walk there daily, but it was in a busy business neighborhood and right on a main street. Hardly the place in which a person could study quietly.

As I grimaced over the information, my phone pinged.

Are you in trouble with Tree Trunk?

I glanced toward Aiden, who was concentrating on the morning traffic ahead of us. From the scowl on his face, I knew it wasn't going to be a pleasant conversation.

Yes, I am.

Her next text made me grin.

Want me to rescue you? I could break you out. He wouldn't know. I'm a seasoned Ninja.

My lips twitched as I tried not to laugh.

No, I will take my punishment. It will be worth it having been able to spend some more time with you.

Her reply was short.

La, you are a charmer.

We pulled into the garage.

La? Now, who's old-fashioned?

Simply using words I thought you'd be familiar with. That was one of my Nana's favorites. You're still a charmer.

I'm pleased you think so. Have a good day, Freddy.

Stay strong, Rigid.

She followed it up with one of those little faces people used with text. I had no idea how to add one. I hated texting and the way people bastardized the English language, so I always kept mine simple and short. For some reason, I wanted to send her something to make her laugh, but it wasn't the time to ask Aiden for texting advice. I was certain the two words he would reply with wouldn't be "for sure."

The office hummed as we strode through the hallway. I stopped by Sandy's desk, Aiden brushing past me without a word. Sandy had been with me since my university days. She was an older woman, refused to take shit from any of us, especially me, and kept the place running. Her gleaming white hair was swept into an old-fashioned chignon, and her hazel eyes, wise. She was tall and imposing; although below the no-nonsense exterior, there was the heart of a warm woman. I'd be lost without her.

She arched her eyebrows. "Someone is in a mood."

"Yes."

"What did you do?"

"What makes you think it was something I did?"

"He only gets like that when you've done something."

I took the small stack of messages and papers she had for me. "I may have given him the slip this morning."

"Bentley."

Her opinion was clear from the way she spoke my name.

"I will apologize."

"You hired him to do a job. Let him do it."

She was right.

"Maddox was looking for you two, as well."

"Okay, let him know I'm in and you can buzz him when I'm done with Aiden." I paused. "Or when he is done with me, I suppose."

"All right."

"Bring us coffee in about ten minutes, please. If you hear screaming, ignore it."

She sniffed. "I intend to."

Rolling my eyes, I walked into my office. Aiden was staring out the window, the set of his shoulders tense, his expression serious. I placed the papers I was carrying on my desk and studied him briefly. He seemed to get more massive as the years went on.

We both showed up to apply as a roommate in a house close to the university campus. I had thought I would try dorm living, but realized quickly I hated it, so I began looking for off-campus housing. Once I met the person who placed the ad and saw the house, I knew I was no longer interested in living there, and I left. Hurried footsteps behind me made me turn, and a huge guy grinned at me.

"Dodged a bullet there, eh?"

I grimaced. "I'm trying to get away from the party atmosphere of the dorms, not live it twenty-four/seven." I indicated the house with a tilt of my head. "I have a feeling it will be party central, daily."

"No shit." He stuck out his large hand. "Aiden Callaghan."

I shook his hand firmly, hoping he didn't crush mine. "Win—I mean Bentley Ridge."

He raised one eyebrow but didn't comment.

"So, I assume you're still looking for a place?"

"I am."

He smiled. "Why don't we look together?"

"I'm pretty private."

"No worries. I'm not looking for a party place either. I need a quiet place to study and a room to put my equipment."

"Equipment?"

"I work out a lot. A basement would be great."

I studied him. He was taller than I was, and broad, his muscles rippling under his shirt. He seemed like a decent guy. I hated it in the dorm, and I could afford to live alone, but I wanted the experience of living with other people.

"At least come have coffee with me, and we can get to know each other before you say no."

I nodded in agreement. "Sure."

I cleared my throat. He turned, arms crossed, and not a glimmer of his usual humor in his eyes. He was seriously pissed.

I started to speak, and he held up his hand, stopping me.

"Why did you hire me?"

I sat down at my desk with a sigh. "Because you're my best friend, and I trust you."

"You trust me?"

"Totally. There's no question about it. You and Maddox are family to me."

"You let Maddox handle all your finances. Millions of dollars. You listen to what he says. No questions asked."

"Of course I do. He knows what he's talking about."

He stormed toward me, stopping in front of my desk. He leaned on the thick wood, hands balled into fists. "And I fucking don't?"

"I never said that."

He tossed a white envelope on my desk.

"What's that?"

"My resignation."

I was horrified, and I pushed the envelope back his way. "I'm not accepting it. Aiden, all I did was go for coffee."

"You deliberately didn't tell me where you were going this morning. You didn't *trust* me with that information. I'm supposedly your *right hand*, and the head of your security."

"It was *coffee*. No one is going to notice if I go for coffee."

"That's not your decision to make."

"Aiden—"

"Bentley," he interrupted me. "Someone is watching you. Someone knows your movements. All they need to see is a pattern. You sneaking out to meet your new fixation for coffee is going to be noticed. It's a fucking invitation for someone to get to you."

"*Don't* call her that. She isn't a fixation."

"Jesus, you don't even know her."

"Sort of the point of taking her on a date—to get to know her."

"Emaline Harris," he stated. "Born in Ontario. Parents deceased. One sibling. Lives alone. No arrests, or convictions. Works part-time in Al's Coffee Shop, and attends Toronto School of Design."

"Is that all you got?" I asked dryly.

"I was in a coffee shop. I'll have more by the end of the day."

I rolled my eyes at his matter-of-fact tone. Even if I told him not to dig, he would do it anyway.

"Those are just facts. That's not getting to know her."

"I'll know more, once I check deeper."

"Leave it alone," I warned.

He shut his eyes as he blew out a long breath. "You're missing the point."

"Which is?"

He tossed a picture on my desk, taken of me yesterday, watching Emmy walk away. She was out of focus, but I recognized her sweater. Did they see me talking to her?

"*Fuck.*"

He bent close, his voice low. "Did you think about the fact if you're being watched, perhaps they'll watch her, too? If I can find that information in twenty minutes, so can they."

I felt myself blanch under his stare. I hadn't thought of that fact. All I had thought of was seeing her again.

"I'm supposed to take her out on a date. On Friday." I shook my head, reaching for my phone. "Damn it. I'll cancel."

"Stop."

I met Aiden's gaze. Some of the anger had gone, but he was still concerned.

"I didn't say you couldn't see her, Bent. I'm asking you to be careful. I'm asking you to trust me to do my job."

"Like going on a date with a chaperone will be so much fun for her. How do I explain it? My security thinks I may be in danger, and therefore you are, as well. Can I see you again tomorrow?" I snapped.

He shrugged. "I can be discreet. All you have to tell her is I'm around." He grinned. "It's not like I want to sit at the table and watch you make kissy faces at her."

"I don't plan on making kissy faces at her."

"Like you didn't plan on giving her your tie? Fuck sake, Bent. That tie was five hundred bucks. I was with you when you bought it. It took me ten minutes to convince you the color wasn't 'over-the-top'."

I shrugged, not giving a shit about how much the tie cost. I had a hundred more at home. And it looked cute on her.

"There's something about her, Aiden. I want to get to know her. She . . ."

"She what?"

"She makes me laugh. She doesn't give a shit about all this . . . stuff." I indicated the luxurious office around us. "She would have no idea how expensive the tie was I gave her."

He studied me for a moment. I pushed the envelope toward him again. "Don't do this, Aiden, please. I'm asking as your friend. Not your boss."

"On one condition. You stop doing shit like today and let me do my job. I'm with you when you're out of the office or the house. Plus, I'm adding more cameras around the house."

I wanted to groan and tell him to forget it. But I knew if I did, he was serious. He would walk away.

"Discreet."

"That's my middle name."

"Funny, I thought it was Joseph."

"Fuck you."

"You first."

He chuckled at our usual banter, then grew serious again. "I mean it, Bent. Until we figure out who took the picture, and what they want, we need to take this situation seriously."

I looked down at the picture. I would have to tell her and give her the choice. It wouldn't be fair otherwise. The thought of her being in danger, because of me, made me feel ill.

I held out my hand. "Deal. Now take back your fucking resignation. Shred it."

He shook my hand, and picked up the envelope, sliding it into the shredder.

He sat down in front of my desk. "So. Where are we going on Friday?"

CHAPTER 5

EMMY

I FLIPPED THROUGH my notes, finally finding the reference I needed. As I was transcribing it into my assignment, a body slid into the chair next to me. I didn't have to look up to know who it was.

"Hey, Cami."

"Hi, yourself."

With a grin, I glanced at my best friend, Cami Wilson. Her long, rich brown hair was thick and wavy, and today she sported purple highlights woven into the curls. I never knew what color they'd be next. She grinned back at me, grabbing one of my carrot sticks, chomping away. Her green eyes danced with mischief the way they always did when she was planning something. Cami was always planning something.

"Friday," she drawled. "I got us complimentary passes to the Art Gallery for the new exhibit. There's a reception too, so free food and booze! And hey—that's not your usual tie with that outfit. Is it new?"

Normally, I'd be excited. I loved going to the art gallery, but I couldn't indulge very often, with my limited budget. I enjoyed walking around on free Wednesday evenings, but it didn't include the special exhibitions.

"I can't go."

She frowned, mid-chomp. "What do you mean you can't go? It's the *art gallery*, Emmy. You can study on Saturday."

"I'm not studying. I–I have a date."

My announcement got her attention. She leaned forward, green eyes huge with curiosity.

"You have a date? With who? Oh God, tell me you didn't finally say yes to that awful Roger guy who keeps pestering you."

I scrunched my nose. "Eww. No. I, ah, met a guy at the coffee shop the other morning. He came back today, and we talked. He asked me out."

"Are you nuts? You're going out with a stranger? Emmy, that could be dangerous!"

I patted her hand. "He is perfectly safe."

"How do you know?"

I sighed and showed her my laptop. "I checked him out."

She gaped at the screen, then me. "That is who asked you out? Bentley Ridge of BAM?"

"Yes."

Her eyes narrowed back on the tie, then to the screen. "Are you wearing his tie?"

I chuckled because of course she would notice a detail like that. She always did.

"I couldn't find my tie this morning."

"Laundry day?"

"Yes." I laughed because that was exactly what he had guessed, too. "Bentley, well, he put this on me as we were saying goodbye." I looked down, stroking the silk. "It was the sweetest thing ever."

"Do you have any idea how much a tie like that costs?"

I shook my head. "No."

"More than your rent."

"*Shit*," I swore under my breath. "I need to give it back."

"I don't think he cares if he gave it to you. You might insult him."

"I can't keep something so expensive!"

"If he gave it to you, yes you can."

I mulled over her words. She was probably right, but I was still giving back the tie.

"He has a bodyguard."

"Really? How exciting!"

"He's massive. His arms are like tree trunks."

"Is he coming with you on Friday?"

"Probably. Bentley showed up this morning without him, and he arrived not long after. He looked pretty pissed."

"Is he cute?"

"Bentley?"

"No, the bodyguard, you idiot. I can see what Bentley looks like."

"Oh. Um, well, he is very tall and big. He has dark, curly hair, and a beard. His eyes are so unique—one green and one brown, and he has a great smile. Although, he wasn't smiling much this morning." I tapped on my keyboard and found a picture of Aiden with Bentley. "That's him."

She stared at the screen. "My dream come to life," she muttered. "Holy shit, he's hot. Look at that tattoo on his arm." She peered at the screen. "Are both arms done?"

I had to think, then shook my head. "No, just the one."

"Hmm. I wonder what it signifies."

I looked at the picture. He was good-looking, but I preferred Bentley. He was classically handsome, while Aiden had a bad boy look about him. Cami always liked bad boys.

"I don't know," I murmured. "I didn't ask."

"I might have to find out."

I chuckled as she continued to stare at the screen.

"Should I get you a napkin for your drool?"

Rolling her eyes, she ignored my remark, and pushed my laptop back to me. "Where are you going on Friday?"

"I don't know. He promised it wouldn't be anywhere too fancy. I told him I didn't have the right kind of dress to wear to the places I think he would normally frequent. He said he wouldn't wear a suit, but I'm still worried I won't have the right thing to wear. I don't want to embarrass him."

She shook her head. "You could never be an embarrassment. Come over tonight. Between the three of us, we'll figure something out."

"I doubt Dee wants me rifling through her closet."

Cami waved her hand. "She won't mind at all. She'll be thrilled to help."

My heart warmed thinking of Deirdre, Cami's older sister. The two of them were family to me. Cami and I had hit it off right away when she came to Al's for coffee one day. We started talking, and that was that. We ended up at the same school a few years later, but different courses. We were in the same business classes, and helped each other get through them. We were a great team.

"Okay, I'll come over later."

She reached for another carrot. "Great."

DEE NODDED IN satisfaction. "That one, Emmy. You look great."

I studied myself in the mirror. I was wearing a brown skirt of mine, and a pretty green blouse from Dee. It was frilly and girly, and I loved it. Cami had added a thick shawl to keep me warm in tones of green and taupe. It was pretty and feminine.

"Wear your ankle boots, and put your hair up," Cami advised.

"Okay."

I slipped out of the outfit, putting my school clothes back on, minus the tie. It was safe at home in a drawer. I looked up the name of the tie maker, and Cami was right. It cost more than the rent on my apartment. I would give it back to Bentley on Friday.

I sat down, sipping the tea Dee slid in front of me.

"I put your stuff in the dryer and threw in the second load."

"Thank you."

Dee and Cami had the luxury of a small stacking washer and dryer in their apartment. The previous tenant was moving into a house and sold them at a low price. They let me use them; although, I took the big stuff like sheets and towels to the laundromat. I could sit and study while my laundry went through the cycles.

Cami took a seat, placing a bowl of grapes on the table. "They had these on special as I went through the market. I couldn't resist."

We all reached for some of the red fruit. They were crisp and sweet on my tongue and a rare treat. The budget I lived on didn't include many luxuries like grapes. Apples were my regular go-to most of the time.

"Delicious," Dee murmured.

I beamed fondly at her. She was eight years older than Cami and me, but a great deal more mature than her years. When their mother died, she had looked after Cami. Their father had walked away when Cami was still young, remarried, and never bothered with them again. When we became friends, she took me under her wing. She was a sister, a friend, and pseudo-mother to us both. She worked in a large law firm as a paralegal and was the exact opposite of Cami. They both had green eyes and similar features, but while Cami had long, dark brown hair, Dee's was a strawberry blonde color, straight, and she kept it chin-length. Cami was like the energizer bunny, never sitting still, and free-spirited, while Dee was quiet, serious, and in a constant state of worry. Cami loved designs and mixing fabrics and styles, while Dee was simple. Smart suits for work, and jeans and tees outside. But they were my family, and I loved them.

"Are you nervous?" Dee asked, studying me.

"A little. He's . . . different."

She frowned. "Different, how?"

I huffed out a breath. "He's very serious. Formal. Then suddenly he says or does something sweet or funny. It's as if he isn't sure how to act around me."

"He's extremely wealthy, and young, to have so much responsibility. Maybe he doesn't know how to act—maybe he's been too busy working to do much socially."

Cami snorted. "He dates a lot."

"What?"

She turned her laptop around so I could see the screen. I stared at the images of him with other women. Lots of other women. They were all beautiful and dressed in expensive clothes. My gaze drifted over to the outfit hanging on the back of the door I would wear to dinner on Friday.

I pushed the laptop back to Cami. "I'm in over my head here, aren't I? I should cancel and go to the gallery with you. I can't compete with his extravagant lifestyle."

Dee shot Cami a glare and patted my hand. "Maybe you're exactly what he needs. Someone real. Dating and being in a relationship are two different things."

"It's just a date," I insisted.

She smiled. "For now."

I finished my tea and left. I still had a couple more things to add before I handed in my project, and my old laptop made everything take longer, but it was all I could afford. I was scouring *Kijiji* and the internet, hoping to find a cheaper one to upgrade to, but so far, no luck.

When I got home, I hung up the outfit, grabbed a glass of water, and sat down to finish my work. The apartment felt chilly, and I pulled a blanket around my shoulders to stay warm. I worked for a while until I was satisfied, saved everything, and put it on the memory stick. I would send it tomorrow. Unable to help myself, I googled Bentley's name and looked at the same images as earlier. He was incredibly handsome, but as I studied the pictures, I noticed the same thing. His expression. Always serious, stern, and unsmiling. There were a few older ones I presumed were taken when he was in university, but even then, a smile was rare. In group pictures, he always stood a little separately, as if he were there, but not really part of them. I understood that—I rarely felt part of groups.

I thought of his words earlier. *"You make me laugh."*

Maybe he needed to laugh. Maybe what he needed wasn't glitz and glamour, but someone to make him happy.

I was surprised how much I wanted to be that person for him. Usually, I was one not to trust people very fast, but I found myself trusting him. I wanted to know more about Bentley. Not the businessman I saw in those photos, but the man who slipped his tie over my head and looked almost shy when he stepped back, pleased with his handiwork. I remembered his mischievous grin when he told me he had ditched his bodyguard to come and see me.

I glanced at my phone, picked it up, and tapped out a text.

I hoped you survived today. Was Tree Trunk very mad?

He answered immediately.

We worked it out. How was your day?

Good. I finished my project. Picked an outfit for Friday. You promised casual, right?

My heart warmed at his retort.

Casual, yes. You'll be beautiful. Why are you worried?

I sucked in a deep breath and decided to be truthful.

I might have checked the internet. You go out with a lot of beautiful, elegant women.

I was startled when my phone rang. "Hello?"

"Emmy." His deep voice greeted me. "Don't look on the internet."

"I was curious."

"Ask me anything. I'll answer you honestly. Pictures are simply that—pictures. I have a lot of friends and business associates who happen to be women. They accompany me to those God-awful dinners, so I'm not as bored. Simple. We do each other favors."

"You haven't been in relationships with any of them?"

"Not for a very long time, no."

"They all look so lovely," I admitted, letting my insecurity show.

"They aren't who I want to spend an evening with. You are."

His tone was so adamant that I knew he was telling the truth. "Okay."

"I ate my scones tonight for dinner."

"Not much of a dinner."

"I had some cheese and grapes with them."

"Oh, I had grapes, too! Cami got them on sale. They were such a treat!"

"Cami?"

"My best friend. I'll tell you about her on Friday if you want."

He chuckled. "I would like to know all about you, Emaline Harris. I look forward to discovering all your likes."

"Tree Trunk checked me out, didn't he?"

"He did."

"And I'm clean?"

"As a whistle. At least so far."

"The whole Russian spy thing hasn't shown up?"

"Not yet."

"Tell him to keep digging."

He began to laugh, and I liked the sound. It was carefree and warm.

"I'll tell him tomorrow."

"Oh, I have to give you your tie back."

"I don't want my tie. I gave it to you."

"Bentley, I looked the maker up on the net, too."

"What did I tell you? Stay off the internet when it comes to me."

"I can't accept the tie. It cost more than my rent!"

"I want you to have it. Please. Accept it. I accepted your scones."

"That's different."

"How?" he questioned. "You gave those to me freely, and I gave you my tie. Because of you, I had a thoroughly delicious dinner. You fortified me. All I did was drape a piece of cloth around your neck."

"Fortified, Rigid? Overkill—even for you."

"It's true."

"It's more than that, and you know it."

His voice became gentle, quiet. "Please, accept the tie. Keep it. Wear it and think of me."

He was too good at this. "Fine. But you don't play fair."

He sounded amused. "But I won."

I grinned into the phone, because he had. And, really, I liked the tie—it reminded me of his eyes. "Okay. I'll see you on Friday."

"It will be the best day of the week for me, Emmy." He paused. "Goodnight. Sleep well."

"Night."

CHAPTER 6

BENTLEY

I SHOULD HAVE told her what was happening in my life. It was the perfect opportunity to inform her what dating me could consist of if she chose to continue.

Yet, I couldn't because I wanted to see her again. To listen to her voice tease me, and hear her laughter. There was something so easy about being in her presence. I didn't have to be anything except *me* with her, and selfishly, I wanted more of that.

I would have to tell her on Friday. It was only fair she knew someone was keeping tabs on me, and therefore, perhaps her. Once the bid on the property was complete, I was sure whoever was behind it would disappear. They would realize I owned the far more valuable piece of land and would arrange to sell to me. I would never know who it was, but I didn't care. I would get the land, and start developing it. It would be hugely successful, and make me even richer. More importantly, it would be my mark. All of it created and designed by my company. BAM.

I grinned every time I thought of the name.

Not long after Aiden and I agreed to share a place, we met Maddox Riley. He was just seventeen, two years younger than we were, but more mature than we ever hoped to be. He was a whiz kid at Math and everything else, but he was also awkward and alone having entered university earlier than most kids did.

He was standing in front of us in line at the student union, waiting to pay for his lunch. He turned when Aiden made some complaint about the high cost of the food compared to the quality and nutritional level of the selections. Maddox was in total agreement, and began a discussion on the benefits of both healthy choices and cost efficiency, by having other options on campus. Soon after, the three of us were at a table in full planning mode. The shy boy persona fell away as Maddox talked numbers and ideas. He became animated, refusing to back down when he was certain about a fact or figure, earning him the nickname Mad Dog by Aiden.

We had been friends ever since.

Together, we'd worked with the university and a willing vendor, and set up a small grocery mart right on campus. Fresh fruits and vegetables, satisfying sandwiches, and healthy premade meals were available; easy to heat up in the microwave, and economical. Tastier in most cases, if you cooked like me. It took a lot of work, some well-placed donations on my part, but we got it started. It was still there, but bigger, and better stocked.

When we had started discussing it, sketching out ideas, listening to Maddox crunch numbers, and finally agreeing on a final plan, Aiden had jumped up, fist punched the air, and yelled, "That's how we do it! *BAM!*"

It stuck. Our initials, our ideas, our brand. My brothers.

I had named my company the same name and brought them on board with me.

There was no one in the world I trusted more than them. Our relationship, which started out as young men, had grown as we matured over the years.

Aiden and I had looked at a lot of houses, dismissing them all. However, one day, we saw a worn-down Victorian house. It was a longer walk from the school, but doable. The owner was moving into a small condo, and the place was big enough we could all live there, and not run over each other. When discussing rent, I made the owner a deal. We would do the various repairs, and he would knock it off the rent. I enjoyed fixing things, and Aiden and Maddox, who had joined in the house hunt, were willing to help. The proprietor was agreeable to my request, and the condition I added that when he was ready to sell, I got first dibs on the property.

We'd moved in the next month, lived there for two years, and I used a part of my inheritance to buy it. I moved us into the smaller place next door I'd had my eye on, and we fixed up the old house, and I flipped it, for a huge profit. I did the same with the next three houses. I quit university and started my own company. BAM Corporation became a reality, and when they graduated, Aiden and Maddox came on board.

Maddox was a brilliant numbers man and handled all the finances and planning. Aiden not only had his business degree but also became a personal trainer. He constantly took courses on computers, security, and physical training. He headed up the security area and was my right-hand man. He had a quirk that allowed him to remember details most people would forget, which often gave us an advantage. We worked extremely well as a team, and the business had made us all very wealthy.

Still, something was missing from my life. I had everything money could buy. I loved my job and the constant challenge it presented. I enjoyed the push and pull of doing deals, and creating new landscapes. I thrived on the challenge of finding the right investors for a project and watching it flourish. However, once the door shut behind me at night, I was alone. I filled in the hours with more work, and I used the gym and pool in the house daily, but aside from business dinners, I hadn't been out on a date in a long time.

My last relationship was three years ago. It ended badly. Since then, I had been on a couple of dates, but they hadn't gone overly well. I was dull, set in my ways, and at times, my temper got the best of me. It wasn't the best of combinations, and as one woman told me, no amount of money could make up for my lack of personality.

I glanced back at my phone and the texts to Emmy. She seemed to bring something else out in me. She made me want to smile and to make *her* smile. Not one given to gestures, or buying gifts, sliding a five-hundred-dollar tie around Emmy's neck had shocked me as much as it had Aiden.

It made me wonder what other things I would do to surprise myself.

FROM THE BACK seat of the car, I scowled at the staircase leading up to Emmy's apartment. Was it safe? It looked rickety to me. I scanned the deserted parking lot. The building was about average for the neighborhood. Somewhat run down, but doing well for the area. The back end faced a derelict garage, with husks of rusted cars scattered on the dead ground. There was one lone light in the corner of the parking lot, its dimness barely covering the small area. I knew Aiden would notice all the details, as well. There was no light by the stairs or over the doors of the three apartments which all faced the empty parking lot. The thought of Emmy walking to her door, at night, alone and defenseless, made me shudder.

The whole thing made me shudder.

"Show up with that look on your face, she'll slam the door on you," Aiden informed me in a quiet drawl.

"This isn't safe."

"Nothing I can do about it right this second. We'll discuss it later. After you see how your date goes."

"Shut it, Tree Trunk." I smirked. "Eyes straight ahead, and mouth on silent when we get in the car, you got me?"

Aiden chuckled from the front seat. He had insisted he come

with me, promising to remain in the background. I still thought he was overreacting, but I agreed in order to keep the peace.

He turned his massive body in the seat, meeting my gaze. "This is her home. No matter what you think, be respectful."

"I will."

"Do you want me to go get her?"

"No," I snapped. "She's not a package for you to pick up." I grasped the small bouquet of lilies I had stopped to get, and opened the door. "I'll be back."

Climbing the steps, I was anxious to see Emmy. She opened the door, taking my breath away with her simple beauty. Her skirt flared out from her knees, and the emerald-colored blouse set off her creamy complexion. She had her hair swept up, showing off the delicate column of her neck. Her multi-pierced ears glinted in the light. However, it was her expression that did it for me. Open and honest, she was as happy to see me, as I was to see her. I held out the small offering.

"You look lovely."

She took the flowers, and rewarded me with one of her soft kisses on my cheek. I resisted the urge to turn my head and feel her lips on mine. I followed her into the tiny apartment and waited while she put the flowers in water.

It was a one-room place. A futon served as a bed and couch. A minute kitchen with a waist-high fridge and the smallest stove I'd ever seen were against the opposite wall. Emmy's desk and bookcase were piled high with books, papers, and her old laptop was sitting on top of a mountain of documents. A makeshift closet and laundry baskets were in the corner. The walls were blue, and she had lots of posters and pictures on them, making it cheerful. It was chaotic and small. The entire place was smaller than my closet at my house. Still, it was clean and inviting, and when I inhaled deeply, I smiled. It smelled like her.

She placed the flowers on the small table beside her futon. She stroked the petals; the tender gesture so her, I had to smile once more. She picked up a shawl, and I hurried forward, taking it from her hands and sliding it around her shoulders.

"Will you be warm enough?"

"Yes."

"I made sure our table wasn't under an air conditioning vent."

Her eyes glistened, and she reached up to cup my cheek. "Thank you," she breathed out. "You are incredibly thoughtful." Unexpectedly, she stood on her toes and brushed her mouth against mine. As soon as our lips touched, I lost control.

I caught her around the waist, held her close, and kissed her back. Her hands slipped around my neck, teasing the hair at my nape and making me groan. Our mouths moved, and I slid my tongue along her bottom lip, sighing in pleasure when she opened for me. Our tongues glided, teased, and tasted. Her hands tightened on my hair, and I pulled her hard to my chest, liking how she fit to me. Even with the height difference, we meshed. I wanted more. More of her taste, of the way her body felt pressed to mine. However, I knew it was too soon.

Regretfully, I eased back, dropping one last kiss on her full mouth.

"Wow," she whispered. "That was unexpected. You're very passionate."

It was unexpected for me, too, but I liked it. "Should I apologize?"

"No."

"Good. Because I'm not sorry."

She beamed up at me. "Neither am I."

"Ready to go to dinner, Freddy?"

"Lead the way, Rigid."

I stepped back, discreetly adjusting myself as she turned to reach for her purse. Rigid was the right name for me at the moment. This woman affected me in many ways.

I saw her hand hover over the straps of her old rucksack, and I frowned.

"Are you planning to study tonight?"

"Um, no. I just . . . I usually take this with me when I go out."

It seemed an odd thing to carry on a date, but she seemed upset at the thought of not taking it with her, which made me wonder what was inside. "We can leave it in the car if that helps. Aiden and Frank will keep it safe."

She hesitated, and I leaned over, picking up the sack. It wasn't heavy, yet somehow, I knew it was important to her to keep it close.

"Thank you." She offered me a smile. "I'm ready."

I held out my hand. "Off we go, then."

I TOOK HER to one of my favorite restaurants. Small, quiet, and tucked away in the neighborhood where Aiden, Maddox, and I had shared our first house. The same family still ran it, the food was delicious, the wine list surprisingly good, and best of all, as I promised, low key and comfortable.

Emmy had chatted with us all in the car, her polite, sweet nature infectious. I enjoyed listening to her talk. She was engaging and smart, making us all laugh at her wit.

Mama Leona greeted us at the door, and after many kisses and exclamations over my "pretty date," tucked us into the back booth. It was private and cozy. Frank was outside in the car, and I knew Aiden was in the kitchen, filling his face while keeping an eye on everything.

Once we were seated, Emmy leaned close, indicating Aiden, who was peering at us from the doorway to the kitchen, trying to look inconspicuous. "Does he go with you everywhere?"

I nodded, winking covertly at her. "He's like a fungus I can't get rid of."

"Are you in danger?"

She was too smart.

"Aiden is cautious. He takes his job seriously."

She pursed her lips and nodded. "Good."

Her easy agreement warmed my chest. It was odd to have someone else, aside from a select few, worry about me.

"You've known him a long time?"

I told her the story of how we met. She laughed over my descriptions of the three of us living together, trying to mesh our personalities. "Thank God for Sandy. She sorted us out."

"Sandy?"

"She lived behind us. She saw what a mess we were, and came over one day to help. We were trying to figure out how to use the washing machine and arguing so loud she heard us." I laughed at the memory. "Two days later, she became our housekeeper/den mother. She ran our lives for us, and when I opened BAM, I hired her right away. The woman is a wonder."

I changed the subject. "Do you enjoy your classes?"

"I love them."

"Did you make a career change and go back to school?"

She shook her head, amused at my awkward question.

"Most people are out of school and working at your age, so I thought perhaps . . ."

She took a sip of her wine. "I always loved graphic design and took some courses. I even got a job as an intern with a big company, but it didn't go anywhere. They did offer me a job, but it was low pay, and mostly the grunt work. It didn't take long for me to see I would never get anywhere unless I had more in-depth training and experience. I needed a degree in my field to get ahead. I did some research—I wanted to go to Toronto Design School, except they're expensive. I had to work and save for a few years to be able to afford to go."

I nodded for her to continue.

"The courses I take are not only for design and graphics work, but business plans, marketing, accounting—everything I need to know about how to run my own business, and how to handle multi-layered projects. There's as much textbook work as there is design."

"How long is the course?"

"It's a four-year course. I'll be done in three and a half. I take extra classes in the summer and carry a full course load."

"And work."

She shrugged. "Just one job now at Al's. I worked several while saving up for school so I could get by with the one now. I knew I would have to devote myself to school completely. It's not forever, and I stick to my budget. When I'm done, and get some real experience, I want to run my own company."

I studied her, instinctively knowing once she had made up her mind, she went for it. "What are your marks like?'

She glanced down, looking self-conscious. "Top of my class."

I knew it. I had a feeling she was extremely bright.

"Don't be shy, Emmy. You should be proud."

Her lips curved upward, cheeks flushing a delicate pink. "I don't like to brag."

I squeezed her hand. "It's not bragging. I asked."

It was her turn to change the subject. "You left school before you graduated?"

I arched my eyebrow. "*Google* again, Emmy?"

She lifted her shoulder. "Actually, my friend Cami told me after she checked you out."

"It's fine. Yes, once I started flipping houses, and realized I wanted to keep investing in the property market, I decided to move ahead. I hadn't been enjoying my classes. To be honest, I was bored all the time. I felt I'd learn more doing it on my own." I picked up my wine. "I was correct."

"You hired your friends?"

"There is no one I trust more. Maddox handles the finances, and Aiden is my right-hand. He's brilliant." I tapped my head. "A memory like no one I have ever known."

"And protects you," she added, a trace of worry in her voice.

I sat back, studying her. "Emmy, I need to tell you something."

"Wow, I didn't even make it to dessert. And the lemon sponge cake I saw go by, looked amazing."

I slipped my fingers under her chin and studied her sweet face. She was incredibly pretty. I brushed a kiss to her cheek. "If you want dessert once you hear what I have to say, it's yours. Anything you want is yours."

She leaned closer, her voice low. "Anything?"

I swallowed, my body reacting to her closeness. "Yes."

"I want your last ravioli."

Her demand was amusing, and I speared my last bite of appetizer, feeding it to her. "You drive a hard bargain."

"You know it, Rigid." She picked up her wine. "Now talk."

I waited until the server took our plates away, and refilled the glasses. I knew the entrees would take a bit longer since they made everything by hand and to order. There was plenty of time for her to leave if she decided, but I hoped she wouldn't go. I was more comfortable with her than anyone I had ever met, aside from Aiden and Maddox.

Except I never wanted to kiss them.

"I'm wealthy, Emmy. It's not a secret. People like me are always targets for some weirdos. I get jibes, threats, and demands for my money all the time. Ninety-nine percent of them are harmless."

"But?"

I sighed, running a hand along the back of my neck. "I'm working on a huge project—one that could potentially bring me millions. I have competition, and lately, it's become a little personal."

"How so?"

"Someone is bidding on the same parcels of property I am. I've gotten some threatening letters, and the last couple included pictures of me." I swallowed before continuing. "One of them was taken the day I met you."

"Was I in the picture?"

"You were in the background, walking away. The picture focused on me," I stressed.

"Did my ass look fat?" she asked, her expression mischievous.

I gaped at her, then began to laugh. I didn't know how I expected her to react, but that wasn't it. She was amazing.

"Your, ah, *ass,* looked spectacular."

She patted my hand. "Good answer." She grew serious. "Aiden is worried?"

"He's wary. The pictures bother him."

"I don't blame him. They would bother me, too." She frowned. "Are you in danger?"

"I don't think so. I think they're trying to piss me off enough, so I'll walk away. I'm not known for my patience," I added with a wry grin. "The two small pieces of land I wanted were bought by whoever is behind this, I think, and I have a feeling they'll go after the next parcel, too."

"What happens if they do?"

"Then I'll have to pay more to buy them back or sell the pieces I have purchased and walk away. It all comes down to numbers."

"I see. You don't plan to walk away, I assume?"

"No. I've invested a lot of time and money in this project."

"So, it's about the money?"

"Partially. It's my mark. My legacy; an entire development that will benefit the city, and change the landscape of the area. All done by BAM."

"And make you richer."

"Yes," I admitted. "There is that."

"I guess money is a good thing."

"It doesn't entirely suck," I agreed, and drew in a deep breath. "I can understand if you would rather not take the risk. They might, ah, bother you, as well."

"You mean, like, take my picture? Or talk to me?"

"I don't know really, but I don't want you to be worried, or feel unsafe."

She pondered my words, then shrugged. "I appreciate you telling me, but I don't think I have much to worry about."

"Aiden is right; it's a possibility you have to consider. We *both* have to consider."

"Maybe it's too late. Maybe they already got to me, and I'm working for them."

My lips quirked at her words. "Are you?"

She sniffed. "As if I'm going to break so easily. I'm an expert undercover agent, you know. I arranged the whole trip over the bag and sit at my table thing."

"And I fell for it—hook, line, and sinker."

"You *fell* for it? Rigid, I'm certain you just made a joke."

I arched my eyebrow. "Maybe."

She surprised me with a quick kiss, which made me want another one.

"I like it." She hummed. "You're adorable when you're being funny."

That was a new one. I had never been called adorable.

"Are you sure?" I asked.

"Bentley, if someone approached me, I would walk away. If I were scared, I would tell you. I'm not interested in your business deals."

"They may even offer you a lot of money."

"Then, I guess you'll have to counter their proposal, won't you?" she teased. "I can be bought with fresh grapes, and Starbuck cards, just to give you a heads up."

I shook my head at her quips. "You should think about this. Seriously think about it."

At my words, she held up her hands. "Are you trying to scare me away?"

"No, I'm trying to be honest."

"And you have been. I'm touched you're worried about someone bothering me, but I think this time you're the one overreacting. I'm an art student, not a businesswoman. They'd have to be pretty stupid to think I would have any sort of influence on you. Tonight is our first date, after all."

"I know."

"I doubt they think some woman you might potentially fuck has any say in your business dealings."

Her words hit me. My cock stirred at her unwittingly sexy remark. I edged closer.

"*Potentially* fuck?" My voice was low as I repeated her words.

"If you play your cards right. Maybe."

"I'm good at poker."

Her giggle broke the bubble. "Another quip, Rigid? *Poke her?* You're just full of surprises tonight."

I shared her mirth. She brought the silliness out in me—even if it was unknowingly.

I conceded to her logic. "Maybe I'm overreacting, but I had to tell you."

"Consider me warned."

"I never let personal feelings interfere with business—ever, by the way."

"Then, there isn't a problem."

"If anyone hassles you, you'll tell me? I'll get Aiden to assign someone to you."

She looked horrified. "I don't want a bodyguard."

"You'll tell me if someone bothers you, though?"

She pursed her lips, not replying.

"Shit," I muttered. "Great first date conversation. Guess I blew that."

Her hand slipped into mine, and I met her dark gaze.

"Thank you for being honest and giving me a choice. I don't want to stop seeing you, and I don't scare easily. If you aren't worried about it, then neither am I." She smiled. "As for first dates, it's a great one, conversation or not."

"Yeah?"

"Yeah. I think we can move on now, though, okay?"

I lifted her hand and kissed her knuckles.

"Yes."

CHAPTER 7

BENTLEY

WE LEFT THE restaurant after a thoroughly enjoyable evening. I put aside my worries and concentrated on Emmy. She was as delightful and engaging as I hoped she would be, making me laugh and enjoy the time with her. She loved to talk about art and her studies and had a keen interest in architecture. She liked to stroll around the many museums and galleries Toronto had to offer. She told me of her love for baking and how much she enjoyed trying out new recipes; although, she admitted, these days her time and budget didn't allow for much of either.

After the whole security issue, we steered clear of anything too deep or personal. I knew her parents were deceased, and she had a brother she wasn't close to, but I didn't push her for that story. I told her my parents were gone too, but I had no siblings. Otherwise, we kept the topics general.

She made me chuckle with her stories of her best friend, Cami, and her sister, Dee. Obviously, she was close to them. I shared more humorous incidents about Aiden and Maddox.

"I think Cami has a crush on Aiden," she told me with a grin.

"How could she? She never met him!"

"She has a thing for muscled guys with tattoos. He was in some of the pictures we saw of you, and I told her about him."

"Aiden doesn't do the personal thing. He's rather closed off when it comes to relationships."

"Like you?"

I thought about it. *"The three of us are close, but I guess you're right. None of us has much outside our lives except the business and each other. I think we're all loners."*

"That's sad."

I shrugged. *"I don't think it bothers any of us."* I huffed out a long breath of air. *"At least until now."*

Emmy's cheeks pinked under my gaze, and unable to resist, I ran my finger along the curve of her face. *"I'd like to try and step out of my comfort zone."*

"Okay," she whispered.

I held her hand as we walked out, then I groaned at the sight of Aiden leaning against the car, talking to Maddox.

What the fuck was he doing here?

I glared at him as we approached. *"Maddox?"* My annoyance was clear in the one word.

As usual, my mood didn't bother him. It never did. He grinned at me, his glasses reflecting his light-colored blue eyes. They were shrewd and sharp, rarely missing anything. He was tall and lean, his clothes hiding the fact underneath, he was all muscle. To most people, he was quiet and laid back. His aura hid the intensity he allowed few to see. It gave him an advantage. What people saw as easy going was his brain ticking and moving faster than they could understand. He preferred numbers to people—they made sense, and he could keep them in order. Maddox liked order. He had gone prematurely gray at twenty-five, and could never be bothered to do anything about it.

Now the gray had tinges of silver, and the scruff he preferred on his jawline was the same color.

He tipped his chin. "Hey, Bent."

"What are you doing here?"

"I followed you here. Been keeping Frank company and enjoying some food Aiden brought us."

"*What*? You followed me? What the hell for?"

"Aiden wanted to see if anyone else followed *you*, so I tailed behind to check for him." He smirked. "I must be good at it since you never noticed."

Aiden clapped his shoulder. "Excellent stealth, Mad Dog."

"And?" I demanded, ignoring their teasing remarks.

"You're good. All clear."

Emmy began warbling a familiar soundtrack. The sound made us all look at her.

"It's like *Mission Impossible*," she crowed. "So exciting!" She stepped forward, holding out her hand. "All of you suck at this, by the way. No wonder you're all single. I'm Emmy."

Maddox snickered, took her hand, bending low over it, and kissed her knuckles. "Happy to meet you, Emmy."

"Oh, another charmer!"

I wrapped my arm around her waist and pulled her close with another glare at Maddox. "You can go home now."

"But I'm having a good time."

I rolled my eyes, knowing my annoyance meant he was enjoying himself. Then, I had another idea. "So, no one followed us?"

"Nope."

"Give me your keys."

"Why?" he asked, as Aiden began to shake his head.

"I'm taking your car and Emmy and I are leaving. You go with Aiden."

"Not a good idea," Aiden growled.

I turned to him and spoke in a hushed voice. "No one is following. I want some time alone to say goodnight to my *date*."

His eyebrows rose, and he nodded in understanding. "I'm driving ahead and checking it out. I won't be far away."

"Just give me some privacy."

"I don't like this, Bent."

"I don't care."

"Stubborn bastard."

Emmy spoke up. "Tree Trunk, he wants to kiss me without you watching. If anyone comes at us, I know karate."

We all gaped at her. Maddox started to guffaw and turned away to hide his amusement.

Aiden looked at her. "What color belt do you have?"

She blinked at him. "Okay, I'm totally bullshitting you. I have no idea, but I can yell loudly, and I think Bentley can handle himself. Frankly, I want to kiss him, too."

It was Aiden's turn to blink. Maddox pressed his keys into my hand and winked. "Good luck with this one. She's a firecracker." He pulled on Aiden's arm. "Let's go."

I grabbed Emmy's rucksack for her. They piled into the car, turning to watch while I held open the door for Emmy and helped her with the seatbelt. As I bent in, she grinned up at me.

"You better make this kiss worthwhile," she teased. "I went against the hulk for you."

I lowered my face to hers, feeling her breath on my skin. "It will be. I promise."

"I'm counting on it. Take me home, Rigid."

I slammed her door and hurried to the driver's side. Suddenly, her tiny apartment held great appeal.

I WAS A perfect gentleman until Emmy opened her door, and I followed her inside. She had left one lamp on, its glow casting a dim radiance on the room. For a moment, we stared at each other, then like mirror images, crashed together. I gripped her waist as she wrapped her arms around my neck. Our mouths met with a bruising ferociousness that startled and exhilarated me. There was no reticence in Emmy's response—she gave as good as she got. I groaned low in my chest as her tongue touched mine—stroking, tasting, and exploring. Her blunt nails scraped the skin on my nape, making me hiss in pleasure. I traced her curves, feeling the delicate bumps and ridges of her spine, then settled my hands on her truly spectacular ass. I cupped the roundness greedily, and pulled her tight to my body, so she had no doubt what she was doing to me.

She whimpered, letting me lift her so her legs could wrap around my hips, her skirt trailing on the floor. Turning, I pressed her into the wall, trapping her close as I explored her mouth. I dragged my lips down her cheek, murmuring her name, discovering the softness of her neck, swirling my tongue on her fragrant skin. It had been beckoning me all night.

"Bentley," she groaned. "You . . . I . . ."

I dropped my face to her shoulder, breathing hard. What was this girl doing to me? I wanted her. I wanted to carry her over to the little futon and fuck her. Drive her deep into the mattress until she cried out my name. Feel the heat that radiated through her skirt encase my cock, until I came inside her in a blaze of intensity.

Except, it was too fast.

Gently, I set her on her feet, kissed her cheeks, the end of her nose, and forehead with soft presses of my mouth. "You're amazing," I murmured.

She looked at me, her eyes wide and dark with desire. Her lips were swollen from mine, and I had messed up her hair, so it tumbled down one shoulder. I liked how she looked.

I traced the edges of her mouth. "Did I make it worthwhile?"

An indulgent, lazy smile curled her lips. "Pretty much."

"Not a stellar recommendation."

"Maybe you need to try again. Redouble your efforts."

I crashed my mouth to hers, yanking her hard to my chest. Wrapping her hair in my hand, I tilted her head and kissed her, controlling every movement, commanding her mouth. She melted into me, succumbing in the most erotic of ways, following my lead and matching my passion.

With a groan, I dragged my mouth to her ear. "I have to stop, or I won't be able to."

"Maybe I don't want you to."

I stood straight, meeting her gaze. It was open, honest, and steady.

"We don't have to rush. I'm not going anywhere."

A shadow crossed her face, but she nodded and stepped back. I felt the shift in her, a small wall coming back between us at my simple words.

"Hey," I said. "Emmy, what is it?"

She smiled, although it didn't reach her eyes. "Nothing. Really."

I let it go. We could revisit it at another time. However, it was imperative I see her again.

"Sunday."

"I'm sorry?"

"Sunday. Brunch," I stated. "Aiden will pick you up at eleven."

Her eyebrow rose slowly in question. I waited for her response, then realized my mistake.

"I apologize. I did it again, didn't I?"

She nodded, looking amused and exasperated.

"Emmy, would you have brunch with me on Sunday?"

"As tempting as the kind offer is, I have to refuse."

My shoulders sagged, as disappointment flooded my body. "Why? Was the date that lousy? I promise not to talk about anything work-related."

"No," she assured me, cupping my cheek. "The date was amazing. Sunday, though, I'm having brunch with Dee and Cami."

"They get you all the time."

She chuckled at my petulance. "It's an important day for them. I promised."

"Important? How?"

"It just is."

"I was going to make you coddled eggs."

"What is that?"

"An old English thing. My father used to make them for my mother when I was young. Sandy grew up eating them and taught me how to make them correctly. They are one thing I can cook that is edible. Trust me; they're worth blowing off your friends for."

"Maybe next week?"

"What is so important?" I pushed. I really wanted to see her again. "Couldn't they wait until next week?"

She sighed. "You are impatient at times, aren't you?"

"When I want something, yes."

"It's my birthday on Tuesday. They take me to brunch the Sunday before—it's our tradition."

AIDEN SHOOK HIS head. "Bad idea."

"Why?"

"You've had one date with her, and you want to buy her a three-thousand-dollar laptop for her birthday?"

I shrugged. "I buy shit like this all the time."

"For yourself. You're used to it. It's too much."

I stared at the screen. It was the perfect laptop for Emmy. Small, light, easy for her to carry, and it was loaded with every feature she would need. She had told me about her studies for graphic design, and how she often used the computers at school since hers was so old. It would make her life easier, and her rucksack lighter. Surely, she would appreciate the gesture.

I had been surprised when she told me it was her birthday. Aiden hadn't mentioned it, and I hadn't thought to ask him the date when we talked. I could understand she wanted to see her friends for their usual get together, but I also wanted to celebrate her birthday with her. Finally, she agreed to have dinner with me on Tuesday, and once again, I promised her a comfortable place.

Then, feeling uncharacteristically excited, I started to plan.

I glanced back at the screen and hit purchase. Maybe I couldn't give it to her immediately, but if my plans held true, she'd be at my place, and she could borrow the laptop. I could figure out a way of gifting it to her at another time. I waited until the confirmation came through, and I shut the laptop.

"What should I get her?"

He shrugged. "How would I know?"

"You emphatically tell me I can't give her a laptop, but have no suggestions what would be appropriate?"

"Flowers?"

I waved my hand. "Cliché."

"Perfume?"

"She doesn't wear perfume." I knew that because I had asked her what fragrance she wore since her scent was intoxicating. She told me she wore a body lotion she had made at a small place that specialized in combining unique fragrances. She wore a blend of honey and lilac that smelled incredible on her skin.

"Dee worked there years ago, and gets a discount. She gives me a bottle every year for Christmas. I make it last."

I could buy her a couple of bottles of the lotion, so she didn't have to stretch it out, if I could find out the name of the shop, but that seemed too easy.

"Women like jewelry," Maddox mused, as he strolled in.

"What are you doing here?"

He grinned, throwing himself on the sofa. "Aiden called and said you were going overboard on a birthday gift for Emmy and I had to come help rein you in."

"Like jewelry isn't over the top?" I said in a snarky tone of voice. The laptop was a better idea.

"I'm not saying buy her diamonds, but what about something useful like a watch."

Aiden shook his head. "Girls don't wear watches anymore. They use their cellphones."

"A bracelet? I think they like those leather bands. Sandy wears one with a bunch of charms. Panda something? Ask her."

I groaned. "Neither of you are helpful."

Maddox met my gaze. "None of us have much experience with this sort of thing."

I huffed out a long blast of air, then sat up as I thought of an idea. "Wait. Emmy told me Cami works at some fashion store. She said she was meeting her today after work. If I could figure out what the store was, I could go and ask her for ideas. She's her best friend. I bet she could help."

"She didn't say the name?"

I racked my brain. "Glad something?"

Aiden tapped away on his phone. "Glad Rags?"

"Yes!"

Maddox stood. "Okay. Road trip—I call shotgun!"

Aiden flexed his muscles. "Look out Cami, here we come."

Groaning, I grabbed my jacket, and followed them out of the room. Perhaps, I should have done the shopping on my own.

Or better yet, went with the laptop idea.

Entering the store, I knew I was right. The laptop would have been much simpler. There were racks of clothes, displays of lingerie, and shelves of accessories. I could smell perfumes and lotions. Plus, there were women.

Everywhere.

They were all staring at us—the only men in the place. "Umm . . . whose idea was this?"

Maddox and Aiden spoke in unison. "Yours."

I raked a hand through my hair. "Shit. We should have just called."

Aiden rolled his shoulders. "Too late, Romeo. Okay, we need a plan."

"Find this Cami, ask the question, and get the fuck out of Dodge," Maddox muttered. "Let's divide and conquer."

"No, safety in numbers," I replied.

We moved forward. I was determined to find the manager, ask

for Cami, and be done. We headed toward the counter, and I made a beeline for an older woman, thinking she'd be the safest bet. Except when she looked up, her frank appraisal made me hesitate. When she licked her lips, I felt Maddox's yank on my arm.

"Abort, abort," he hissed. "Cougar."

Like a well-oiled machine, we veered to the right, stopping in front of a pretty brunette with purple streaks at the ends of her hair, sparkling green eyes, and who looked amused.

Desperate, I gasped out the one word I could think of. "Cami?" I asked, hoping she could direct me to her.

"Yes?"

"You know her?"

"I *am* her." She smirked. "Bentley."

"You know who I am?"

"I do."

Aiden pushed himself between us. "How?" he demanded.

Cami rolled her eyes, appraising him. Her gaze took in his form in a long, slow pass. He was casual today, his preferred rugged jeans, and tight T-Shirt showing off his muscles and ink. Her stare was open and frank, and even I felt the heat of her gaze. Aiden stood taller, his shoulders flexing under her scrutiny.

"Relax, Tree Trunk. My source is safe."

I grinned at her use of Emmy's nickname. Aiden grunted.

"Nice tattoos. They mean something?"

"Yes," he snapped.

"Want to share?"

He crossed his arms over his massive chest and glared. "Not today."

I was fascinated watching them. I had never seen Aiden so defensive with a woman. She wasn't the least put out by his tone. If anything, it made her bolder.

She shrugged. "You can save it for another time then, perhaps when we're alone. I look forward to your explanation."

His only reply was another huff.

"What are you doing here?" she asked me, even though she was still looking at Aiden.

"Emmy's birthday. I need a gift."

"Do you always travel in a pack?"

"Pardon me?"

She met my gaze, her eyes dancing, and she played with a purple-colored curl. "Does it take three men to choose a gift?"

"Ah, well . . ."

"We're headed to the gym after we're done here. We thought we'd take care of this first," Maddox explained smoothly. It was a great cover.

"Right."

Her tone told me she didn't buy it. I cleared my throat.

"I bought her something, but I was told it was inappropriate."

She tore her gaze away from Aiden. I was surprised to see the splash of color on his cheeks and the intense expression on his face. I had never seen him look that way with a woman. I glanced between them. Was he attracted to her or annoyed? I couldn't decide.

Cami's voice interrupted my thoughts.

"What did you get her? Some sort of racy lingerie?"

"Of course not!" I sputtered. "I bought her a laptop."

"A laptop?"

"Hers is old. I thought I would replace it with something more functional."

"Who told you it was inappropriate?"

I indicated Aiden, hopeful she would berate him about his opinion, tell me it was a great gift, and we could get the hell out of the store. I could feel all the attention we were attracting, and I didn't like it.

"At least one of you has some sense."

Damnit.

"Well, since it appears I have been outvoted, I thought perhaps you could advise me."

She bit her lip, trying not to show her amusement. "Emmy's right. You are a bit overstuffed. So formal."

Aiden's lips twitched, and Maddox glanced away to hide his amusement. I ignored her overstuffed comment. "Can you help?"

"You want me to pick something?"

I was going to say yes, just to get it over with, but I changed my mind. "No, perhaps you could help me choose? Point me in the right direction?"

"Do you have any ideas at all?"

I had nothing. I was about to admit that when my eye caught the flutter of something behind her. A scarf moved in the breeze of the air conditioning, and I had an epiphany.

"She's always cold. I noticed she wore a pretty shawl last night. Maybe she could use another one—something light and warm?"

Cami's face changed from uncertain to happy. She beamed at me—there was no other way to describe the way she smiled. Laying her hand on my arm, she nodded. "Perfect. Come with me."

She led me to a display, Aiden and Maddox following behind. "These are cashmere and silk," she explained. "Light, warm, and so luxurious. Emmy looks at them every time she comes in."

"Why doesn't she have one?"

Cami turned over the price tag. "They're $450.00. Even with my discount, she couldn't afford one," she spoke softly. "Neither can I."

I lifted the end of one, feeling the silkiness of the weave. "This will keep her warm?"

"Beautifully so. Yes."

I lowered my head. "Will it offend her if I get her one?" I asked quietly.

Her bright eyes softened. "No, I don't think so. She'll be overwhelmed with any gift, but I know she'll love it."

"Which color?"

"She'd get most use of the black, probably."

"I don't want to give her what she needs. I want to give her something she wants."

I could feel Aiden and Maddox staring at me.

"Blue is her favorite color."

I nodded because it was beautiful and the one I kept looking at due to its intense color. Bright and bold, it reminded me of the tie I gave her. I liked how the blue looked on her.

"She'd like the blue one; although, she would wear the black more."

"I want both."

Her eyes widened.

"I won't tell her where I got them."

She giggled, shaking her head. "You are too cute, aren't you? She'll know, Bentley. Trust me."

"I'll tell her they were on sale."

"Like a BOGO!" Aiden piped up.

"A BOGO?" I asked.

"Buy one get one," he explained. "It's common sales terminology."

"Thanks," I stated dryly.

Maddox arched his eyebrow, peering over his glasses at Aiden.

"What?" he snapped.

"Just impressed with your shopping lingo." Maddox grinned. "And I was checking to see if your vag was showing."

"Fuck you, Mad Dog," Aiden growled, grabbing his crotch. "I'll show you my vag, asshole. All nine inches of titanium."

Maddox burst out laughing.

I rolled my eyes, even though I was used to them. Glancing at Cami, I mouthed, "Sorry."

She shook her head and chuckled. Although, I noticed her gaze lingered on Aiden's crotch a few seconds too long.

"You guys are funny." She turned to me. "You really want both of them?"

"Yes."

"Okay." She agreed happily. "I'll get those from the stock at the back. Would you like them wrapped?"

"Yes, please," I responded, relieved. "I'll give them to her on Tuesday. We're having dinner."

"Okay."

I had an idea. "Would you and your sister like to join us?"

She hesitated with a frown. "We wouldn't want to intrude."

"No, Aiden and Maddox are coming, too. Birthdays are meant to be celebrated, right?"

She studied me. "Have you discussed this with Emmy yet?"

"Ah, no. I wanted to surprise her."

"Surprised everyone, I think," Maddox mumbled.

"Where?" she asked.

Aiden spoke up. "The Taquito on Smythe."

I shot him a glance. Mexican was his favorite, and he could eat vast amounts of it. He met my gaze steadily, challenging me to refuse, but knowing I couldn't. I roped them into this, so he was picking the restaurant.

"You like Mexican?" Cami squealed. "That's one of Emmy's favorites!"

I gave in. If Emmy liked it, I was okay with it.

"So, you'll come?"

It was a spur of the moment idea, but I realized a good one. I could see Emmy, get to know her friends, and celebrate her birthday. I knew, without a doubt, it was important for Cami and Dee to like me. Emmy could get to know Aiden and Maddox more, and I had a feeling Cami would enjoy getting to know Aiden. The thought of watching the two of them spar amused me. Maddox would come along because we were there, plus the added bonus of beer and tacos.

"Yes. We'll come. What time?"

I handed her my phone. "Why don't you give me your number and I'll text you the information? I can have you picked up, so you don't have to worry about driving."

She grinned as she took my phone. "Make it a big, fancy car, and you have yourself a deal."

I laughed at her honest bluntness. I was surprised I didn't find it offensive. In fact, it was somewhat charming.

"Done."

CHAPTER 8

BENTLEY

EMMY AND I had texted and spoken on the phone several times over the weekend and Monday. I liked hearing her voice and enjoyed the amusing stories she shared about her days. My stories were definitely less entertaining, yet she listened to them, and I found I wanted to share with her. It was the first time, in many years, I could recall the desire to talk to someone outside my small circle. Somehow, my day didn't seem complete now without hearing her voice or at least getting one of her funny text messages, silly emoji included.

I had told her Tuesday's dinner would be casual, and there was no need to get dressed up. I explained I would pick her up after a meeting I had to attend ended. I casually mentioned the location, and when she told me it was right around the corner from Cami's, where she would be studying, I suggested picking her up there, to save time.

Cami and Dee helped keep the evening a surprise. We arrived in a huge limo I had Frank arrange. Emmy's eyes were large when she came outside and saw the car. They grew bigger when Cami and Dee came out and slid into the limo first.

I bent down to meet Emmy's confused gaze. "I thought you'd like to share the evening with your friends, as well."

She beamed up at me, stretching on her toes to press a hard kiss to my mouth. I caught her around the waist, pulled her tight to me, and dropped another kiss onto her waiting lips.

Even casual, she was lovely. Her hair fell in a heavy wave of golden wheat down her back, and I itched to feel its softness under my fingers again. She wore dark pants and a long-sleeved sweater in a pale pink tone. She had on a scarf of a deeper hue draped around her shoulders. She carried a large bag, and I knew without looking, it contained her small rucksack. From what she had said on our date, she never went anywhere without it.

"Hey, we're starving!" yelled Maddox, pounding on the roof. "Keep the PDA for later!"

She smiled against my mouth. "Maddox is here?"

"Aiden, too."

"You just made Cami's week."

I slipped my fingers under her chin and met her gaze. "I'm hoping I made yours, to be honest."

She grinned as she listened to the pop of the cork from the champagne I had waiting and the merriment inside the car. She kissed me again before sliding into the limo. "You already did."

I GLANCED AROUND the table, inwardly shaking my head. If someone had told me a week ago, I'd be sitting in a Mexican restaurant, wearing a sombrero Aiden insisted we all wear as part of the birthday celebrations, drinking Margaritas, kissing a beautiful girl, and enjoying myself, I would have told them they were crazy.

Yet, there I was.

Emmy's friends were hard to resist. The three of them were so different in appearance and personalities, yet there was a common bond between them. Emmy was quietly pretty with her bohemian style, while Cami's looks were more flamboyant with her darker color and bright highlights. Dee was sedate and classy; her look polished and professional. Cami was droll, her wit and sarcasm equal to Emmy's. Listening to the two of them was like a ping-pong match, and at times, my sides hurt from laughing so hard. I couldn't remember feeling that carefree. Dee was quieter, and obviously the mother figure, but she held her own. The affection they had for Emmy was unmistakable, and she clearly felt the same. They were to her what Maddox and Aiden were to me: family.

Aiden was mesmerized, caught in Cami's spell. Somehow, when we sat down, we ended up like couples, and that was how the evening progressed. Maddox and Dee seemed to have hit it off; their heads often bowed toward each other as they conversed. She was older than he was, but as Emmy mentioned, only by three years. Maddox was always the most mature of us, and they seemed to bond together.

Something about those three women seemed to draw us all out of ourselves. It was as if they breathed life into our little bubble, expanding it with their joy. The laughter was constant, the teasing never-ending, and the jokes grew worse as the tequila flowed. Emmy and I started sipping water about halfway through dinner, but the rest of them carried on. Luckily, no one was losing control—or at least, they hadn't yet.

When the birthday cake arrived, we all sang happy birthday. Emmy's eyes filled with tears she blinked away before blowing out her candles. Cami had told me Emmy's favorite cake was vanilla with white frosting, and she loved flowers decorating the top, so that was exactly what she got. After the cake, a small pile of presents appeared, and once again, I watched Emmy struggle to hide her emotions. Cami and Dee gave her a book of homemade vouchers for things she loved. Aiden and Maddox each got her a gift certificate for a different store. I held my breath as she opened her shawl. I'd had Cami wrap each one separately, and I planned to give her the other one when we were alone.

She fingered the rich weave of the black shawl, not saying anything. I swallowed nervously, looking toward Cami.

Had I made a mistake?

She shook her head, biting her lip as she watched Emmy.

"You can exchange it," I assured her. "Pick something you like."

Her eyes met mine, glossy and radiant. "There isn't anything I could pick I would like better."

"Yeah?"

"Why did you buy this for me?"

"Because it's beautiful and warm. Like you."

She flung her arms around my neck, a quiet sob escaping her lips. "Thank you."

I looked up and met the stares of Cami and Dee. They smiled and nodded their approval.

I stood and shook out the shawl, draping it around her shoulders after she shrugged off the scarf she was wearing. It settled like a cloud around her, wrapping her in softness. She ran her fingers over the plush wool, then reached for me. I sat and wrapped my arms around Emmy, feeling the warmth of the shawl, but even more importantly the warmth of *her* as she burrowed close. Everything and everyone else faded away, and all that mattered at that moment was her—*us*.

"Happy birthday, Emmy."

WE WAITED FOR the limo, still laughing and enjoying the night. I leaned close to Emmy's ear. "Come home with me? Please?"

She looked at me, nervous.

"I want a little alone time with you. I'll make sure you get home safely later."

"Okay."

I moved closer to Aiden. "Drop Emmy and me off at my place first, then make sure the girls get home safe?"

He nodded. "Done."

"Thanks."

A short ride later, we exited the car. I knew Aiden wouldn't leave until we were inside, so I escorted Emmy up the stairs and punched in my code. Once the door shut behind us, the car pulled away.

"What if there had been a Ninja waiting?"

"Then I guess your karate skills would have come in handy."

She chuckled, followed me into the hall, and waited as I pushed the elevator button.

"How big is this place?"

"Four stories. I live on the top three."

"What's down here?"

"My houseman's apartment, the garage, and some office and storage space."

She shook her head. "Houseman—like a butler?"

I chuckled. "Far less formal. He is very low key, but he keeps me and this place in order."

"Only you, Bentley."

We stepped into the main living area. I observed her reactions as she walked around. She seemed overwhelmed. "This floor has the living room, kitchen, my den, and the gym. Upstairs are the bedrooms."

"And the fourth floor?"

I shrugged. "A theater room, a few empty spaces, plus the sunroom, and pool on the back half."

"You have a pool?"

"A small one."

She snorted as she looked around. "I bet your bathroom is bigger than my entire apartment."

It was too much for her to take in, and I wanted to distract her. I crossed the room, stopping in front of her. "Do you want to compare square footage or get to the real reason I brought you here?"

"Which was?"

I slid my hand around the back of her neck, tugging her close. "I haven't kissed you properly since Friday. It's been too long."

"You kissed me at least four times tonight."

"Not like this."

Our mouths melded together, obliterating any more coherent thoughts. I kissed her with all the pent-up energy I had felt since Friday night. Her texts and voicemails weren't enough, and her sitting beside me all evening didn't ease my tension. The brief kisses we had shared only ramped up my desire for her.

I didn't understand it, and I didn't care.

I wrapped her hair in my hands, pulling her close. I stroked her tongue and explored her mouth, our breath mingling. Her essence was erotic; her mouth hot, wet, and sweet. She tasted like silk and sin. All I could think about was how she would taste everywhere. How much I wanted her under me. I wanted to hear her cry out my name as I pleasured her with my tongue, my fingers, and my cock. I dropped my arm, gripping her hip, and grinding myself into her. She moaned low in her chest, fisting my shirt so tight, I felt the material begin to give on my shoulders. I pulled up the fabric of her sweater, spreading my hand across the expanse of her back, stroking the soft skin. She whimpered, pressing closer.

I knew one more minute, one more sweep of her tongue on mine and I was going to push her to the sofa and have her naked in a flash.

With a frustrated groan, I stepped back, gasping.

She stared at me, confused.

"Bentley?"

I bent forward, clutching my knees, breathing hard. "Fuck me."

"Why did you stop?"

"If I didn't, I'd have you on my bed right now. If we made it that far."

"I wasn't asking you to stop."

I straightened, studying her. Her face flushed, eyes wide with desire. I cupped her cheek. "I don't want to rush you."

She turned, brushing my thumb with her lips. "You're not."

"I honestly didn't bring you back here to get you naked."

Her right eyebrow rose. I found the slow way she arched it sexy.

She said so much with a simple gesture and no words.

It said bullshit.

"I have something else for you."

She frowned, confused.

I led her to the sofa. "I'll be right back."

EMMY

I LOOKED AROUND the massive room in awe. It had high ceilings, dark hardwood floors, huge windows, and immense proportions. There were three sofas in a U-shape, all wide and deep, covered in the softest tan leather I had ever felt. The walls were creamy colored, and the tables and accents done in more dark wood. Wall to ceiling bookcases flanked the fireplace, and two massive wingback chairs in a deep ebony fabric graced the front of the hearth. A heavy, antique dining table sat by the windows, with six parson chairs neatly tucked around it. A matching sideboard sat on one wall, holding trays of gleaming crystal decanters and glasses. I noticed all the side tables and a few other pieces were also antiques. Hallways ran from opposite ends of the room, and a swinging door by the dining table most likely led to the kitchen. There were a few pictures on the walls, some carefully placed pieces of art on the shelves and walls. It was an eclectic, unique collection, yet it all blended.

Unique—like Bentley himself. He looked every bit the modern businessman, but his well-bred manners and formal persona hid an old soul. To the outside world, he was stern and rigid, but once he relaxed with me, he was sweet and fun.

As I took in the room, I noticed the richness of it all. The vastness. It was flawless, not a thing out of place. No magazines on the coffee table, no shoes by the door. Its perfection screamed emptiness. It was as if someone created the room, yet it wasn't used, lived in or shared. I tried to picture Bentley stretched out on the sofa, relaxing, or sitting with his friends in the room. I couldn't imagine it.

I wondered if, aside from Maddox and Aiden, he had anyone to share it *with,* or he spent his time alone. I had a feeling the latter was the case most of the time.

He came back from down the hallway with a bag in his hand, looking excited and nervous. He sat beside me, his leg bouncing as he laid a large, flat bag on my lap.

"You already gave me my gift." I fingered the shawl, knowing exactly where it came from and how much it cost. It was already too much.

"That was for Emmy." He grinned, looking boyish.

"And this is for?"

He leaned close and brushed a kiss on my lips. "*Freddy* needs something, too. It's her day, as well."

His thoughtfulness made my chest ache, but his teasing made me smile. He was impossible to resist.

"Bentley . . ."

He shook his head. "Emmy, it's a gift. Something I want you to have."

"I can't compete with"—I waved my hands—"all this."

"All this?"

"This house, the limos, and cars. Your bodyguard." My voice dropped to a whisper. "Your wealth. I have nothing like that to offer you."

"What you have to offer is so much greater."

"I don't understand."

"Do you know when the last time I went out with people and had a meal? Just a fun, enjoyable night out with friends?" He shook his head. "I can't even remember. Back in university, I think."

He looked around. "This is simply a room. A house. My cars take me to meetings and the occasional boring business dinner. I know I have a lot of money, but it hasn't given me one second of the happiness I have shared with you this past week. You have made me smile more since I met you than I have in years." He tapped the bag on my knee, anxious. "These gifts are tokens of my thanks. Accepting *them*, is accepting *me*." He hesitated, meeting my eyes. "Please accept me."

"You spent so much already."

Bentley huffed out a long breath. "Do you want me to explain how I see this in basic, honest terms?"

"Yes."

"The gifts I'm giving you are the same value to me as when you buy a cup of coffee, Emmy," he stated. "It is not a great deal of money in my world."

"Wow." I couldn't find any other words to say. I couldn't imagine that sort of wealth.

"My wealth is part of who I am. I will buy you things because I want to, because it makes me smile to see you happy." He held up his hand before I could say anything. "And yes, I know you cannot reciprocate in the same fashion, but it doesn't matter to me. The scones you gave me the other day were one of the nicest things anyone has ever given me. Because of who they came from, not their value, but what they represent. They represent you, and your caring ways." He studied me. "Can you understand my thinking?"

His words and the way he spoke them rang of nothing but the truth. His eyes were gentle as he looked at me but filled with anxiety. He was asking me to accept and understand him. Not to allow our differences to come between us.

"Yes," I replied. "Let's be clear, though. I think *you're* the valuable commodity, not your money."

"Then, we're on the same page." He nudged the bag. "Now, open your gifts, Freddy."

I slid a box from the bag and opened it. There was a messenger bag, the leather luxuriant and pungent, in a rich shade of cappuccino. Bentley watched me intently. "I picked it out," he explained proudly. "I know you have a rucksack, but this would hold your things so much better. Your papers wouldn't be all scrunched up. You'll find it easier on your neck."

I traced the stitching on it. I had wanted one of these, but I'd never been able to afford it—especially one of such good quality. He was right; my rucksack was old, the clasp broken, and one of the straps almost torn. I had hoped it would make it through the end of the year and I could find one on sale. For him to have noticed my unspoken need said a lot.

"Thank you. It's beautiful."

"Will you use it?"

I met his gaze. "Yes."

His smile was wide. "Good. There is something inside, too."

Curious, I opened the bag and pulled out a flat box. I set aside the messenger bag and opened it, gasping when I saw the bright blue shawl like the black one he had already given me.

"But—"

"I liked the color. Trust me, Cami had to stop me from buying you one in every color. I couldn't resist this one, though. I think I showed great restraint, don't you?" He reached over and took it from me, draping it over my shoulders with the other one. "I love this color on you against your skin." He tucked the edges under my arm. "It will keep you warm."

My throat felt thick. I cupped his face, feeling the scruff on his chin under my palm. He leaned into my caress, smiling into my kiss.

"Thank you. This has been the best birthday I can remember."

"Good. Mission accomplished." He tapped the end of my nose. "Can you stay a little longer? We could watch a movie or something?"

I nodded. "I have no class until one tomorrow."

"Great. I'll get us a drink."

BENTLEY

SHE ACCEPTED THE gifts. I had seen the way her face paled when I compared what I spent to something she could relate to, but I had to make her understand. I meant what I said: I would buy her things, and

I didn't want it to be a constant battle. I knew she lived very modestly, and although I didn't want to overwhelm her, I did plan to make her life a little easier wherever I could.

I uncorked and poured some red wine. In the fridge was a plate with some snacks Andrew had prepared at my request. I put it all on a tray and went back to the living area. Emmy was wandering around, investigating the room. She stood by the sideboard, studying the array of decanters.

"The antiques belonged to my parents. They brought them over from England. I asked the designer to incorporate them into the room."

"They're lovely."

I bit back my smile. I noticed she didn't say the room was lovely. I had to admit that I found it too much at times. I rarely used it.

"I thought we'd go to the theater room. It's more comfortable."

"Okay," she agreed.

She giggled as we went back into the elevator. "I've never been in a house with an elevator until today."

"I bought the property and designed the house to fit it. The lot was narrow, and so I built long and up. My architect designed the place to maximize the square footage, and the elevator is a plus. Some days I don't feel like climbing all those stairs." I chuckled. "Especially when I forget my glasses in the den and have to go up and down three flights to get them off my desk."

"Makes sense."

"I lucked out on the lot, but it took me a while to get a design I liked."

"Oh?"

"It's the corner, on a dead-end street, with a ravine all around it. The property had been vacant for a long time since it was such an odd shape. My neighbors next door are an older couple and all they were worried about was that I didn't tear down the trees on the property line we shared. I was happy to comply."

"You like it here?"

"Yes. It's a quiet area—sort of a hidden treasure in Toronto. It's about twenty minutes to the office unless there is traffic, and another short drive when I go other places I frequent."

"You said there was a garage?"

"Yes, I built one for convenience that holds my personal car. I house my other cars off-site. Frank drives them to me as needed."

"Your personal car?" she asked, confused.

"Sometimes I like to drive myself. However, there was no room for a big garage," I explained. "I was lucky to get one car in there. The house takes up the entire lot. No garden, no backyard. I built it as far to the edges as we could legally go."

"Not much for gardening?"

"I wouldn't know how if I tried. There're a few pots of flowers around the pool, but Andrew looks after them."

We walked into the movie room, and Emmy's eyes grew large in delight. "Oh my God! This is amazing!"

I had four elevated rows of movie recliners in the room, all in a dark red leather. Wide, deep, and comfortable, they were great to relax in and watch a game or movie. The walls were a soft taupe color, and the room had its own popcorn maker and a small kitchen area. The back wall held all the electronics and floor to ceiling shelves housed hundreds of movies and TV shows. The screen itself took up an entire wall and the surround sound rivaled any theater.

I spent a lot of my downtime in this room.

"What do you like to watch?"

She looked around in awe. "Anything is good. What do you normally watch?"

"At this time of the night, usually the news, but we can do better than that."

She surprised me. "No, I haven't seen the news for a bit. It would do me good to catch up."

"Are you sure?"

"Yep."

I turned on the TV and sat back in my recliner. She curled up in the one beside me, giggling as I showed her how to use the remote and recline back.

I tried to concentrate on the screen, but my gaze kept drifting over to her. More times than not, when I would look over, her eyes were riveted on me. Then she would look shy and glance away.

She looked tiny in the chair, and I realized it was the first time I had ever had a woman in my theater room. It hadn't been built when my last relationship ended. Aiden and Maddox took up considerably more room than she did.

She stood from her chair. "Washroom?"

"Across the hall."

I watched her leave, smiling at the fact she still had both shawls wrapped around her. I watched the TV, and glanced at my watch. She'd been gone longer than I expected and I worried she was unwell. Hearing her footfalls, I relaxed. She hurried in, and without warning, slid onto my lap.

I wrapped my arm around her. The chair was big enough for the two of us, and I wondered why I hadn't thought of sharing until now. "Well, hello."

She hummed and burrowed into me. I reached down to tug her closer, and my hand froze as it touched the bare skin of her thigh. I inhaled sharply, and looked down, meeting her steady gaze.

"What are you doing?"

"Being spontaneous."

"I think in your spontaneity, you forgot your pants."

With a slow leer, she grabbed my hand, pulling it higher. There was more skin. *All* I could feel was warm, supple skin.

"I lost my shirt, too."

I spread my fingers wide across her back, pulling her flush to my body. "Emmy," I warned.

"It's my birthday. You said you wanted it to be a good one."

"So, sitting on my lap almost naked makes it one?"

She traced her finger along my jaw, running the tip of it over my bottom lip. "It depends on how much more naked I get."

My cock twitched, swelling and pressing against the confines of my pants. I sucked her finger into my mouth, swirling my tongue around the tip. She watched me with hooded eyes, her breathing picking up. Goosebumps broke out on her skin.

"If I take off your shawl, you'll get cold."

"Unless you can figure out a way to warm me up."

She was impossible to resist, and I didn't want to.

I hit the remote, turned off the TV, but left on the low voltage lights to see. I gripped her hips, shifting her easily, so she was straddling me in the chair. I groaned when I felt her heat pressing down on my growing erection. She slid her fingers through my hair, as I held her hips and my mouth fused with hers.

Instantly, everything else faded away and there was only her. Only us. The feel of her wet, sweet mouth. The slide of her tongue with mine. How she felt pressed to my chest, and the slow motion of her undulating over my cock. The low, erotic sounds she made as we sank deeper into our kisses, cranked me up. I couldn't get her close enough, taste her enough, or feel her enough. I slid my hand down her back, across her hips, and delved my fingers under the silky waistband, cupping the swells of her ass, then gliding into her heat. She gasped in my mouth as I circled her clit, moaning at how ready she was for me.

"*Jesus.* You're so hot, Emmy. So wet for me."

"I want you," she pleaded. "I've wanted you all night. I want to see more of the passion you showed me last week."

"You're going to have me." I licked and nipped at her neck. "All of me. But first, I want you to come, here, *right now.*"

"Yes . . . *Bentley* . . ." She whimpered as my fingers continued to work her.

I eased one inside her, then another, using my thumb to keep the pressure on her clit. "I want you to come for me, Emmy. Come on my hand, and I'll take you to bed, and we can start all over. Only next time you can come on my cock."

"Oh God—"

Watching her fall apart was incredible. Her head fell backward, her back arched, and she uttered a long, low cry as her pussy clenched around my fingers, and she rode out her orgasm. Her shawl fell away, exposing her gorgeous, lace-covered tits. I sucked one tight nipple into my mouth, lapping through the satin, biting down gently as she cried my name. My weeping cock strained at the confines of my pants. I needed her naked and under me. I needed to feel her tight pussy milking my cock, and the way her body would slide against mine as I took her.

Claimed her.

Made her mine.

I felt like a damn caveman, but I didn't care.

I stood, gripping her ass as she wrapped her legs around me. I strode down the stairs, hissing when I felt her tongue and teeth on my neck. In my room, I laid her on the bed and stepped back. The moonlight flooded the room, showcasing the way her creamy skin stood out against the navy blue of the duvet. Her golden hair spread out around her head like a halo. My clothes disappeared, discarded carelessly on the floor. Emmy sat up, shrugging off her shawls, and pushed them aside. I saw the delicate shiver that raced through her body.

"Are you cold?"

"No," she assured me, voice trembling with need.

Our eyes locked as she removed the wisps of lace that covered her, and she lay back, opening her arms. "I need your warmth, Bentley."

I covered her body, the sensation of her bare skin on mine superb. Our bodies molded together, her softness conforming to my hard angles perfectly. I felt the coolness of her skin warming under my touch. I caressed and stroked her, learning her body—what made her shiver, gasp, and call out my name in a longing voice. I trailed my lips over her skin, tracing the dips and curves, discovering her ticklish ribs, laughing with her as she squirmed and giggled. She groaned when I found her, wet and warm, teasing her with my fingers, and then my mouth, until she arched under me, her fingers grasping at my skin.

My cock ached with the need to be inside her. The feel of her hands exploring me, the touch of her mouth on my skin, and the sound of her whispering my name were undoing me. Her touch was gentle, making me tremble in anticipation. I had never felt that way about someone. Never been affected the way Emmy did it for me. The walls I built, the guard I kept up, fell away completely. My entire focus was on the tiny woman under me, and her pleasure.

"Please, Bentley, I need you," she pleaded, her eyes bright in the dull light. "Please."

I grabbed a condom from the night table, rolling it on. I hovered over her, sheathing myself inside her inch by inch until we were flush. Her legs wrapped around my waist, anchoring me to her body, her tightness surrounding me.

I dropped my face to her shoulder. "*Jesus*, Emmy. You feel so amazing wrapped around me."

"Please," she whimpered.

I began to thrust, groaning at the responsiveness of her body. Gradually, we built our rhythm, our bodies attuned to each other, moving as if we'd done it a thousand times. Her hands clutched my shoulders, and her nails dug into my skin. Sweat raced down my back, as the sensations increased. I sat up, pulling her hips with me, slamming into her harder. She cried out, her voice hoarse with desire. My balls tightened, my nerves snapping with electricity as my orgasm built.

"Come with me, baby." I slipped my hand between us, teasing her clit. "I need you to come."

She stiffened, her body bowing in a taut arch as she shattered.

I followed, my orgasm tearing through me as I rode her hard, and came inside her.

I fell forward, my weight pressing her into the mattress. I covered her mouth with mine, kissing her until we were breathless. I rolled from her, discarded the condom and tugged the duvet over her rapidly cooling body. I slipped in beside her, tucking her to my chest. She burrowed close, her gentle breaths drifting on my skin.

"Are you all right, Freddy?"

I felt her smile. "Yes, Rigid. I'm more than all right."

My next question surprised me. "Will you stay?"

"If you want me to."

"Yes. I do."

"Okay." She sighed. "I'd like that." She pressed a kiss to my scruff. "Best birthday ever. Thank you."

I lifted her chin, needing to kiss her again. "I think I should be thanking you, Emmy."

"Let's call it even."

I tucked her close. We'd never be even.

She was so much more than I could ever be. And she had no idea.

CHAPTER 9

EMMY

WARM KISSES WOKE me. Again.

The more formal, rigid Bentley apparently disappeared once we were alone and naked. He was rigid in a totally different way. His guard fell away, and the open, sexual man he kept hidden revealed. He was a passionate, sensual, and giving lover. He made me feel beautiful and wanted. His need for me was empowering.

We made love twice in the night, his desire for me seemingly endless. Being with him, surrounded by the dark with his body pressed to mine, was a surprisingly intimate act. It felt as if we were the only two people in the world. I loved how his voice became raspy; the way he uttered my name as he came, and his hissed curses. He was incredibly gentle, yet his touch was possessive and sure.

As if, I belonged to him.

"Emmy, baby," he murmured, his lips at my ear. "I have to go to the office."

I struggled to open my eyes.

He chuckled low in his throat. "No, stay in bed. Andrew is off today, so the house is empty. Look around, and make yourself at home. Frank will be here at noon. He'll take you home so you can change, get your things, and he'll drive you to school."

I was so tired, I couldn't argue with him. More sleep sounded great. His bed was far more comfortable than mine was, and it smelled like him. The sheets and duvet were soft, cozy, and inviting. The one thing missing was his long, strong body. I wound my arms around his neck, pressing my lips to his throat over the stiff collar. He was clean-shaven today, and his jaw hard under my tongue.

"You should come back to bed."

He groaned, kissing me hard. Morning breath was no deterrent for him, it seemed. "I want to, but I have a meeting."

I slid my hand down his chest, cupping his growing erection. "I could persuade you. Staying here would be so much more fun than a meeting."

He stepped back, straightening his tie, trying to look affronted. "I cannot blow off business for sex."

I arched my eyebrow. "I could blow *you*."

He bent forward at his knees again, the way he did the night prior, and inhaled deeply. "*Jesus,* Emmy. What you do to me."

Lifting his head, he met my gaze, his stare intense. "I love the fact you're so open with me. That you tell me what you want. God, I want to get back into bed with you and fuck you until you scream my name . . ." His voice trailed off, and he shook his head.

It was my turn to inhale deeply. I loved hearing him talk dirty to me. It was such a contrast to the formal front he showed to the world. "Something to look forward to then."

He lunged, pressing me into the mattress, and kissing me until I was breathless. His own breathing was heavy when he pushed himself away, eyes hooded. "Yes."

He straightened his tie again and smoothed down his suit jacket. I noticed his hair wasn't as perfect as usual. I had sort of messed it up.

It suited him, so I didn't say anything.

"You look hot," I teased.

He shook his head. "Such a troublemaker. Now go back to sleep and Frank will be here to pick you up. He'll text you when he is downstairs. The door will lock behind you. Deal?"

I smiled at him. "Deal."

"Stop it."

"What? I'm just smiling and agreeing."

"You are fucking me with your eyes."

"The term is *eye-fucking*, Rigid, and at least my eyes are having fun."

He turned and strode out of the room without another word. I heard his footsteps echoing as he descended the stairs. No elevator this morning for him, which made me wonder if he needed the physical release before getting into the car. Giggling, I rolled over, inhaling the scent of his pillow. It really did smell like him. My phone buzzed from the bedside table, and I picked it up, unable to contain my grin when I read it.

I'll make sure the rest of you has fun tonight.

I dozed in Bentley's bed but didn't fall back to sleep. I groaned when I checked my phone and saw it was only 8:30 a.m. Usually, I slept in on Wednesdays, but today wasn't my usual Wednesday. Obviously, Bentley was an early riser, no matter how little sleep he got the night before.

I sat up and looked around the room. Large, with more big windows, it was more inviting than downstairs, but still felt empty. The walls were a simple white, the same as the soft sheets on his bed, with navy and gray accents. The furniture was heavy and masculine, and the headboard was padded and thick. His closet was bigger than my apartment, never mind his master bath suite. There was a walk-in shower with six jets, and a huge, freestanding infinity tub calling my name. The heated floors under my habitually cold feet added to the decadence. The closet and bath were connected at the back for easy access. One could get ready and not disturb their slumbering partner, which was what happened this morning.

I felt my chest tighten as I wondered how many other women Bentley hadn't disturbed in his bed.

I shook my head—I wasn't going to dwell. I would ask him directly. He seemed to appreciate my forwardness. I only hoped I was prepared for the answer. Despite his reassurances, I knew he wasn't a monk. He was far too skilled in the bedroom and too good-looking not to have had a lot of female companions.

I squealed when I discovered a tiny alcove at the back of the room. There was a waist-high refrigerator tucked under a counter with a Keurig machine, and all the fixings needed for coffee. Obviously, Bentley had drunk one; the mug still sat on the counter. Without hesitation, I used it, somehow liking the fact his lips had pressed against the porcelain earlier. Back in his closet, I grabbed a discarded T-shirt, slipped it on, found my pretty, blue shawl, a pair of his thick socks, then coffee in hand, I went exploring.

I started back on the main floor, finally trudging up to the top level. His addition of an elevator was a good idea. There were a lot of stairs to climb.

His kitchen was a dream with gleaming stainless steel, glossy cupboards, and rich quartz on the counters. The gym was well equipped with a variety of machines and weights, and the thought of him working out, building up a sweat, made me heat up. I peeked in his den, not going in. His desk must have been another antique from his parents. The bookshelves and the rest of the room were modern and clean. There was a large model of something in the middle of the space, but I didn't go in and look.

The guest rooms were simple and sparse, and most of them appeared unused, a couple still empty. I bypassed the theater room and entered the sunroom, my breath catching in my throat. Entirely encased in glass at the back, it was heaven. Tiled floors, well-used, comfortable furniture, and a games table graced the space. A large TV hung on the wall. Fans overhead moved the air.

At the end, behind glass doors that folded flat to the wall, were steps that led down to an indoor pool. As Bentley stated, it wasn't huge, but it was still amazing. Pots of flowers hung in the windows, growing large in the sun. I dipped my toe in, sighing at the feel of the heated water. The view was lovely with the ravine and towering trees. It was the one room I had seen to appear lived in. There were a couple of books beside an armchair. A pair of reading glasses sat on them. A well-used blanket draped over the back of the chair. This room was the private Bentley. The one no one saw. He could be comfortable and himself. I could picture him reading, relaxing, or napping. Floating in the pool and staring up at the night sky under the glass dome.

I wanted to see that and to share it with him.

I moved to his chair and sat down. I felt the way the chair was molded from his body, and I curled into the cast left by him. I shut my eyes and drifted, thinking of the day he would be here with me, curled around my body for real.

BENTLEY

I COULDN'T CONCENTRATE. For the first time that I could ever remember, my mind wasn't on business. All my thoughts were with the person currently asleep in my bed or probably exploring my house. She was a woman after all, and surprisingly, I didn't care if she snooped. I wanted her comfortable in my home because I wanted her to spend a lot of time with me there. Especially, after last night.

I struggled to stop the thoughts that kept drifting through my head and failed miserably. I thought of her warmth. The way her body felt pressed to mine and the way she tasted. How she looked when she came, and the sound of my name as she cried out.

I remembered how she looked this morning, sleeping like a contented kitten in my bed. The drowsy look on her face, and the way her eyes danced as she woke up and teased me.

"I could blow you."

My cock hardened, thinking of being in her mouth. I had been tempted. So tempted to shrug off my responsibilities and stay with her. Dive back into the bed and let her do whatever she wanted, then have her all over again. I still wanted to do that. I glanced at my watch, surprised to see it was only 9:30. Normally the day raced by for me, but today it felt as though time stood still. I could go home and have an hour with her. Maybe longer. Perhaps if I showed up, she would skip school, and we could have the whole afternoon together.

"Bent?"

I shook my head and met Maddox's eyes.

"What do you think?"

"Sorry, I was, ah, thinking about something I forgot to do."

"Like brush your hair this morning?" Aiden quipped. "Looks like someone's fingers have been in it."

Instinctively, my hand flew to my head and he grinned.

"Gotcha."

I narrowed my eyes. "Fuck you."

"No thanks. You're not my type. Besides"—he grinned—"I think that's been taken care of."

"Don't you—"

Aiden held up his hands, laughing. "Not doing anything, except stating the obvious."

He knew Emmy had spent the night. He hadn't said anything at first, aside from one raised eyebrow this morning when I got in the car, but the silence hadn't lasted long. As soon as we arrived at the building, he disappeared into Maddox's office. The two of them were like old women gossips, sharing information over the fence.

I glared at him, then spoke to Maddox. "You were saying?"

He chuckled. "I asked if you thought the numbers were good."

I glanced down at the papers in front of me. "I'll go through them this afternoon."

"There's another first," Aiden observed.

My phone buzzed before I could flip him off. However, I couldn't contain my grin when I saw Emmy's message.

> *Class was canceled so Frank doesn't need to drive me. I'll grab the bus in a while. Just enjoying your sun for a bit longer.*

She attached a picture she had taken, curled up in my favorite chair. I squinted at the screen. She was wearing one of my shirts, and unless I was mistaken, she was holding the mug I used this morning.

I stood, already dialing as I strode into my office, almost slamming the door in my haste. I cut off the loud guffaws that followed me.

Emmy's voice was slow and lazy when she answered. "Hey."

"Hey yourself."

"This room is amazing."

"Stay."

"What?"

"Don't go home. Stay and be there when I'm done for the day."

"Bentley, I have to do some school work. I need to go home and get my laptop, so I'm not going all the way there and coming back. And before you can say it, I'm *not* having Frank take me either."

I grinned for two reasons. Her stubbornness, and the way she might have helped me find the excuse for her to start using the laptop I had purchased.

"Do you have your project backed up?"

"Yes, it's on the memory stick in my, ah, bag."

I *knew* she had her old rucksack tucked into her purse. I let it slide, knowing she wasn't yet ready to tell me why she carried it everywhere.

"Go to my den, and look on the credenza."

"You want me to go into your private den? Aren't you afraid I will dig up some secret stuff to report on? I get a bonus if I'm fast."

I tried not to laugh. "You aren't much of a spy, Freddy. You missed the secret vault in my dressing room. I highly doubt your bosses are going to be very impressed with my shirt and mug as your haul for the day."

She began to giggle. The sound was light and feminine, and it made my smile wider.

"Damn, you noticed."

I lowered my voice. "I liked how my shirt looks on you."

"I liked drinking from your mug. It was as if I was kissing your lips every time I took a drink."

I groaned and let my head fall back. My body tightened and my cock lengthened at the thought of kissing her. The way her lips felt, full and plump, the feel of her tongue sliding with mine, the erotic way her sweet breath filled my mouth.

"Did I lose you?"

"You are making it damned difficult not to call Frank and have him take me straight home."

"I'd like that. I'd like to spend more time with you."

I paused at the honesty in her tone. "If you stay, I'll come home early."

She inhaled quickly. "I'm in your den."

"There's a laptop on the right. Blue cover."

"Got it."

"Plug your memory key in there and use it. I think you'll find it has everything you need to do your work. The password is Scone1, capital S."

Aside from the typing of the keys, there was silence for a moment, until she spoke. "Why does this laptop have all the software I use on it?"

"I use it, as well."

"Yet, this one looks brand new. There are no files saved on it, no work done." I heard a few more keystrokes. "It *is* brand new. Winston Bentley Ridge, tell me you did *not* buy this laptop for me."

I gaped into the phone and adjusted myself. Was it incredibly wrong I found her full-naming me a turn on?

"It is new because I got it yesterday. I haven't had a chance to bring it into the office to have it set up. I thought you could use it today—or whenever you're at my place, to save you from carrying yours back and forth. It, ah, looked heavy."

Her sigh told me she knew I was lying.

"It's a laptop, Freddy. One of many I have. Use it today and stay."

I waited, then went in for the kill. "Please."

"I'm not keeping this laptop, Rigid."

"Of course not."

"I'll only borrow it today."

"Or whenever you need to."

"It *is* very light."

"It's fast, too. Super-fast. It will help you get your work done easier."

"Are you actually going to come home early?"

"If you're there, yes."

"Can I make us dinner?"

"I would love that."

"Then, it's a deal. See you later, dear. Go make some more millions."

I hung up, smiling. Strangely enough, that was how I seemed to act when it came to Emmy. I glanced back at the door to the boardroom, knowing what was waiting for me. Aiden would pounce as soon as I went in, and Maddox would lean back with a knowing smirk on his face, and again, they would tease me mercilessly. I knew they were gossiping away again, anxious for my return.

I straightened my jacket, tugged on my sleeves, and prepared my game face.

That was how we showed that we cared—we gave each other a hard time. I could handle them.

Emmy was worth it.

I FOUND HER in the kitchen, the laptop open, her hand a blur holding the mouse as she created something on the screen. Music played from the speakers, the beat a low hum. The kitchen was warm, the air was pungent with garlic and spice, and whatever she was cooking contained a heady red wine. It was mouthwatering.

She was concentrating so hard, she didn't hear me come in, and

I took the time to study her. My shirt hung past her thighs revealing her shapely calves. Her small feet were encased in a pair of my socks. Both shawls were draped around her body for warmth; although, one side had slipped, pulling down the material of my shirt, showing her skin. She had her hair piled high on her head, exposing her delicate neck. Curls escaped from her messy updo, hanging around her face. She pushed them aside as she muttered to herself, and colors appeared on the screen as her design took shape. The light glinted off her ear piercings, and her musical tattoo was a dark image on her pale skin behind her ear. Her exposed shoulder showed the butterfly tattoo I had discovered last night. I remembered tracing it with my tongue, making her shiver. She had told me it was a tribute to her grandmother.

"She loved butterflies," she whispered.

I slid behind her, wrapped my fingers around her shoulder, and dropped my face to her neck, to kiss the soft skin. At the same time, I placed the flowers I'd picked up across the laptop. She startled briefly but melted back into me. I held her tight, then she turned, throwing her arms around my neck, and pressed her mouth to mine.

I needed no further encouragement, kissing her thoroughly. It was even better than I remembered; the softness of her lips, the feel of her tongue and the taste that was just *her*. She grasped my shoulders, and I slipped my hands under her shirt, feeling the delicate ridges of her spine as I ran them over her skin.

I eased back, holding her to my chest.

"Welcome home," she murmured.

"Best welcome I've ever had. Usually, by the time I get home, there is a plate ready with dinner on the counter and an empty house."

She gazed up at me, her dark eyes sad. "I don't like that."

I stroked the skin of her cheek.

"It's fine."

"I guess I'll have to change it."

"Oh, yeah?"

She nodded, turning her face so she could kiss my hand. "Yeah." Then, trying to lighten the mood, she grinned. "Your laptop is awesome."

"Ah, always second to the laptop."

"Sorry, Rigid. The hard drive is pretty impressive."

My already aching cock swelled. Her voice, her teasing, the way her eyes expressed the emotions she felt. They all turned me on. I had been hard for her since I left that morning.

I turned her to the laptop. "Save your work, Emmy."

"Oh?"

I leaned down and nipped her neck. "I'll show you an impressive hard drive."

She tapped a few keys. "Done."

I swept her into my arms. "Good."

CHAPTER 10

BENTLEY

WE BARELY MADE it out of the elevator. By accident, my groping fingers hit the top floor, and I went with it, carrying her to the sunroom and laying her on the deep sofa. I had pulled the clip from her hair at some point, and the waves cascaded over the cushion, almost reaching the floor. The sun glinted in the strands casting a burnished gold around her head.

I crouched over her, my erection pressing into the zipper of my dress pants, painful and needy. "As much as I like my shirt on you, it needs to come off."

She shimmied, the shirt and shawls disappearing. Her skin was pale, the only color showing was the small peek of the butterfly wing over her shoulder, and the tiny set of teardrops tattooed over her heart. Four splatters of red, each symbolizing a person she lost, she had explained when I asked her. They spoke, without words, of the sorrow she carried. She etched her heartache onto her skin, embedding the pain there forever. She kept all her tattoos private. Even her musical tattoo was hidden most of the time. That one, she informed me, was for her. She loved music and constantly had it playing everywhere.

Bending low, I kissed the ink, then slid my mouth down, covering her nipple, and sucked, teasing the peak with my tongue. She gasped, arching up, and used her hands to push off my suit jacket. Our mouths met in a series of blistering, intense kisses. Hot, wet, mind-blowing caresses. I needed more of them. More of her. Everything she could give me.

She yanked and pulled on my tie, fumbled with my buttons, and tugged on my belt. Unable to break from her mouth, I helped her, until we were at last naked and pressed together, our bodies melded. Cradled in between her legs, she was slick and ready. She lifted her hips, as the blunt head of my cock rubbed against her. The searing heat of her, made me groan—I wanted her so fucking much.

"Condom," I gasped.

"Where?"

I wanted to scream in frustration. "My room."

"Why aren't you a typical bachelor who hides condoms all over his house in case?"

"In case?"

"In case of situations like this!"

Her words made me stop. They broke the intensity of the moment and made me grin. "I'm not your typical bachelor, Freddy. I've never encountered a 'situation like this' before now."

"Never?"

"No. You're the first woman who has stayed here."

She leaned up, kissing me hard. "I like that. I hope you're fast then."

"I was first in the hundred-yard sprint in high school."

"I want to see a repeat. I need you inside me."

I was certain I broke the record. I was back and on her in thirty seconds flat. I held up the condoms.

"Six?" she asked, lifting that sexy eyebrow of hers.

"In case," I replied, covering her mouth, getting us right back to the moment.

Seconds later, my sheathed cock was inside her. She cried out my name, her fingers yanked on my hair, and her legs wrapped tighter around my waist. I gripped the cushions beside her head, needing to kiss her, craving the constant connection. Her sweetness wrecked me. The sounds she made and the way she tugged me close as she moved with me was addicting. Her hands slipped over my ass, gripping and kneading the muscles that bunched under her touch.

"Oh God . . ."

"*Yes.* Come for me, Emmy. Let go, baby."

I buried my face in her neck, letting the intensity overtake me. My cock swelled as she came, fluttering and tight around me. Pleasure tore through me, my balls tightening, and I pushed her legs apart, slipping in deeper and coming hard. I cursed and shook with my orgasm. She gripped my hair, and our mouths joined, deep and desperate at first, then slowly becoming gentler. Sweeter. Light.

I rolled, taking her with me, and pinned her between the back of the sofa and my chest.

She sighed, laying her head on my shoulder. Silence surrounded us, the room light with the afternoon sun. The woman I was holding, sated and content. I was the same.

It was an odd feeling, and yet, I liked it.

EMMY LOOKED RELAXED as she drifted in the water. After we rolled from the sofa, I had convinced her to stop getting dressed, and that a swim would feel good.

A naked one.

She didn't bat an eye, dropping my shirt and racing to the pool. I had turned up the water heater the previous night, so I knew it was warm. Add in the sun shining through the glass, the room was comfortable for her, and she was enjoying herself as she relaxed.

I was enjoying the view. I pulled the floating lounge closer and kissed her tempting mouth.

"Cami wants to have coffee before class tomorrow," she said, running her fingers through my damp hair. "No doubt she will pump me for information." She looked shy suddenly. "She was rather surprised to find out I was still here today when she texted me."

"Oh?"

"I don't usually move this fast in a relationship."

That information pleased me; once again making me feel like a caveman.

What was it about this girl that brought that out in me?

"If it makes you feel better, neither do I. I think, perhaps, it has something to do with the person."

Her eyes widened, and she smiled. "You were so amazing last night."

"I thought we were amazing together." I chuckled. "I think I should be insulted you sound so surprised."

"No! I didn't mean it that way. It's just . . . you're so . . . um, uptight and formal, but you were so passionate, and giving. I just . . . oh God, I screwed that up. I'm sorry."

She gasped as I pulled her off the lounger and tugged her tight to my body. I loved how she felt against me. Small, soft, and supple.

"You didn't screw anything up. I am uptight, and I am formal. It's how I was raised. It's how I conduct myself daily. How I have always conducted myself. Most women find me dull, yet when I'm with you, I feel . . ." I struggled to find the right word. " . . . lighter. Like I can be me. You're the first person I have felt like that with in a very long time."

"Oh," she breathed out. "Really?"

"Really. I don't rush into anything—business or personal—yet with you those rules have gone out the window."

She regarded me with those espresso-colored eyes. They were wide and sincere, and I loved how they looked at me. "Why?"

I bent closer. "I think, maybe, it has everything to do with *you* and the person you are, Emmy."

"I don't understand."

I pressed a kiss to her forehead. "Your words." I swept my lips across her closed eyes. "Your beautiful heart." Another caress of my mouth went across her lips. "Your smile." I nuzzled her neck. "Your actions." I dragged my mouth up to her ear. "Your reactions to me."

She whimpered, drawing my face to hers. "Only for you," she murmured.

"Good."

A SHORT WHILE later, I grinned at her, replete and satisfied.

"That was the best Beef Bourguignon I have ever tasted. I can't believe you made bread."

She popped a grape into her mouth, chewing slowly. The small bunch of flowers I brought her sat beside her in a small vase. I had remembered her musing of loving grapes, and the small corner store where I got the flowers had them on display. I might have bought too many, judging from the large bowl of them between us.

"Stew. It was just stew. Not Beef Bourguignon."

"Still amazing. Like the bread."

"It's a fast bread. It's so dense, it's great with the stew." She glanced around the room with an almost forlorn expression. "Your kitchen is so well-stocked."

"You can use it anytime you want."

"Do you cook?"

"I can do the basics. And by that, I mean toast, canned goods, and frozen pizza."

"And coddled eggs."

I winked. "Only on special occasions."

"What did you do when you all lived together?"

I chuckled, thinking about those days. "I was in charge of the laundry. Aiden did the yard work and Maddox cooked. The rest we sort of split up. And I paid Sandy to give the place a good clean once a month. We survived."

Her eyebrow rose. "*You* did laundry?"

"I did it very well."

She picked up her glass and took a sip. "I can't see it, frankly."

"It made the most sense to me. Sandy showed me how the machines worked, and I was very organized. Lights, darks, whites. Bleach, no bleach. I had a system."

"Everything in its place."

"Yes."

"You like it like that."

It wasn't a question, but a statement.

I filled my glass and topped hers up, draining the bottle of wine. "I like order."

"Does change bother you?"

I furrowed my brow while mulling over her question. "It takes me time to adapt. Aiden goes with the flow, but Maddox is more like me; although, he rarely shows it. There are times, I admit, I have to have space to adjust."

"Is that because of the way your parents were while you were growing up?"

I met her gaze, answering her quietly. "My parents died when I was five, Emmy. I was raised by my Uncle Randall and Aunt Jane."

She wrapped her hand around mine. "Oh, Bentley, I didn't know."

"I know. I don't talk about it much." I paused. "Yet, I find I want to tell you. I think you need to know to understand me."

Lifting my hand to her mouth, she kissed the knuckles. "I'm listening."

"I don't remember much about my parents. I remember the eggs my dad used to cook every Sunday for my mom. How they danced in the kitchen, and my dad would pull me from my chair and spin us both around. Mom and I would laugh." I sighed. "My mom always smelled like Lily of the Valley. Every time I smell them during the spring I think of her."

"Those are good memories."

"There are only a few others. I was so young. Mostly vague images and thoughts."

"Can I ask how they died?"

I stiffened, trying not to react to the feelings that flooded my chest when I thought about the past.

"My mom loved the theater. Musical theater in particular—she always had scores playing in the house, and she sang along. They went to a lot of shows. One evening, they went out." I stopped, taking a large sip of wine for fortitude. "They were late and parked farther away than normal. They were mugged leaving the theater, and according to the story, something went awry." I met her eyes that were brimming with emotion. "He had a gun, and they were killed."

She tightened her hands around mine. "*Bentley.*"

"I don't remember much. I think, perhaps I blocked most of it. One day they were there, and suddenly, my life changed. Everything changed. I was taken from my home, everything that was familiar, my parents were gone, and I was sent to live with my aunt and uncle."

"Were your aunt and uncle . . . *nice?*" she asked hesitantly, knowing there was a reason I was telling her my history.

"They were good people. I was fed, had the best education, a nice place to live. However, they were different from my parents—distant and cold. Their marriage was more for convenience than anything. They were very austere people. There was no affection between them"—I met her gaze—"or for me. Coming from a home where there was a lot of love, it was very unsettling, but eventually, it became my life, as well."

Understanding dawned in her gaze.

"My life was vastly different after my parents died. Very structured. Children were meant to be seen and not heard. I had my lessons, and later, school. My grades had to be perfect. The activities I was part of had to be done for a reason, not for fun. Manners were drummed into me. Responsibility above all else. Decorum and good breeding. How I dressed. Spoke. Thought. It was all exceedingly exacting. Sensible.

Reserved. There was little room for emotion."

She frowned, not speaking. I drank more wine.

"My mother wore a string of small pearls. She wore them every day. My father had given them to her when they were married—they weren't expensive, but they were sentimental. I remember how they felt when she would hug me. The cool feel of the beads as they pressed to my cheek. If I sat on her lap, I always played with them. I liked how smooth they were." I sighed and ran a hand over my face.

"When they were robbed, there must have been a struggle. I don't know if they fought back or what happened, but not long after their death, my aunt got a small box of their belongings. There wasn't much since most of it was evidence, but somehow a few pearls were found in the pocket of my mother's coat. I assume the necklace was torn from her neck and they scattered." I reached into my pocket and pulled out the four pearls I carried everywhere I went. "There was a small fleck of blood on one, and my aunt was disgusted they would have sent them back, and she threw them away."

"You found them."

"Yes. I heard her telling my uncle, and I saw her toss them into the trash. I got up after they went to bed and found them. I washed and hid them." I shrugged, feeling self-conscious. "They were all I had of hers. I carry them with me everywhere."

"She loved them, so of course, they meant something to you."

"They still do."

Her eyes met mine. "I understand."

"Thank you."

"She shouldn't have thrown them out."

"Keeping them would have been a sentimental act. That wasn't in her nature."

"Cold," she murmured.

"Yes. Like me."

She moved a little closer, so her knees pressed to mine.

"You think you became like them."

"I *did* become like them. I am reserved. Formal. Cold."

"Formal, yes. I don't find you cold. You're incredibly kind, generous, and sweet."

"You seem to bring that out in me, Emmy. No one else does. Not for a very long time."

"I think Aiden and Maddox see a different side of you."

"They do, to a point. It took me a while to relax with them, to *allow* myself to relax. The truth is, I will never be as easy with the world as other people are."

"You don't have to be."

I leaned close, earnest. "I want to be for you. You have such a light, and when I'm with you, I feel it. I feel different. You make me laugh. You make me want to be silly just to see you smile."

"You do make me smile." She cupped my face. "I like your old-fashioned ways, Bentley. I like how you are when we're alone. You're funny and passionate, and you make me feel as if I matter to you."

I laid my hand on top of hers. "You do matter. That's why I'm telling you. I am rigid and formal. I am blunt and outspoken at times, and I have a temper. A bad one. It doesn't come out often, but when it does, it's ugly."

"I'll have to try not to make you angry."

I brought our clasped hands to my chest and kissed her. "I can't imagine you doing so."

She lifted one eyebrow. "Should I remind you of our first meeting?"

I chuckled. "That was annoyance, not anger. I was being my usual snotty self."

"I don't think you're snotty."

It was my turn to arch an eyebrow at her. "Everyone thinks I'm snotty. Yet, I feel differently with you. I don't want to lose that."

"I'm not going anywhere."

Relief flooded my chest. "Good."

"Are your aunt and uncle alive? Will I meet them?"

"No. My aunt passed away from a heart attack when I was nineteen. Six months later, my uncle choked on a piece of London

Broil one night at his club."

"Oh."

"I inherited everything. Plus, I already had a trust fund from my parents."

"So, you're telling me you're even richer than I thought?"

"I don't know how rich you thought I was, but perhaps."

"Rich enough to buy five pounds of grapes at once. Enough for me to wonder if you'll get bored with me."

"The grapes are a treat for you—that's another new thing for me. I enjoy spoiling you. As for getting bored . . . frankly, Emmy, I cannot even imagine that happening. I never know what you are going to say or do next. It's part of your charm."

"I don't think anyone has ever thought I had charm until now."

I traced my finger over her cheek, wrapping a wayward curl around my finger. I rubbed the silkiness of her hair on my skin, then watched as the curl unfurled, wild and soft against her face. "They weren't looking hard enough."

"Why aren't you taken, Bentley?"

I cocked my head to the side. "I rather thought I was . . . *now.*"

Her eyes crinkled in merriment. "I meant before I waylaid you."

"Caught me in your web?"

She nodded imperviously, lifting her chin. "Trapped you as per my devious plan."

"Right." I sucked in a deep lungful of air and blew it out. "You are not devious, Emmy. That I know for a fact."

"Oh?" She studied me. "Did you know someone devious?"

"While we were in university, I met a girl. Lucy seemed . . . lovely. Great. A bit shy, and quiet. She lived off campus, and she liked her privacy, the same way I did." I snorted. "Or so she led me to believe."

Emmy reached out, covering my hand. "What happened?"

"She told me her parents were extremely strict. They didn't allow her to date. They kept her on a tight budget, and she worked in the admissions department to help make ends meet. We would meet for coffee or dinner in small places, off the beaten path. I liked her." I met

Emmy's steady gaze. "I liked her a lot. She said all the right things, did all the right things."

"But?"

"I never talked about money. Ever. My aunt and uncle drummed that into my head. It was private, something a person didn't show off. It wasn't right to boast about what I had, and we never discussed it. I always paid for coffee or dinner simply because that was how I was raised. A man should treat a woman like a lady. One day, she was upset because she had somehow lost her wallet and it had all her money for the next week in it. Without a thought, I handed her fifty dollars and bought her a new wallet. A few days later, she mentioned a CD she wanted, and I bought it for her. Then, she showed me a dress she desperately wanted to buy so she'd 'look good for me'."

"You bought that, too?"

"Yes. Anything she asked for, I bought. Every time she was short of cash, I handed it over. She never asked outright, but I found myself giving her more and more. She had a way of demanding without even saying the words. It was expected."

"You never questioned it? You never wondered how she knew you had the money to hand over?"

"No. I was stupid, young, and for the first time, imagined myself in love. I never questioned the secrecy or the constant requests. Maddox and Aiden didn't like her. They thought she was odd. Untrustworthy. I ignored it, thinking they were jealous I found someone and they were still playing the field. We became even more secretive. When Maddox found out about the money I was giving her, he almost lost it. We had a huge fight, and I stormed out, all indignant and self-righteous, defending the woman I loved."

"He was right, though?"

I swallowed the last of my wine. "He certainly was. I marched over to her place—unannounced—something I never did, since she always told me her parents might be around, but I wanted to see her and tell her what had happened. Instead of finding her alone and studying the way she told me she did, I walked into a party.

A big one, with her real friends, and her boyfriend. She had been scamming me. I guess she accessed my financial records through the university database. She had arranged our first meeting. She knew exactly what to do and say." I shook my head. "I was such an idiot. Uptight, reserved Bentley who fell for the biggest con artist on the campus. She was anything but shy or quiet. Her friends had a good laugh at my expense."

"I'm sorry."

I shrugged. "It was bound to happen. We had a huge blowout fight, and she said plenty of nasty things once she realized there was no way out for her. I went home, and got trashed." I shuddered. "Really trashed. That was the last time I lost control or allowed someone to get close. It was also the last time I didn't listen to Maddox and Aiden."

"What did they do?"

"They showed me their loyalty. They got drunk with me and made sure I was okay. And, of course, stated repeatedly they told me so. Then the next day, they made a lot of noise, making sure the suffering continued. Bastards."

She bit back her grin. "Of course."

I opened a new bottle, filled my wineglass and studied her over the rim. "That is how I know you're not devious, Emmy. I've met devious. I was stupid enough to believe devious."

"And you haven't found anyone you felt something for since then? That's a long time to be alone."

"I like my work. I've put forth a great deal of effort to get where I am today. I haven't made time for relationships, nor particularly wanted one. The last woman I had what you would call a relationship with walked away. She said I was too self-absorbed and boring, and she hated the fact I worked so much."

"I wouldn't call you boring. I don't think she knew you very well."

"I think perhaps she wasn't the right one for me. I preferred working to her company, so I guess that should have been my biggest clue. I have met other women, dated a few, and ah . . . enjoyed their company . . ." My voice trailed off, and I cleared my throat.

Emmy lifted her eyebrow slowly with a grin. *"Enjoyed their company?* So proper. Hardly news, Rigid. It's pretty obvious from your moves, you're not a monk."

"My 'moves'?"

She met my gaze directly. "You're an amazing lover. Giving. Passionate." She huffed out a breath, the air lifting her bangs. "Hot as fuck, actually. I didn't think you got that way through osmosis."

I laughed at her words. "Not even a little bit jealous, Freddy? I think you've wounded my pride."

"Oh, I'm jealous all right. But I'm the one sitting in your kitchen, wearing your shirt."

"Yes, you are." I leaned forward, wrapping my hand around the back of her neck. "You're also the one I want to have a relationship with. The only one."

"Ditto."

Her gaze lowered, then she met my eyes. "I'm on birth control. I haven't been with anyone for a very long time, and I've been tested clean."

I knew what she was saying. I had told her the six condoms were all I had, and I would have to get more. Lots more.

"It's been a while for me," I confessed. "As much as you think I've been with a lot of women, I need you to know, I am always monogamous, and always safe."

"When you're ready, you don't have to buy more condoms."

Merely the thought of being inside her, of being able to feel *all* of her, made me hard. I wanted that with her, more than I had ever wanted it with another woman.

I stood, taking her with me. "Let's go see what else I've learned through osmosis."

She laughed against my mouth. "Okay, Rigid."

CHAPTER 11

BENTLEY

I HEARD MY name yelled, and I turned to see Emmy racing across the street. I paused at the door to Greg's building wondering why she wasn't in school. Glancing at my watch, I noted it was past nine. Since the school year started back, she was always in class at this time of the day.

"Oh, shit, she's been waiting," Aiden muttered. "Brace yourself."

I barely had time to throw him a glance when Emmy was in front of me, hands on her hips, and a scowl on her face. I tried not to notice how sexy she looked this morning. She was wearing some sort of lacy dress that fluttered around her knees and was cinched in at her waist with my blue tie. Tights covered her toned legs, and the blue shawl I had given her wrapped around her shoulders. Despite her anger, she was gorgeous.

"Hey, Emmy," I greeted her cautiously. Casting a glare toward Aiden, who started to pull open the door and disappear, I bent to brush a kiss on Emmy's cheek.

She stepped back avoiding my caress and addressed her voice to Aiden. "Not so fast, Tree Trunk."

He turned, flashing her a smirk. "What's up, Emmy?"

"What do the two of you know about the sudden construction going on at Al's?"

Judging from the frown on Emmy's face, deflection was the word of the day.

I crossed my arms, trying to appear casual. "How would we know what your boss is up to regarding his property?"

She snorted. "Al is so tight, he squeaks. He never spends a penny unless he absolutely has to. Today, he tells me I need to find a place to stay for a few days while they install new doors and locks on the apartments, new steps, and security lighting out back. This smacks of you, Rigid."

"Perhaps, he is simply doing what is best for the upkeep of his building. If he upgrades the structure, the property value will go up."

At least, that was what Aiden told Al when he offered to have the upgrades done—at no cost. We even covered new doors for the coffee shop since I knew Emmy worked in there alone in the early morning hours. Al couldn't sign the paperwork fast enough, but obviously, his cover story didn't work.

I stepped forward. "I, for one, am glad he is looking at making the entranceway to your place safer. You're welcome to stay at the house while the work is being done if that is what concerns you."

"What concerns me is the fact you're making a mountain out of a molehill again. The *entranceway* was fine."

This time I couldn't help my derisive snort. "The stairs were rickety at best. A child could pick your lock, and there wasn't adequate lighting out back at all."

She poked a finger into my chest. "A-ha! So, you admit it!"

I threw up my hands. "Yes! I admit it. I'm an awful person for being worried you might trip on the uneven stairs, get mugged at night, or have your home invaded! Sue me."

"*Sue you?* For what? More wasted money?"

"It's not wasted! Yell at me, then. Stop giving me scones. It's still going to happen."

Aiden spoke up. "The stairs were in bad shape, Emmy. I showed Al the report I had, and we offered to help him out."

"You had a report? Oh my God! I can't believe you people."

Aiden smirked. "You people? That's what you think of Bentley? He's just *people?*"

"Don't change the subject. What exactly did you get in exchange for this *help?*"

I blinked. "Nothing. I expect nothing and want nothing. Only to know I made you a bit safer."

Her anger deflated, and her shoulders slumped. "What am I going to do with you, Rigid?"

I caught her around the waist and tugged her close. Dropping my head to her neck, I rained kisses on her skin, swirling my tongue behind her ear on the spot she found so sensitive.

"I had to do it, Emmy."

She studied my face and shook her head. "You overstepped."

"I'm aware," I admitted. "I did it because I care."

"It's still overboard."

"Let it go."

"You are such a pain in my ass."

I bit down on her tender earlobe. "We haven't explored your ass yet, but if you insist . . ."

She pulled back, fighting a smile, and slapped my chest. "Dream on. I'm still mad at you."

"Why?" I asked softly. "Al is thrilled. Your place will be safer, and no one is hurt. Why are you so upset?"

"Because, once again, I can't compete."

I tightened my arms. "It's not a competition. Even if it were, I am still way behind."

"How can you say such a thing?"

"Because I get you. That is worth more than any amount of

money."

She leaned up and pressed a hard kiss to my lips. "I give up."

"Good. So, you'll come to my place tonight? The work should be done by the end of the weekend."

She rolled her eyes. "I'm not talking to you, though."

"That's fine." I winked at her. "We can think of other things for your mouth to do."

Shaking her head, she turned away, pausing at the curb. "You are such a wimp, Aiden," she called out. "Such a big, bad security guy letting Bentley take all the shit."

"I was allowing you privacy."

"Whatever."

"You could have brought some scones with you!" he yelled in return.

She flipped him the bird and raced across the street. I gaped as I watched her cross the road. The sway of her hips in the dress she wore was mesmerizing. I wanted to follow her, trap her in a corner, and really apologize—with my cock.

Not that I was sorry.

Aiden groaned. "Well, that went better than I expected."

I pushed past him. "Emmy's right—you are a wimp. I think my girlfriend actually scared you."

He chuckled as he followed me. "Your little *girlfriend* is fierce."

I pushed the button for the elevator. "That she is."

And she's all mine.

I LOOKED OVER the numbers, frowning in concentration. I handed the documents to Aiden to look at and met Greg's steady gaze.

"Is it enough?"

He drummed his fingers on the desk. "It's way over the estimate. It's enough."

"I want it."

"I know that, Bentley."

"It's the last piece. I need it to have the project work."

"Then sign it, and I'll submit the bid. We'll know soon."

Aiden handed the documents back with a nod of his head. I scratched out my signature, and handed the documents to Greg. He presented me with a stack of paperwork.

"I need your signature on these, as well."

I sat back and glanced over the various forms. They were all things he was working on; a few other land deals, a building I had my eye on—nothing major, but they were all lucrative. As usual, all completed to my specifications and done with his precise attention to detail. As I was signing, he gave me back the first set.

"You missed a couple of places."

"Really?"

He nodded, already looking at the stack I gave him back. "Updated forms—more places to sign." He smirked. "The city loves new paperwork. More signatures mean more money."

"Sounds like lawyers," Aiden quipped.

I snickered as I added my signature where Greg indicated.

He reached for a folder. "I came across a few interesting land parcels. I had Mrs. Johnson print them for you."

I glanced through the papers, then watched as he added his signature to the bid, affixed the seal, and slid it into the envelope.

"I'll have it couriered this afternoon."

"Great. Hopefully, soon, we'll celebrate."

He regarded me, appearing amused. "Looks to me as though you've already been celebrating."

"I beg your pardon?"

He tapped his lips, a knowing grin on his face. "I never thought of you as a pink kind of guy, Bentley."

I swiped at my mouth and looked at my hand. A smear of soft pink lipstick was on my thumb.

Emmy.

Aiden chuckled, and I knew the bastard had purposely not said anything. I shot him a dirty look and cleared my throat.

"Thanks."

Greg reclined in his seat. "Seeing someone?"

I never discussed my personal life with Greg. I knew nothing about his, aside from the fact he was divorced twice, and never seemed to lack a woman on his arm, or from the rumors, in his bed. I shrugged, not really wanting to talk to him about Emmy. We didn't have that kind of relationship, and it made me uncomfortable.

"I am."

"Serious?"

"Why would you ask that?"

He held up his hands. "Lately, you've been, ah, different."

"Different?"

It was his turn to shrug. "Happier, maybe? Content. Something. I thought, perhaps, it was because you were in a relationship. I'm pleased for you."

I paused. Greg was astute, but I didn't think I had changed very much. Obviously, Emmy was having a bigger impact on me than I realized.

Aiden leaned forward, clapping his hands. "Oh, great. Is this the part where we all spill our guts and talk about our feelings? This should be fun. I can go first. Because, right now, what I'm feeling is nauseous. Can we get back to business?"

A dry chuckle escaped my mouth, and I glanced toward him. He seemed tense and out of sorts, not his usual cheerful self. His shoulders were tight, and the folder bent under his grip. Greg seemed to be annoying him more than usual today.

I stood. "On that note, I think we're done."

Greg buttoned his jacket and shook my hand. "I'll be in touch. Let me know if there is anything in the file you want me to pursue. Perhaps, we can work on a venture together. Something different from the usual."

"I will."

I followed Aiden to the elevator in silence. Once the doors shut,

I barked out a laugh. "What the hell is up with you today?"

He shook his head. "What's with the personal comments? He never talks private shit."

"There's more to it than that. What's going on?"

"Why the hell is he finding you leads? We find the leads."

"He's not stepping on your toes, Aiden. So, he found a couple of things for us to look at—he's done it other times. No big deal." I flipped through the few pages in the folder. "Nothing major in here. Relax."

He crossed his arms. "You heard him. All of a sudden, he wants to collaborate with us. Be part of the projects. Worm his way in."

Is that what he was worried about? Greg invading our group, so to speak?

"We've discussed this a couple of times already. I offered him the chance to be part of the company in the past, and he refused. Case closed. It's the three of us. Besides, if I changed my mind, you know very well before that happened, I would give you and Maddox the opportunity to say no."

"And if one of us did?"

I had the largest share in the company and could outvote them, but I valued their opinions, and we discussed everything. I met his challenging gaze steadily and spoke in a firm voice. "Then the answer would be no. You and Maddox are my partners." I laid a hand on his shoulder, feeling the tension. "My family."

He huffed out a breath, his shoulders loosening. "Okay."

We stepped outside, and Aiden moved to call Frank just as a kid slammed into me, causing me to drop the folder and stumble back.

"Shit, man!" The kid gasped. "Sorry!" He bent and picked up the pages that fell from the folder, shoving them back inside. "My bad."

"Watch where you're going next time!" Aiden growled, stepping in front of me.

I took the folder from the kid and held up my hand to Aiden, stopping him from doing anything else. "No problem. It was an accident."

The kid ducked his head and nodded, then turned and took off running.

I watched him disappear around the corner and exhaled. "Crap, I feel old. Do they all dress like that now—the hoodie and baggy jeans? The ball cap with glasses and their headphones jammed in their ears all the time?"

Frank pulled up to the curb and Aiden opened the door for me. "Yep, old man. Just like that."

I sighed and looked across the street at Al's, wishing Emmy were hurrying back across the street with a scone for me. I'd even take her scowl if I could kiss her again before we left.

Sadly, the door never opened, and the street remained Emmy free.

Still, it made me grin when I remembered she'd be at the house when I got home later.

It was something to look forward to, at least.

⟲⟋

THE DAY COULDN'T pass quickly enough, and finally, my last meeting was over. I waited impatiently for the car, almost pushing Aiden out of the way in my haste to open the door and clamor inside.

He slid in, shutting the door. "Anxious, Bent?"

I loosened my tie. "Just want to get home. Long day."

He leaned back with a grin. "Expecting an equally long night?"

I lurched, punching his arm, dislodging the files sitting beside him. "Watch it."

He chuckled, and I bent to grab the papers that had fluttered to the floor. As I gathered them, a square, manila envelope, which looked oddly familiar, fell to the carpet.

"What is that?" I asked.

Aiden held out his hand, stopping me from touching it. He slipped a hand into his pocket, producing a latex glove.

I cocked an eyebrow. "Planning on a murder spree on the way home, Aiden? Do you seriously carry one of those around with you?"

He shot me a serious look. "You never know."

He picked up the envelope and studied it. It was the same type as the other pictures had arrived in previously. The sight of it made me anxious.

"This wasn't in the file when Greg gave it to you."

"No," I agreed.

"Has the file been on your desk all day?"

"Yes. No one has been in my office other than you, Maddox, or Sandy."

Realization hit, and our eyes locked. "The kid this morning."

Aiden nodded. "It wasn't an accident."

He opened the envelope carefully, and pulled out a picture, handling it by the corner. He studied it, then handed it to me. "Only touch it with the glove."

The photo was simple. Me, outside Greg's office this morning. Aiden wasn't in the picture. The person who was made me stiffen with alarm.

Emmy was walking away from me; her head turned as she spoke. I was staring at her, a slight grin on my face.

I looked up at Aiden. *"Fuck."*

"Stay calm. You're the focal point."

"I didn't see anyone."

He shook his head. "No one does, Bent. Everyone has a damn camera phone now, taking pictures of everything. It's so common we don't even notice it. From the angle, I'd say they were across the street. Five minutes later, they would have had it printed and were waiting for you to leave the building." He tapped his knuckles on his knee. "Which means, they're still watching."

"If they're watching me, they're watching her." I felt the panic stirring in my chest. "I need to break it off with her until this is settled. They'll leave her alone."

He snorted. "Wow. Overreact much?"

I dug my hand into my pocket, running my fingers over the pearls hidden inside. "I can't risk her. I can't lose her. I fucking can't."

He leaned forward. "And you won't. Don't do anything stupid, Bentley. I won't let anything happen to her, or to you." He lowered his voice in understanding. "You won't have to go through that again."

Aiden and Maddox knew my history. His look told me he understood.

"I told Emmy about my parents."

He nodded. "Then I know how much she means to you. I'm sure they're doing this to piss you off, but I'll put someone on her. They will be discreet, but you need to tell her, so she doesn't panic if she spots them." He grinned. "She's pretty freaking smart, and she *will* spot them, I'm sure."

"I don't want to worry her."

"Did this morning not teach you anything?"

I dragged a hand through my hair. "Maybe Al's a bad liar. If I don't mention it, it's not a lie."

He shook his head. "I spoke to him. He stuck to the script, but she knew instantly. Your girl is clever." He held up the picture and snapped a copy on his phone. "I'll send you this. I'm taking the original to have it dusted for prints, not that I expect to find anything." He slipped the photo back into the envelope and laid it aside. "Take my advice, Bent. Lying by omission is still a lie. You're better than that. Tell her the truth. You don't have to overreact and dump her like an idiot or make her panic, but you should tell her. Let her know we're simply being cautious."

The car stopped, and I looked up at the house. "Okay."

"Make sure the system is armed at all times. If you're going out, let me know, and I'll be here. You want me to move into the first floor?"

I thought about it. There was a comfortable room there, and Aiden had stayed in the past. There was a complete set-up security wise, too.

"I'll think it over."

"Okay. I have my code. No going out without me, Bentley—I'm serious."

"Yep. Got it." I wasn't taking chances with Emmy.

I got out of the car and headed inside. Andrew greeted me at the elevator with his usual pleasant expression.

"Good evening, sir."

"Andrew. How was your day?"

"All is well. May I fix you a drink before I depart?"

"No. Is Miss Harris here?"

"Yes." He chuckled, his brown eyes crinkling in his round face, and the light gleaming off his bald head. He was a short man, who took his job seriously. He kept my house immaculate, and on occasion, joined me in a game of chess we both enjoyed. He had been with me since I moved in. He had come highly recommended, and I would be lost without him. He came from a much larger household, but due to health issues, hadn't been able to keep up. My quiet lifestyle worked well for him. Emmy had charmed him in about three seconds flat, and he clearly adored her.

"She insisted on cooking your dinner."

"Commandeered your kitchen again?"

"She did." He patted his stomach. "I guarantee you will enjoy it. She made me a plate, as well."

I chuckled. "Excellent."

"Also, Mr. Tomlin was here earlier."

My eyebrows shot up. "Greg? He was here?"

"Yes. He left you something on your desk. He received a call and couldn't stay."

"All right. Did he, ah, see Miss Harris?"

"Briefly. He introduced himself as she was heading up the stairs. Was I wrong to let him in your den?"

"No, of course not. I'm sorry I missed him." I clapped him on the shoulder. "Have a good evening, Andrew."

I headed to my den, surprised to find a bottle of Courvoisier on my desk, and a note from Greg.

Bentley
I felt I crossed a line with you and Aiden this morning. My apologies.
I had hoped to share a drink with you, but have been called away.
Perhaps next time. Share with Aiden. Enjoy—G.

I stared at his handwriting—bold, dark, firm, just like the man. I frowned. It had been an odd day. Aiden's sudden outburst, Greg's apology and unexpected gift, and Emmy's anger. Not to mention the photograph. I rubbed my temples in vexation. I wanted to stop thinking about it, and relax.

Grabbing the bottle, I headed upstairs.

Emmy was curled into the corner of the sofa in the sunroom, busy working on the laptop. She had changed into one of her comfortable, warm shirts, and a sweater with yoga pants. She liked this room the best. She said it felt like "me" the most out of all the rooms in the house. I wasn't sure what she meant by that statement, but it was also one of my favorite rooms. Setting down the bottle, I bent over the back of the sofa, dropping a kiss on her head.

"Hey."

She looked up, tired but smiling. "Hi. I didn't hear you come in."

"Your head was buried in your work. How goes the project?"

"Good. It's so much easier with this laptop. I have everything I need right here instead of having to work off memory sticks or wait until I go to school to finish something."

I sat down across from her. "Good. I'm glad it's coming in useful."

"I'm taking good care of it. I'll return it as soon as I'm done."

I waved my hand. "I told you not to worry about it. It's one I bought and didn't use. I'm glad it was something that helps you."

She regarded me suspiciously. She still wasn't convinced by my explanation.

"I hear you met Greg."

She smirked. "He introduced himself as Mr. Tomlin. He wasn't exactly Mr. Warmth."

"No, he isn't, but he's good at what he does."

"You trust him?"

It seemed an odd question, and I shrugged. "He's never given me any reason not to. He does a good job on my behalf."

Her eyes dropped back to the laptop. "Good."

"Did he upset you?"

She glanced up. "No. He was cool, and didn't seem overly interested. Dismissive, I suppose." She shivered. "He laughed when I said I was making you dinner. It seemed to amuse him. It was a peculiar sound."

I nodded in agreement. His laugh was a little strange, as if it were forced and not real.

"He's different. Don't worry about him, though. You won't see him very often. We don't do the social thing."

"Okay."

I sighed. "Are you still angry with me?"

"No."

Shrugging off my jacket, I leaned back. "So, that's it? No yelling or silent treatment?"

"Neither."

"Not that I'm complaining, but can I ask why?"

She shook her head and stood, closing the laptop. Straddling me on the chair, Emmy pulled my tie loose and unbuttoned the collar. She ran her hands along the base of my neck, her touch gentle and soothing. "I don't think I want to know the kind of women you dated if that's what you were expecting."

I gripped her hips, enjoying how she felt on my lap. "You were pretty mad this morning."

"I was. I said my piece, and it's done." She ran her fingers through my hair.

With a long exhale, I leaned into her caress. "That feels good."

She tugged on the strands. "I like your hair so much better when you leave it natural. It makes you even hotter."

I chuckled at her statement. She had informed me I was too young for a comb-over and hid the gel I used to keep my hair in order. I had to admit I liked the feel and ease of simply toweling it dry and leaving it alone. It was freeing, and Emmy liked to run her fingers through it, so I left it. She also liked me a bit scruffy, and I had stopped shaving every day to please her. Although, at times, it felt strange.

Aiden and Maddox had nailed me to the wall about becoming a pussy. I had flipped them off and walked away. Emmy's opinion was more important. Her pleasure came with benefits that resulted in my pleasure—frequently.

She spoke quietly. "I know you worry because of what happened to your parents. I talked it through with Cami, and she convinced me it was a totally romantic gesture."

A smile tugged at my lips. "I guess I owe Cami."

I met her gaze. It was soft, concerned, and a little confused. "I'm not used to being worried about."

"I can't help it when it comes to you," I confessed.

"I know. I feel the same about you."

Our eyes locked, and I sucked in a long breath.

"I have something to tell you."

She frowned. "That doesn't sound good."

I pulled out my phone and showed her the picture Aiden had copied.

"That was this morning!" she exclaimed.

"Yes."

Her lips pursed. "Well, that isn't happening again."

My chest tightened. "Oh?"

She nodded, looking serious. "That pattern makes my ass look huge! I am not wearing that dress again—ever."

I gaped at her. "Your *dress*? You're worried about your *dress*? Someone was stalking us, Emmy."

She shrugged. "You, I would say."

"Still, this involves you and your safety. It's the second time."

"I think I'm just in the shot. Looking less than fashionable, I might add."

I slipped my hands over her ass and squeezed. "For one thing, your ass does not look huge. And second, it's not the point of the conversation."

"What is?"

"I wanted you to know what was happening." I huffed out a

heavy sigh. "And to tell you, Aiden is going to assign someone to watch over you."

"No."

"Yes. It's important."

"It's not necessary."

"Then we can chalk it up to me being overprotective, and get rid of them later. Do this for me, please. Give me the peace of mind. I need it right now."

She looked down at the photo and shoved my phone into my chest. "Fine. They had better not interrupt my day, or I'll go ballistic on them."

"They'll only be observing. I'll make sure they blend in and not bother you." I stroked her cheek. "Thank you."

"You owe me."

"More than I could ever repay you."

"Are you hungry?"

"Yes."

"Then let's have dinner."

"Great idea. Dinner, some wine, and a little time with my girl." Her eyes glowed. "Okay."

I winked. "Good."

TWILIGHT WAS DESCENDING, the room aglow as the sun set. We devoured her delicious pasta, drank the wine, and I had swum my laps as she finished her work. After swimming, I doffed my wet trunks and wrapped a towel around my hips. I felt Emmy's gaze follow my every move, and knowing she was watching, I moved leisurely, my erection kicking up just thinking about her heated gaze. I poured myself a generous dollop of the brandy Greg had dropped off, and got a smaller one for her, thinking she might enjoy it. I handed her the glass and sat beside her.

"I've never had Courvoisier." She eyed the glass.

"You sip it," I explained. "Swirl the glass in your hand like this." I demonstrated. "The warmth of your skin heats the brandy and brings out its flavor. It's delicious."

She followed my instructions, then sipped at the amber liquid. She wrinkled her nose a bit, making me chuckle.

"Not to your taste, Freddy?"

"Maybe it's not warm enough." She wagged her fingers. "My hands are never very cooperative that way."

I wrapped my hand around hers, not surprised to feel the coolness of her skin. She was rarely warm to the touch, unless we were holding each other.

I offered her my glass. "Take a sip of mine. Roll it around on your tongue. Taste the difference."

She tasted my brandy and swallowed, her eyes closing in pleasure. "Oh, you're right. It's lovely when it's warmer." She ran her hand through her hair, bunching it with her fingers through a sigh. "Decadent."

She was sexy in her artless mannerisms and low voice. I hated the fact her hands were too cold to warm the liquid; although, I had no problem sharing my brandy with her. I glanced down at my glass as an idea sparked. I took her glass and poured the liquid into mine, swirling it around.

"The warmer it is, the better the flavor."

"I can't imagine how you can improve the flavor."

"I have an idea."

I shifted, turning to face her, and tugged her closer. Our eyes locked, hers widening as she felt the intensity of my gaze and the way the air around us shifted. I stared at her as I lifted the glass and filled my mouth with the amber liquid. I pressed my lips to hers, smiling as she opened for me, allowing the warm liquid to pass into her mouth. She swallowed deeply, a groan low in her throat as I pressed my tongue to hers, savoring the taste of the brandy mixed with her flavor. She slipped her hands up my shoulders, her fingers moving restlessly on the nape of my neck, playing with my hair, making me shiver. Her touch was gentle and light. It always stirred such emotion in me. I deepened the kiss, holding her tight and devouring her mouth. She whimpered, the sound muffled and needy.

In seconds, she was under me on the sofa. I pushed away her sweater and yanked down her yoga pants, covering her with my body. She tore off my towel, and our bare skin slid together, warming us both.

She wrapped her legs around my hips, cradling me with her body. I groaned at how ready she was for me, the heat of her enveloping my aching cock. I drew a plump nipple into my mouth, teasing it with my tongue until it was hard and glistening. I ran my lips to her other breast, repeating the action. She arched her back bringing her breasts closer to my mouth and gasped my name. I teased and nipped at her flesh, then buried my hands in her hair and captured her mouth again. Moments passed of only her taste. The feel of her lips, the silkiness of her hair gripped in my hands. The exquisite torture of her pussy as it slid against my cock, coating me with her desire.

"Every time," I moaned against her skin, "every time with you is so amazing."

Her feet pressed into my ass. "Inside me, Bentley. Now."

I sank deep, the sensation of being bare inside her still new and intoxicating. The heat and wet of her surrounding me, pulling me in, milking my cock as I moved was like nothing I had ever experienced. I braced my arms by her head, driving into her as desire took over. My hips pounded into hers, our sweat-soaked skin sliding together. She met my thrusts, crying out in her passion. I buried my face into her neck, breathing in her unique fragrance. My balls began to tighten, and I turned my face to her ear, sliding my tongue around the sensitive flesh.

"Come with me, baby. I need to feel you coming around me."

She arched, crying out my name. My release followed as I emptied inside her, groaning out in pleasure. I collapsed, rolling to the side, dragging her with me. I pinned her between the back of the sofa and my body, knowing she would need the heat. I snagged the blanket and draped it over her to be sure.

She sighed in my arms, nestling her head on my chest.

"You were right."

I traced my fingers around her shoulder, my touch lazy and indulgent.

"About?"

"The brandy. It tastes better from your mouth. The warmer, the better."

I grinned against her head. "I think it was you who made it taste delicious."

I felt her smile.

"Probably not a good idea to share one in public, though. We might get thrown out of the restaurant if this is what happens to you."

I started to chuckle.

"Good plan, Freddy. We'll keep brandy sharing for our private time."

"I wonder . . ."

"What?"

"How it tastes when you lick it off skin. *Your* skin."

I tightened my grip. "Emmy . . ."

She looked up at me, her eyes filled with mischief. "I was just thinking. A mouthful of brandy . . . a mouthful of you . . ."

I stood, taking her with me.

We were going to need more room.

Plus more brandy—*lots* more brandy.

CHAPTER 12

EMMY

BENTLEY SHIFTED, MUTTERING something as he moved. His arm tightened around me reflexively, then loosened as he drifted back into sleep. Early dawn spilled through the glass, and I could study his face in the wan light. Relaxed, without the serious countenance that people saw him wear, he looked younger and oddly vulnerable. His light brown hair, without the product to tame it, was wavy and fell over his forehead. I liked how it looked on him. The stubble was thick on his chin, and I knew I would find evidence of his passion on my skin. Slight red blemishes his rough beard left behind. He allowed the scruff because I liked it, even though I knew he preferred to be clean-shaven. He did so many things to please me, but he couldn't see how wonderful he was.

I inhaled, content and lazy, yet not sleepy. The bed smelled like Bentley, like me, like us. There was the faint aroma of brandy and sex, making the scent unique and heady.

Unlike his serious, stiff persona he showed to the world, when we were alone, Bentley was open—a passionate, giving lover. I adored his playful side and loved his hidden, ardent nature. He made me feel free to express my wants. He loved it when I was vocal with him, and he had no qualms about giving me everything I asked, or demanding what he wanted, *needed*, from me. I'd had other relationships in the past, but nothing close to what I shared with him.

He was a constant surprise to me. The day I met him in the coffee shop, I thought he was bigger than life. It hadn't taken me long to see past the haughty exterior, or his snotty remarks—they were simply a cover. His eyes told a different story. Exceptional in color, they were a vivid blue, with dark circles around the irises, setting off the hue. They spoke of sadness and pain, and they drew me to him. I hadn't expected to see him again, and when he had shown up, my heart flew into my throat; although, I had acted calm. His bumbling attempts at asking me to dinner, only cemented my first instincts that there was more to the man than he ever let anyone know.

The lengths he went to for my birthday, the way he included my friends had been the nicest thing anyone had ever done for me. Since then, he had bent over backward to be part of my world. He had let me drag him bowling, once again bringing Aiden and Maddox along. The six of us had the two end lanes, splitting up into boys versus girls. While he'd appeared horrified at the idea of wearing shoes someone else had worn, and informed me tossing a ball down an alley was hardly a sport, once he relaxed, he proved not only to be a good bowler but joined in the trash-talking and amusement as much as Aiden and Maddox. They looked shocked at his antics, but laughed hard when he slapped my ass after his third strike and dragged me into his arms, kissing me hard and informing me, "That's how it's done."

We also hosted a movie night, and everyone came to the house. We made homemade pizza, teasing and arguing over toppings and how long to bake them. Afterward, we watched movies, and I curled up in his lap, enjoying the closeness. Aiden started a popcorn fight between movies, and we were all laughing and breathless as we collapsed into the comfortable recliners when it was finished.

Bentley had pressed a kiss to my head, breathing a quiet, "Thank you," into my ear. I knew what he was thanking me for—a night of fun and friends, instead of another night alone. I hated the thought of his life before we met, and the loneliness he endured all the time. I curled up closer to him with a silent promise he would never be alone again.

I couldn't help noticing our friends had paired off again. Aiden and Cami were in the back row, and I was certain I had seen their hands clasped together at one point. Dee and Maddox seemed to be in constant private conversation; their heads close as they spoke.

I had laid my head on Bentley's shoulder, content and hopeful the future would have many nights like those for us.

I thought of his reaction when I surprised him one night with a pair of plaid lounge pants and a thermal top with matching trim. They weren't expensive, but the blue in the plaid reminded me of his eyes, and I wanted to give him something since he gave me so much. His smile had been big and honest, his delight genuine, as if I'd given him a designer housecoat instead of a silly set of pajamas. He had kissed me soundly, then as soon as we'd washed them, he pulled them on and struck a pose, asking me in a teasing voice if he could pass as a couch potato now. I tackled him to the sofa, proving how sexy a potato he was. He made a point to wear them often, which made me happy.

Then there was the business dinner I attended with him. He had surprised me with the invitation and a dress he had Cami help him pick out. It was deep blue silk, and the simple cut suited me perfectly. His declaration that he needed me with him had touched my heart, and when I presented myself to him that night, the look on his face made me warm all over. His deep kiss spoke of promises of "later," and he had more than lived up to them when we returned home.

As he looked at me, he frowned and reached out, running his finger over my ear. "Where are your earrings, Emmy?" He lifted my hands. "Your rings?"

"I thought it best I take them off for tonight," I admitted. "I don't want to embarrass you."

He studied me for a minute, then unbuttoned his jacket and sat down.
"I'll wait."

"For?"

He smiled, the tenderness on his face, and the gentle tone he used,
touching me deeply.

"For you to put them back in. I want my Emmy with me—all of her.
Nothing about you could now, or ever, embarrass me. Go finish getting ready,
then we'll leave."

I did feel naked without them. Bending low, I kissed him with my own
promise and hurried up the stairs to do as he asked.

Watching him in business mode was fascinating. Cool and in control,
he worked the room, his posture stiff, his shoulders tense, never stopping long
or being personal with anyone. He shook hands, discussed projects and bids,
traded business cards, and never once left my side. At the table, he pulled my
chair close and leaned over often to murmur something sweet or dirty into
my ear, his voice and manner completely different to the one he used with
everyone else. I saw the glances and felt the glares of a few women there,
but I didn't care. I was the one he wanted there beside him, and that was
all that mattered.

He was all that mattered.

Breaking out of my memories, I glanced at the clock and sat up,
stretching. Bentley groaned, opening his eyes.

"What are you doing?"

"I have to go. I'm meeting Cami to study."

"Why didn't you have her come here?"

I chuckled as I slid from the bed, escaping his attempts to stop
me. "Because she'll want to use the pool, watch a movie, and bake
cookies in your ridiculously impressive kitchen. We'll get nothing
accomplished, and I want it done. I have a ton of other projects I have
to do, as well. I'm meeting her at Al's, and when we're finished, I'm
already at my place."

He followed me to the bathroom and crowded me in the shower.
"I don't want you to go. I like it when you're here." He trailed his
hand down my arm and clasped my fingers. "You could stay, Emmy."

I gazed up at his serious face. He'd been dropping not so subtle hints the entire time I had been there. I had a passcode, a key, and he constantly referred to his house as our home. Still, it was too soon. My place wasn't much, but it was mine, and I had control there. That was important.

"You'd be sick of me in a week," I teased, trying to lighten the moment.

"I'll never be sick of you."

I stared at him, feeling the panic well in my chest. I wasn't ready for that conversation. Not yet. "Bentley . . ."

"It's too soon?"

"Yes," I breathed out. I hoped he wasn't going to argue and push the subject.

"So, it's not a no forever? Just for right now?"

"Just for right now."

"When will you be back?"

"I have classes Monday and another project due Wednesday, so maybe Thursday?"

He pursed his lips, crestfallen. "I have to wait until Thursday to see you? That's a long time."

"You used to not see me *ever,* so I hardly think four days is an eternity."

He pulled me close, his lips hovering over mine. "It's going to feel like it."

"I'll stay for the weekend."

His mouth was hard on mine. "Good."

CAMI GRINNED AT me. "Which one is it?"

I glanced over my shoulder. "The muscle-bound one in the white T-Shirt. That's Simon."

She pursed her lips. "He looks about twenty."

"The other guy, Joe, looks even younger, so they blend in with the crowd. According to Aiden, though, they're lethal. Black belts, trained in all sorts of deadly force." I sighed. "So excessive based on a blurry photo."

She lifted one shoulder. "Aiden takes his job seriously."

I quirked my eyebrow. "Know him pretty well, do you?"

She sighed, sipping her coffee. "Not as well as I'd like."

"You looked pretty cozy on movie night."

"I thought so. We had a great time." She scoffed. "Of course, we had a great time at your birthday, bowling, and every other time we've been together."

"And?"

"I don't know. He's amazing. Smart, funny, sexy as hell . . ." Her eyes softened, her expression dreamy. "Never mind how talented that mouth of his is. The man can kiss like there is no tomorrow."

"But?" I prompted again.

She sighed. "But nothing. He shuts down. As soon as we get close, it's as if a curtain falls, and he pulls away. He's . . . hot and cold. It's very frustrating."

"You really like him?"

Her gaze skittered away. "More than I should."

Cami always fell hard and fast. She put everything she had into relationships. All of them. Lovers, friends, groups at school. She only knew one way to be involved, which meant giving her entire heart and soul. I had watched her suffer many times because of it. I didn't want to see her suffer again.

"Bentley told me relationships weren't Aiden's thing. He never said why, but I get the feeling something in his past scarred him. I think all three of them had difficult pasts." I covered Cami's hand. "I don't want you hoping for something that might never happen."

"What if I think he's worth the risk?"

"Do you feel that strongly?"

She looked away, not speaking. It was something I admired about her. We teased and joked, but when there was a serious question or topic to discuss, she never rushed into an answer, but always gave it her full concentration. I sat back and waited, knowing not to push her, but I was already dreading the answer. I could sense her feelings.

"I think Aiden could be the person to change my life."

My eyes widened. "*Cami.*"

"We fit. When he's just Aiden, we mesh so well. He makes me laugh. I feel"—she tilted her head—"cherished. It's as if I'm the only person in the world."

"Until he shuts down."

"He's hiding something. I want to help him get over it. I think I can. I think I might be the *one* person who can help him. The way I catch him looking at me . . . I can't explain it, Emmy. It's a risk I have to take."

"I don't want you hurt."

"I'm a big girl, and it's my decision."

"Have you–have you slept with him?"

"No. We've come close, but he always stops." She sighed. "He says I'm not a one-night stand girl, and that's all he is capable of."

I frowned. "I think Aiden is capable of much more. The way he looks out for Bentley? It's not only a job. He cares."

"I think he cares deeply about a lot of things. He's afraid to show it, though. The big man hides his true self behind a wall of muscle and humor."

"He *is* big."

She arched an eyebrow at me playfully, letting me know she was done with the serious talk. "I can vouch for that. I've felt how 'big' he is."

I couldn't help my giggle. "TMI, Cami. TMI."

"I'm just saying. He is packing, and I'm certain he knows how to use it. His mouth and hands are dangerous. Add in his cock, I bet the man is lethal."

We started giggling and making sarcastic, sexy remarks about men. It was us, laughing and joking together. Finally, she sighed and wiped her eyes. "We need to study."

I grasped her hand. "Can I do anything?"

"No. He adores you. He thinks you're the best thing ever to happen to Bentley. Just be you and let Aiden and I work this out." She paused and shrugged. "Or not."

"I won't keep inviting you over if it's too much."

"No, it's fine. We're both adults. Besides, we have a lot of fun on those nights. Everyone does."

"What's going on with Dee and Maddox?"

"That's the million-dollar question, and she's not answering."

"I haven't imagined the chemistry between them then?"

"God, no. She lights up like a lamp when he's around. He seems very attentive."

"They're always talking."

Cami arched an eyebrow. "That's not all. I caught them in the kitchen when I went to grab something on movie night. Unless my sister needed mouth-to-mouth resuscitation—that was another kind of in-depth conversation they were having."

I chuckled. "She's older than he is."

Cami shrugged. "It's a number."

"Bentley says he is the most mature of them all. That he always has been. He's also the most private and intense."

She snorted. "There's the pot calling the kettle black. Mr. Rigid himself."

"I think he means he is old beyond his years."

She pulled out her laptop. "Well, I like him, and I think he's good for her. She smiles more."

"I guess time will tell."

She nodded. "For all of us."

"Who knew all this would happen the day Bentley tripped over my rucksack and told me off?"

"I know. Your millionaire is pretty awesome."

I scowled. "He's more than a millionaire."

"I know that. I was only teasing."

"He's so much more than his money."

"He is with you." She sighed. "The way he came to me and asked for a dress for you. He was so"—she waved her hand—"*earnest* and worried. He wanted you to feel pretty, but not overwhelmed. He wanted to make you happy."

"He did. He does—all the time." I glanced to the side. "Except for the escorts."

"At least they aren't obvious."

"No," I agreed. "They stay in the background. They make sure I'm okay, and nobody bothers me." I sighed. "I just think it's unnecessary."

She shrugged, opening her laptop. "Once this blows over, you'll go back to normal."

I took her cue and grabbed my notes.

I wasn't sure with Bentley there was such a thing as normal.

CHAPTER 13

BENTLEY

WE PULLED UP in front of the house, the entire drive silent. I was fuming, my mood dark, and the scotch I had slammed back souring in my stomach.

Aiden eyed me warily. "You want to talk about it?"

"No," I snapped. "I don't even want to fucking think about it right now."

"Bent, it's a deal that didn't work. It's not as though we can't afford to absorb the loss."

I threw open the car door. "Not the fucking point."

"I know the project meant a lot to you, but we'll regroup and figure out our next step. We'll find the right spot for your vision."

"That was the right fucking spot, and someone screwed me over." I stepped out of the car. "I'm going to find out who it was, if it's the last thing I do."

He started to follow me, and I held up my hand. "Not now. I

don't want to talk about it, and I don't want to see anyone tonight."

"Emmy's here."

"She's different." I was glad she was there. She would distract me. We could have dinner, and then I would spend the rest of the night inside her. That was always a good distraction. I'd think about the entire fucked up deal tomorrow. There had been too many lately.

"Try to rein in your bad mood. It might help."

I flipped him the finger and left him at the car. I didn't care where he went as long as it wasn't with me.

In the elevator, I rubbed my eyes, and let my head fall back. I hadn't felt that amount of rage in a long time. It bubbled and prickled at my skin, and I yanked on my tie, loosening it. I wanted to forget about the entire fucking day. I stepped off the elevator, focused solely on finding Emmy. I paid no attention to where I was going and found myself on my knees after tripping over something on the floor.

Cursing, I grabbed at my throbbing knees and glanced behind me. Emmy's old rucksack sat on the floor as if she'd dropped it there in haste. My dark mood grew exponentially blacker. I hated that rucksack with a passion, and even more, I hated what it symbolized. She took it everywhere with her, and she always left it close to the elevator if she didn't plan on staying—which meant she didn't intend to be here long tonight.

I stood, brushing off my pants, and cursing again. There was a tear in the fabric of one knee. I had just bought the suit. I liked it, and now it was ruined, all because of that goddamn rucksack. Without thinking, my foot shot out, and I kicked the offending bag across the floor where it hit the table leg, causing a small piece of sculptured glass to scuttle over the edge, and smash on the wooden floor.

"Fuck!" I roared.

Emmy appeared around the corner, a knife in her hand. "What on earth—" Her words dried up when she saw me. "Bentley, what's wrong?"

I stalked over and picked up the bag. "Do you have to fucking leave this by the elevator? I have closets, you know. You could act like a responsible adult and actually put it away. How many times do I have to trip over this piece of shit?"

She grimaced and took the bag from my fist. "I'm sorry. I was running late, and I dropped the bag when I came in with my arms full. I meant to put down the groceries and come back to get it. I wanted to have dinner ready for you." She smiled tentatively. "I'm sorry you tripped."

"Ruined my new suit." I snarled, not ready to let it go.

She glanced down. "Oh, God, Rigid. I'm so sorry."

"My name is Bentley. Not fucking Rigid! Knock it off with the nicknames. I hate them."

She stepped back, studying me with a scowl. "You never mentioned that. I apologize. Maybe it would be best if I went back into the kitchen and finished dinner, to give you a chance to calm down a little. Maybe have a drink and a shower before we eat."

Her calm demeanor only angered me further. I poked at the bag. "Why are you still carrying that crap? I got you a new one for your birthday!"

"I have it with me, as well. My hands were full when I arrived. I dropped the rucksack, and as I said, forgot to go get it. I apologize—again."

"Why the hell do you need two? What is so fucking special about this one? Why do you always have it with you?"

She drew in a deep breath. "I'll answer your questions when we can discuss it calmly."

"I want to discuss it *now*."

She shook her head. "Too bad. I'm making dinner, and you can go cool off somewhere. I don't like your tone."

"And I don't like my suit being ruined because you're too lazy to pick up after yourself!"

Her eyes narrowed at my ire. "Well, you're in a mood." She turned and walked away, leaving me fuming. I followed her into the kitchen.

"What is that smell?"

"I'm making tacos."

I grimaced. "Tacos? I don't want *tacos*. Why didn't you let Andrew make dinner? It's what I pay him for, and at least it would be something an adult would eat."

She whirled around. "I think you need to leave the kitchen."

"It's *my* kitchen."

"You're acting like a child."

I knew I was. I was acting like an asshole. The truth was, I liked it when she made tacos. In fact, I liked everything she made. Tonight, nothing was going to be right. Not even, it seemed, Emmy.

I stormed out of the kitchen. "I need a fucking drink."

I grabbed the decanter of scotch and poured a healthy shot. I downed it in one swallow, the liquor burning its way down my throat and into my chest. I refilled the glass and stomped upstairs to my room, pulling off my suit. I swallowed some more of the liquor and stepped into the shower. The sting of the water on my knee made me hiss and looking down I saw a gash from where I fell.

I was going to burn that piece of shit rucksack when I got hold of it.

I turned on all the jets and closed my eyes as the hot water poured over me. The steam billowed around me, and the heat worked its magic on my stiff muscles. Bracing myself on the wall, I huffed a deep sigh and let the water rain down. I had no idea how long I stood there, but finally, I lifted my head, no longer as tense as I had been.

I reached for my shampoo, and my fingers encountered the buff thing Emmy liked to use. I picked it up, studying it, remembering her reaction to the shower the first time she used it with me. Her excited giggles and the delight as the water poured all around us. The way she had added her body wash to the puff and scrubbed herself, then me. I thought of her joy and laughter, and the way I had taken her against the tile. A smile tugged at my lips at the memory.

My head fell back with a groan. What had I done? I had been a complete ass to her. My day was shitty from start to finish, and the one thing I had wanted was to be in her company. Instead of brushing off the stupid rucksack incident, I had attacked her over it and picked a fight with her so my shitty day could get even shittier.

What a fucking moron.

My only consolation was she refused to rise to the bait. Still, I owed her an apology. A big one. Quickly, I finished up, stepped out of the shower and dried off. I swallowed the rest of the scotch, pulled on the silly lounge pants and shirt she had given me, and hurried back toward the main floor.

As I went through the living area, I noticed the broken glass was gone, and Emmy's messenger bag was tucked by the sideboard. The rucksack wasn't anywhere to be seen.

I sighed in relief, knowing she was still there. I had fully expected to find her gone after my behavior. I would have gone after her because I didn't want the incident to fester for either of us. She wasn't in the kitchen though, and the tacos she had been making for dinner were obviously off the menu, since the kitchen was spotless, and the food I had seen earlier, put away.

I raced up the stairs, taking them two at a time, finding her in the sunroom. She was sitting in my chair, her legs drawn to her chest. The rucksack was on the floor beside the chair. I tried not to glare at it. She regarded me silently as I burst into the room.

I went to the bar and grabbed a bottle of wine and glasses. I had a feeling we were going to need it. I set them on the table in front of her, and filled the glasses, offering one to her. She reached for it, but before she could take it, I grabbed her hand.

"I owe you an apology."

"Yes, you do."

"I didn't know if you'd still be here when I got out of the shower."

She pulled her hand away and reached for the wine. She took a long sip and sighed. "I almost left. I even had my 'fucking rucksack' in hand and was going to walk out the door, when I realized if I did, that made my actions seem as childish as your outburst. So, I decided to act like a grown up and stay to see if you wanted to talk, or continue to fight."

"I don't want to fight with you."

Her eyebrow rose. "I must have imagined that part."

My shoulders drooped, and my head fell forward. I stared down at my clasped hands, trying to find the right words.

"I have a temper, and sometimes I lose it."

"You told me that once. I thought you were exaggerating."

I looked up. "I wasn't. It's rare that it gets the best of me, and I'm not proud of what happened." I huffed out a breath. "I had a spectacularly shitty day."

"You lost the land bid, didn't you?"

I blinked at her. "You remembered that was today?"

"Of course I did. I know you don't like to talk about it, but I do pay attention." She leaned forward, patting my leg. "Bentley, I'm sorry. I know how stressed you were about the entire situation."

I grabbed her hand, not wanting to lose contact with her. "I was stressed and now I'm furious. I don't understand what happened or why things are going to shit businesswise. Still, I shouldn't have taken it out on you. All I wanted was to come home and see you. You were going to be the good thing about today."

"Then you tripped over the bag, hurt your knee, ruined your suit, and became even angrier."

"I don't care about the suit or my knee," I confessed. "It's the bag. What it represents. It was as if it hit me in the gut, and that was it. I exploded."

"What it represents?"

I leaned forward, gripping her hand. "I love your independence. I love how strong and vital you are. It's that bag—you carry it everywhere. I know when I see it by the door, you're going to leave. I feel as though you're always ready to run."

Her next words shocked me. "I am."

"What?" I ran my hand over the back of my neck, the nerves prickling under my skin.

She wanted to run?

"It's because of my childhood, Bentley."

"Why, Emmy? I don't understand. You never talk to me about

your past. I told you about my childhood and my messed-up state of mind, but you never share that part of your life."

She sighed and picked up the rucksack. "This was my brother's. It's all I have left of him."

I was confused. "Isn't he alive?"

She shrugged. "I think so. I have no idea."

"I don't understand."

"I didn't have a normal childhood. My parents were, for lack of a better term, gypsies. They hated to stay in one place. My grandmother stayed with us since they were always off on some adventure."

"She's the one who taught you to make scones?"

A glimmer of a smile tugged at her lips. "Yes. She was the one constant I knew." Emmy's smile faded. "She died when I was young."

"I'm sorry."

She pulled out a tattered book from her rucksack. "This was hers."

I took the handmade cookbook and looked at the pages covered in writing, notes and sketches. I glanced up, nodding at her to keep talking.

"After she died, my parents were forced to stay home more. I was ten, and Jack was fifteen. For the next two years, they were miserable. To this day, I don't know why they had kids. They were lousy parents, and more concerned with what quest they were missing out on than how their actions affected us. They would disappear for a few days, sometimes longer, leaving us alone. When they were home, they'd move us around constantly. I never had any friends, or stability. Jack tried hard to be the responsible one. He was older than me, and I relied on him for everything."

"That must have been difficult."

She nodded. "When Jack was seventeen, my parents left, and never came back. They walked away from us. I was twelve."

"*Jesus*. They just left you?"

"Yes. They left money and a note. Told Jack to look after me, and they disappeared. We never saw them again." She sighed. "We were informed they died in Asia on some expedition. Their bodies were never recovered." She reached into the rucksack, pulled out a small frame, and handed it to me. "That is the last picture I have of my family."

I studied the faded snapshot. Her parents were young and smiling into the camera. A child version of Emmy and a taller boy stood beside them. His arm was around her protectively. Her parents were dressed in hiking apparel, and Emmy looked sad.

"My parents' behavior taught us to never rely on anyone else but ourselves. I learned early on not to depend on others. Even Jack. He drummed it into my head never to let my guard down. Always be prepared to leave. Be the first to go. Never trust anyone. Be responsible for yourself."

"That's one hell of a lesson for a young kid."

"We had to stay ahead of everything until Jack turned eighteen and could legally care for me. We were constantly on guard." She sighed, her fingers stroking the worn leather. "He kept everything important in this bag and never let it out of his sight, in case we had to leave."

The significance of the rucksack became clearer.

"What happened?"

"We never settled in one place for long. When people started asking questions, we moved on. Once he turned eighteen and I was a bit older, we came here. Big city, not a lot of people ask questions. No one looked for parents. He found a job and looked after me until I turned seventeen."

"And?"

Her voice dropped, saturated with sadness. "Jack and I are two very different people. He had more of my parents in him than I did. He hated being in one place, the same way they did. He didn't want roots. He, at least, had enough of my nana's teaching to be responsible and care for me, so I didn't end up in foster care. Still, when I turned seventeen, he decided I was old enough to be on my own. He'd done his duty, and it was time. I woke up one morning, and he was gone. Just like my parents."

"Emmy," I groaned, aghast.

"He warned me all my life. Never trust anyone—never rely on another person. He emphasized that above everything else. I never realized he included himself in that statement. He walked away, and all he left behind was this rucksack."

"You must have been gutted."

"I was. I was terrified. I grieved, and then I got angry."

I felt a fission of pride at her words. "What did you do?"

She tossed her hair. "I spoke with Al, and he agreed to let me rent the smaller apartment in the building."

"That's where you lived with Jack? Over Al's?"

"Yes. We lived at the other end of the hall in a larger apartment. I had the bedroom, and Jack slept on the couch. I talked to Al, and he let me move to the smaller place and gave me a job. I finished high school and took more courses. I got another job—the one I told you about. I kept working at Al's and added a couple other part-time ones to save as much money as I could. I decided what I wanted to do, and I worked my ass off to get into the school I wanted. The one really good thing that happened was I met Cami and Dee, and I made my own family."

"And you trust them?"

"As much as I trust anyone."

"What else is in your rucksack?"

She pulled out more pictures, a few trinkets, a broken watch, and some paperwork. There was a small worn box she laid on top.

"The watch was my dad's. He gave it to Jack, but it stopped working. He always wore it anyway, but he left it the day he left me."

My throat tightened at the pain in her words.

I indicated the box. "What is that?"

"My nana's wedding ring. It's the only thing I have that holds any value. If I was desperate and needed cash, I could sell it."

I lifted the box and flipped open the lid. A thick band of gold was nestled in the dusty velvet. Highly sentimental, yes, but hardly worth much if sold.

I sat back, looking at her. I stared at the few possessions she held most dear. None of them, even the ring, was worth anything, but they were all she had left of a lonely life and childhood. Small mementos of people who never loved her enough to stay. They were a reminder of what she had lost.

Understanding dawned on me.

She was terrified of losing her rucksack because if she did, she was going to lose them all over again. That was why she clung to it so fiercely. She felt it was all she had in the world and the small items she had defined her.

The way she saw it, she had never been enough for any of them to stay. She wasn't enough to be truly loved.

She had to be the one to leave.

But she was wrong.

I shifted forward and held out her things. She slipped them into the bag and placed it by her feet. Reaching out, I grasped her hands in mine.

"Emmy, I'm sorry. I'm sorry for what you went through, and I'm sorry about my outburst earlier." I shook my head before she could speak. "I know what your rucksack represents to you now, and I understand. I won't give you a hard time about it anymore."

Tears glimmered in her eyes.

"I need to ask you something, though. Please be honest with me."

"Okay," she whispered.

"Do you trust *me*, Emmy? At least as much as you trust, say, Cami?"

She hesitated, then nodded. "Even more."

"Does that scare you?"

"Yes."

"I want to tell you something, and I want you to listen, okay?"

She squeezed my fingers, and I lifted her hand to my mouth and pressed a kiss to the skin.

"You are such a light in my life. You have brought me so much . . . *joy*. I can't imagine my life without you anymore. I'm *not* going anywhere, and I don't want you to either. I want you here, with me, as much as possible."

Her hands began to tremble.

"I know it's difficult for you to believe, but it's true." I inhaled a long breath. "I never want you to leave. Ever. You *can* rely on me because I am *not* leaving you."

A tear ran down her face.

"I know you're not ready, but when you are, I'll make you a place where you can put your rucksack, and it will be safe. You'll never have to carry it with you because you'll know you never have to run."

"W-why?"

I slid my hands up her arms to her face, cupping her cheeks. "Because your home will be with me, Emmy. Always," I murmured, as her tears fell thicker. "I love you."

She stared at me, blinking and shocked.

"I love you so much, the thought of you leaving me makes me crazy. I want you here."

She began to shake her head.

"I know you don't think you're worthy of being loved, baby, but you are. You're more worthy than any person I know. How your brother and parents acted was wrong. You didn't deserve that. No child deserves that." I wiped her tears. "One day I'll make you see how much you're loved. And maybe you can love me back." I held her face tighter. "Because that would be the greatest gift I ever received. You."

"I have n-nothing to . . ."

I shook my head, knowing what she was trying to say. "Yes, you do. My wealth doesn't make me deserve your love, Emmy. The kind of man I am, that I *want* to be for you, does. I'll keep you safe; you can keep me grounded. I'll buy you lots of shawls, and you can make me scones. We'll take care of each other." I smiled at her tenderly. "We could build a great life together, baby. No one gets me the way you do. I need your loving, forgiving heart in my life. *I need you.* And I think, if you let yourself feel it, you need me, too."

"I'm scared."

"I know. I am, too. I never thought I could love someone like I love you. I do, and I want you to know it."

"If you walk away, I'm not sure I'll survive it," she confessed. "Not this time."

"You will never have to find out. I swear to you."

Her breath stuttered out of her throat, nervous and tense.

"I-I love you, too, Bentley."

Her words filled me with hope, and I felt everything else drain away. They banished all else in the world, making all of it unimportant. I had her, and that was all that mattered. Not a business deal gone bad, or a shitty day. *Her.*

I pulled her to my lap and kissed her. It was a kiss filled with adoration and hope, one that promised something we both needed. Love.

I tucked her head under my chin. "We'll figure this all out, Emmy. One step at a time. Just promise you'll talk to me. Don't run. Don't ever run."

"I promise."

I sighed, holding her close, needing to break the intense bubble surrounding us. I wanted to make her smile and find her feet. "I have one more thing to ask of you tonight."

She tilted up her head. "What?"

"Can we go downstairs and have tacos now? I'm starving."

She grinned, her dimple popping on her cheek, her response simple and perfect.

"Yes."

CHAPTER 14

BENTLEY

I DIDN'T GO into the office the next day. I decided not to return the rest of the week. I texted Aiden and Maddox, told them to take time off, and instructed Sandy to get one of the interns to man the office and take the days off, as well. We all needed to regroup.

When I told Emmy, she flashed me a grin and said she was taking advantage of my "un-rigidness" and staying home with me. She would get her classmates to take notes and would do her work online. I called down to Andrew, telling him to have the entire weekend off, too. I knew he'd love the time to spend with his daughter and grandkids, and it would give me the time alone with Emmy. At least, so I thought.

I answered some emails, shut the laptop and sat back, wondering if I should take Emmy away for the weekend. Maybe a break would do us some good. She walked in, holding a steaming mug of coffee and a plate piled high with pancakes. She had a bottle of syrup tucked under her arm. She set the plate and mug on the desk with a grin, then crawled onto my lap.

"I brought you breakfast."

I slid my hand along her leg. "You or the pancakes?"

She chuckled, drowning the pancakes in syrup. "You already had me in the shower, so you'll have to make do with the pancakes."

I nipped at her ear. "I bet you'd taste damn good with some syrup."

"Messy."

"But so sweet," I whispered, swirling my tongue on her skin, sliding my hand higher.

"Not happening," she replied in a singsong voice.

I pulled back with a frown. "Why?"

"Because Aiden and Maddox are in the kitchen eating pancakes. I doubt you want them witnessing your, ah, *syrup* fantasies."

"Why are they here?"

She cupped my cheek and lifted a mouthful of pancakes to my lips. "Open up."

I chewed the sweet, thick offering, licking my lips in appreciation.

"They were worried about you, Rigid. They came to check on you, and I offered them breakfast."

"That's like feeding a stray cat. They won't leave."

"I promised them brunch on Sunday if they ate, checked on you, and left." She fed me another mouthful and took a smaller one for herself. "For the record, when they saw I was here, they offered to leave."

A dribble of syrup leaked down her chin, and I grasped the back of her neck and licked it off her skin, fighting the groan when she whimpered. My already hard cock twitched at her breathy sound.

"Why didn't you listen to them?"

She tilted her head. "Because I wanted you to see you have people who care about you. Not your business, but *you*. They're here because they love you."

"Is that why you're here?"

She traced my jaw, her touch feather-light and warm on my skin.

"I love you very much."

"Good. They need to leave, though. I want you alone." I traced over her lips with my tongue, tasting her and the syrup. "I want you to show me how much you love me. Then I'll show you. It's going to take all day, Freddy. All damn day."

She grinned. "One track mind."

"Two track actually. I want more pancakes, then I want you."

She slid off my lap, taking the coffee cup with her. "Eat up then."

I watched as she moved around my den. She rarely came in, and I had to admit her lack of curiousness was a surprise. She never snooped or pried. When we talked about my business, it was more concern if I was working too hard, or was too stressed. She listened when I ranted on occasion, and always seemed interested in the projects or meetings, but more about me in the scope of it all, not what I did. It was as if I was more important than my money or work. A feeling I found strange, yet endeared her even more to me.

She paused by the concept model of the project that was now dead. She studied the display for several moments, not saying a word. Finally, she spoke. "This is quite the project. The scope is enormous."

Wiping my mouth, I stood and crossed the room to stand beside her.

I ran a finger over the mock-up. "*Was*, you mean."

"Are you going to sell the land?"

"If the offer is fair, I think so. There is no point in sinking more money into a project that hasn't panned out."

"Won't you know who is behind the scenes once they start building?"

"No. I'm certain they'll pass it all along to various companies they own, all numbered and anonymous, and finally, sell it to a holding company that will build. The layers will be too costly to peel away and figure out where it all started. Walking away makes the most sense now."

"Is that your only option?"

"I could still build condo towers once the land is cleared. It wouldn't be what I envisioned, but could still be profitable."

She made a funny noise and scowled.

"What?"

"Nothing."

I grew impatient. "Emmy, you obviously have something to say. Just say it."

"How rich *are* you, Bentley?"

That wasn't what I expected from her. She never asked or seemed to care about my wealth.

"Rich enough."

"Are we talking millions?"

I rubbed the back of my neck. "Hundreds of millions, actually."

"Huh."

I narrowed my eyes. She was going somewhere with her line of questioning, but I wasn't sure what point she was trying to make. "Huh, what?"

"Can you spend it all?"

I shook my head. "Only if I were an idiot. I have enough if I never did another day's work I could live very well, as could my children and even their children."

"So when is enough—*enough*?"

"What are you getting at?" I demanded, not understanding.

She indicated the design. "You said this was about making your mark first. Money second."

"It is."

"Then change your design."

"What are you talking about?"

Maddox spoke up from the doorway. "This I want to hear." He sauntered in, sipping his coffee, looking relaxed. However, I knew him, and I saw the interest in his eyes.

Emmy hesitated, and I squeezed her hand. "It's okay. We want to hear what you have to say."

"This piece . . ." She pointed to the end of the property. "It's not developed yet?"

"No. It's all trees and wild growth."

"What if you built a condo tower here?" She indicated the land close to the road. "Then instead of adding a second one here, made it into a private park?"

"What? What good would that do?"

Maddox edged closer. "Keep talking."

She worried her lip. "I saw something once, on TV, about a building where all the units face frontward; the only things on the back of the building were the hallways. If you designed it like that, then every condo would have amazing views of the park and the water, right?"

She kept going. "And if the park was private to the condo tower, it makes it even more exclusive. You could have woods, a playground, barbeque areas. Make it a real family kind of place."

"Family?" I questioned.

"Even rich people have children too, Bentley. Think about it. Has anyone ever done something like that?"

Maddox set down his coffee cup. "No," he replied, excitement filling his voice.

"No one has." Aiden's voice suddenly joined in the conversation as he appeared beside us.

I leaned forward, looking at the mini structures. "They could do the same thing."

"They could, but we have the advantage," Aiden mused. "They wouldn't have the park. Or the views. They either look into the city or the back of our building."

They both began to speak.

"With the bylaws, they can't build higher than ten stories, so they're screwed."

"Even if they got it changed, we could, too. We could build higher."

"We need to get the building designed, so it's one of a kind. All front facing, individual towers with separate entrances, and elevators. Custom layouts for different sized families."

"Single people would like it, too," Emmy offered. "The park setting would be a huge draw in the city."

"We'd lose revenue without standard sized units and plans. Expensive to build," I ruminated.

"No," Aiden said. "What we'd lose in the number of units, we'd make up for with the price on the uniqueness of it." He chuckled. "I bet our profits go up. We add all sorts of amenities."

"Underground parking," Emmy offered.

"Two pools. Other family activities only residents have access to," Aiden stated.

"Like a resort on a daily basis." Maddox grinned.

"Let's not get carried away," I protested, but I had to admit, it was an intriguing idea.

Aiden winked at me. "Not billions, but we'd kill it."

"And we keep it," Maddox stated firmly. "BAM owns it. No investors. Just us."

"Or I sell it and walk away."

They looked at me.

"You could," Aiden drawled. "This is an interesting concept, though. We can find other land to develop the original concept. Try something totally distinctive."

"We could lose our shirts."

Maddox shook his head. "No, Emmy is right. Lots of wealthy families love condo living. Give them the best of both worlds, and it will explode. I'm sure of it."

"We would have to make the back of the building into something unique. Eye-catching."

"Mosaics."

I glanced at Emmy.

"Use stone, hire artists. Make it beautiful. A focal point." She beamed. "Your mark."

I returned her grin. She was glowing, her dark eyes excited.

"I can see it. A haven inside the city." Maddox's eyes combed over the model, nodding. "An escape without leaving home."

Aiden pointed to the layout. "We could build up this area here, like an embankment. It would cut off noise from the road and offer even more privacy. Add trees and flowers to make it scenic."

Emmy giggled, and I looked at her. "Like a ridge," she explained. "You can call it Bentley Ridge Estates."

I started to laugh, remembering her remarks the first day. "Where the living is easy."

"That's not bad. We could fine tune it."

I shook my head. "It's a joke."

"No, Bent." Aiden shook his head. "It could work."

Emmy grabbed a piece of paper and sketched furiously. "If you made three separate towers with arches between them for the entrances and elevators, you could name them."

"Name them?"

"Towers B, A, and M."

Aiden grinned. "I like it."

I LOOKED AROUND the room, only to realize Emmy was gone. She must have slipped out at some point.

Aiden followed my gaze. "I think she thought we needed some privacy."

I shook my head. "This is *her* idea."

"I don't think she thought you'd take her seriously."

"I think we should," Maddox observed. "This is what we needed. Fresh eyes." He met my glance. "She's totally amazing."

"She is."

I glanced at my watch, shocked. It was past three. We had come into the den at ten. Where had the hours gone? I glanced around to notice the piles of paper, and notes we all scribbled, assembled together. It had been a productive planning session.

"You really think this could work?"

Aiden nodded. "It's a great concept. We need the right architect and planner."

"It would be easier to sell and walk away."

"When have we ever done the easy thing?"

I looked back at the mock-up. Aiden followed my glance. "We can do that elsewhere, Bent. Let whoever bought the other land develop it without this piece. They won't get the impact they wanted, and in fact they might end up selling and moving on. Whatever idiot develops around us can have the hassle of figuring it out. We can do this and sit back and relax. The more I think about it, the more I like it." He grinned. "Think about it—this will piss off whoever thought they could get the better of you."

I smirked at the thought. "Greg expects me to tell him to sell the land this week."

"Too bad. Change of plan." He tapped the pile of papers beside him. "It's a good plan. A brave one. Something we can all be proud of."

I nodded in agreement. He was right.

"This nightmare would be over. No more extra security. Back to business as usual."

"I think I'd be cautious a little while longer," Aiden advised.

"If I do this, if we do this—*we* won. I lost the battle, but I won the war. They don't get what they wanted, and there is nothing they can do about it." I warmed to the idea. "We go with the new plan, we get the best design and soak some serious cash into it, and go for it. They'll want to sell to us."

Maddox laughed. "Fuck them, right?"

I smirked. "Not interested. Unless the price is deeply discounted. Then I might take it off their hands."

Maddox chuckled, but Aiden looked concerned. "Let's not invite trouble."

"What can they do? They can't stop me from building, and they can't touch the land."

"They can touch you."

I shook my head. "No. It's over, Aiden. They pissed me off, caused some chaos, and they bought the land, but we came back stronger.

We won."

I stood and stretched. "I think you guys need to go start your weekend."

Maddox chuckled and grabbed Aiden's arm. "We've been told."

Aiden frowned. "Emmy promised brunch Sunday."

I waved him off. "Fine. But I want you gone until then."

He made a kissy face, and I flipped him the bird. I walked them to the door, shutting it firmly behind them. I took the stairs two at a time.

I needed to find the girl responsible for the idea and thank her. I knew exactly where to find her.

She was in her favorite spot. Sunlight was streaming in the windows, making the room warm. Still, she had her shawl wrapped around her shoulders. Her head rested on the arm of the chair, a book open on her lap, and her full lips were pursed as she slumbered peacefully.

Bending low, I brushed a kiss to her tempting mouth, grinning as she pouted and stretched, then curled back up like a contented kitten in the sun. She opened one eye, peering at me.

"I was asleep."

I ran a hand over her curls. "I know. You looked adorable and I had to kiss you."

She sat up, yawning and lifting her arms over her head. Her shirt lifted, exposing a sliver of stomach, the skin soft and inviting. I wanted to kiss it, as well.

"Finished reconquering the world?"

"Thanks to your brilliant idea, I think we've regrouped."

She shook her head. "It was simply a thought. You three jumped on it and created the whole concept."

"It was more than a thought. You amazed me. You amazed all of us."

She lowered her eyes, shyly.

"Hey."

She met my gaze.

"Your idea was fresh, innovative, and helped us find a new path.

I'll be forever grateful. I was too pissed to look at it objectively. We all were."

"So, you're not selling?"

"Nope. Next week I'll put my team on it, and when I meet with Greg, tell him to reject the offer."

"Will he be pissed?"

I laughed. "No. He gets paid no matter what I do. He has no vested interest in the land, either way, so he won't care. He'll send me a sizable bill for his time, and we'll move onto the next project."

Her fingers smoothed over the edge of the cushion. "Why isn't he a part of your crowd?"

"My crowd?"

"Your business. You have Aiden and Maddox. I'm surprised he isn't part of the company. You must need a lot of legal advice."

"We have a legal consultant in the company. Greg had always been a lone wolf—never wanted to be a partner in any company, even right out of school. He went at it alone and earned his reputation. He has never expressed any desire to be anything other than what he is, and the one time I made him an offer, he turned me down. His company is his life. He's put it above everything else—including his failed marriages and countless relationships."

"Would you consider him a friend?"

I thought before I responded. "I think so. Not like Aiden and Maddox, but more a business friend. We have the occasional drink, sit together if we're at the same function, but we don't spend time together as personal friends."

She nodded and hummed.

I crouched in front of her chair. "Now, do you want to keep talking about my lawyer, or can we move on to something else?"

Her eyes glittered in the sunlight. "Such as, Rigid?"

Pulling her knees apart, I slid between them, yanking her body close. "About your reward for being so fucking brilliant. And sexy."

"Oh, a double reward?"

"I promise double." I slipped my hand under her shirt, touching the skin that had tempted me earlier. "Since I owe you for breakfast too, if you play your cards right, I think you should get triple the reward."

"Oh," she whispered, wrapping her arms around my neck, her breath hot on my skin. "I fold."

I had her out of her clothes fast, and mine disappeared thanks to her nimble fingers. I made sure to drape her shawl around her shoulders. It always shocked me how she reacted to temperature. She felt the cold so easily, so the shawl kept her back warm while my mouth and hands warmed the rest of her. Her nipples perked under my tongue, her head falling back as she moaned my name. I explored her curves, tracing them with my knuckles, making her squirm in my arms, her heat pressing on my cock trapped between us. I teased her clit, stroking and circling it, then slid two fingers inside, hitting that spot that drove her crazy with lust. She cried out, her muscles fluttering and tightening around my fingers as I wrung out her pleasure.

"That's one, baby."

She leaned forward, fusing our mouths together, her tongue sliding sensuously along mine. She lifted her hips, and guided me to her, then slowly sank down, inch by inch until our bodies were flush, the tightness and heat of her enveloping me. I grunted my approval into her mouth as she began to move. She used the arms of the chair as leverage, making her movements fluid. Dropping her face to my neck, she began to nibble at my skin, small bites that she eased with a touch of her tongue, driving me insane with need.

Need for her.

I gripped her hips, pulling her down harder as I rose to meet her, our skin slapping against each other, the sound of our joining filling the room, and raging in my head. She arched back, and I bent to worship her full breasts. Her fingers slid into my hair and yanked on the strands as she whimpered and shuddered.

"Coming!" she gasped. "Oh, *God* . . . Bentley . . ."

She cried out, stilling as I kept working her. As my orgasm hit me, my balls tightening, the pleasure surged through my body as I emptied deep inside her. With a low groan, I yanked her to my chest, both of us shaking, quiet, and sated.

"Two," I murmured.

"Not sure I can handle three."

"Maybe a dip in the warm pool will change your mind."

She snuggled closer, her head tucked under my chin. "Or maybe we can stay here like this for a while. I like being in your arms."

Her words bled into my chest.

"You're far too easy to make happy."

"You make me happy—that's all I need."

Tenderness only she could make me feel, filled my heart, causing it to beat faster. I tightened my arms, making sure her shawl was in place.

"Whatever you want, Freddy. Today, tomorrow, the rest of the weekend. Ask me and it's yours."

"Hmmm."

"Did you want to go away? Get out of the city?"

"No, I just want the time with you. Us, alone all weekend."

"Then that's what you get."

"At least until Sunday."

I chuckled. "At least until then."

⟲∿

I GLANCED THROUGH the papers Greg handed me, noting two things: the numbered company and the offer. Surprisingly, it was near market value, but considering how long I had held onto it, and my new plans, I wasn't interested.

I shook my head. "No."

"You want to counter?"

"No, I've decided not to sell, no matter the offer."

He paused, tapping his pen on the desk, his words measured. "To this company or in general?"

"It's not for sale to anyone."

Greg stared at me, the office filled with stony silence. "What are you playing at, Bentley?" he finally asked.

"*Playing at?* Nothing. I've decided not to sell the land. I'm going to develop it with a new plan in mind."

"And what plan is that?" He threw his pen on top of the papers.

"A new concept."

His fingers drummed on the desk. "That's not what you said when you left here last week. You were done with this project. You were damned vocal about it. I could hear you cursing in the elevator."

I shrugged. "Things changed. I calmed down. We regrouped, and we've decided to keep the land, and we're going to build on it ourselves. I already have my team working on it."

"Why?"

I leaned forward. "I don't know who these people are, but I am *not* bowing down to them. They fucked with the wrong guy. They've been fucking every deal I have tried to make the past while and I am *done* with it. They could offer me double what the land is worth and I wouldn't sell it to them, even if my life depended on it. They can develop, sell, or do whatever the hell they want to the rest of the property around it, but I'm keeping it."

He stared at me pointedly. "Are you certain this is what you want?"

I lost my temper. "Stop *questioning* what I want. It's my fucking business. I pay you to handle the legal aspects, not for your opinion on what I should or should not develop."

He held up his hands. "I'm simply asking. You haven't shared your plans, so I have no idea what you're thinking."

I pushed the folder toward him. "Once it's finalized, I'll tell you. Until then, tell them no deal. Ever."

He slid the folder closer to him, running his finger along the seam. "You know two pieces of the land are still zoned for industrial. I know you planned to have them rezoned, but what if they don't? What if they build industrial sites there? Will that impact your plans?"

I stood. "If that is the game they decide to play, I will fight it. I'm not going to be blackmailed into changing my mind. The zoned areas are small, and with everything I have going for me, I guarantee you, I will win that battle. They can fucking bring it on." I studied him. "Whose side are you on, Greg?"

"You're my client," he replied promptly. "It's my job to point these things out." He leaned forward, his eyes narrowed. "This is what you pay me for, Bentley. My *expert* advice. My advice that has gotten your company out of a bind a time or two, I would like to remind you."

I wasn't in the mood for his lectures.

"Yes, you did your job," I snapped. "And got paid—well paid, in case *you* forgot that fact."

We glared at each other, then he shrugged. "This entire project has been tempestuous at best. I thought you'd be glad to see it done, cut your losses, and move on. But it's your choice."

"Yes. It is. It's *my* company. There will be no losses once I'm done, trust me. Reject the offer and tell *them* to move on—whoever the fuck they are. The land isn't for sale."

"I'll do that."

I picked up my coat. "Good. Let's go, Aiden."

Aiden said something to Greg, then met me at the elevator.

"That was quite the show," he stated, as the doors shut. "I've never heard you snap at him like that before now."

I rubbed my face roughly. "He annoyed me. I hate being questioned when I make a decision."

"That was obvious." He sighed heavily. "He is right though, Bent. They could try to throw up some roadblocks and delay what we want to do, just to be assholes. The delays and problems could cost us a lot, especially if you're doing this on principle or for revenge. We could walk away and cut our losses now."

We walked outside into the dreary day. I slipped on my coat, my mind wandering to Emmy. I hoped she was warm enough today—the past couple days had been cooler and the nights downright cold. The jacket I saw her wear this morning didn't look thick enough for her, given the level of warmth she always needed. Maybe I should take her shopping for a new one, or surprise her with a gift. Maybe another visit to Cami was in order. She could help me pick out something suitable.

I brought my mind back to the problem at hand. "Maybe at first it was the principle or revenge, but Aiden, the more I think about this project, the more excited I am. I haven't felt this way about a new development in a long time."

He flashed me a grin. "I was hoping you'd say that. Maddox and I feel the same. It's gonna be cool, I think. Worth the risk."

I laughed and clapped him on the back. "At this point, there isn't any risk. So, it's full steam ahead."

Frank pulled up to the curb, and we climbed into the car. Aiden stared out the window.

"What's wrong?"

"I'm still concerned."

"About?"

"I think we still need to be vigilant with security. Until we make sure they've faded into the background."

"Emmy was hoping it would be done. She hates it."

"She said as much to Simon this morning. She was surprised to still see him there when she got to school." He paused, thinking. "It's a precaution I feel strongly about. Something in my gut is telling me to keep things as they are. I know she hates it, and you want to make her happy, but it's only for a while longer."

Aiden was often right with his gut instincts. If he felt that way, I needed to trust him.

"If that's what you think. Just pull back as much as you can. I'll talk to Emmy."

He nodded, staring out the window. "I'll think it over. I don't want someone to approach and bother her."

"Nor do I."

"It's easier when she's at your place. I know she's safe in the house."

"Trust me; I'm trying to make it full-time. She's—"

"Independent? Stubborn?" He finished for me.

"Both," I agreed. "She needs to understand I don't want to change her. I don't want to take her independence away. She has to figure out that part."

"Cami mentioned a couple of things about her upbringing. I get that."

I arched my eyebrow. "Oh, did she? When did that happen?"

His gaze went back to the passing scenery. I was surprised to see the flush of color around his neck. "We were, ah, just talking."

I laughed as Frank pulled up to the office.

"Talking. Right."

He brushed past me, shaking his head. "Leave it alone."

In the elevator, I met his suddenly vulnerable eyes. "It's fruitless to resist, Aiden. Those girls are headstrong. She's been interested since the day in the boutique. Before even."

"I'm not in the market for what she is looking for."

"You mean a relationship?"

"Yes."

"Neither was I. Emmy proved me wrong." I stopped him before he exited the elevator, my voice low and serious. "She's a great girl. You like her; she likes you. I think she'd be good for you. Don't cut yourself off again. What do you have to lose?"

"You know the answer to that."

"Give it a chance. You deserve to be happy."

"No, I don't deserve anything of the sort." With those words, he hurried past me.

I watched his retreating figure with sadness. He did deserve it. I wasn't sure how I could make him see it, yet I knew I had to try.

I ARRIVED HOME late, and Andrew met me at the elevator.

"Sir."

"Andrew—how was your day?"

"Excellent. Miss Harris is upstairs."

"Buried in her books, I imagine?"

"Since she arrived home. She refused dinner, but I have made a tray of sandwiches, and there is a thermos of coffee on the counter."

"You are amazing."

He tilted his head in acknowledgment of my words. "Have a good evening, sir."

"You, as well."

I hurried upstairs, changed, then jogged to the kitchen and grabbed the sandwiches, coffee, remembering to grab a mug.

I paused at the entrance of the sunroom. Emmy sat quietly, a pile of books scattered around her. She was concentrating so hard that she didn't even hear me approach.

"Can you take a break?"

Startled, she glanced up from her notes, her eyes bleary with fatigue. "Hey."

"Hey, yourself."

"My test is tomorrow."

I held up the plate I was carrying. "Just something to eat, Freddy. I made the sandwiches myself. Twenty minutes and you'll feel better."

With a sigh, she stood, and I took her hand, tugging her to the sofa.

"You've been working too hard."

She lifted one shoulder, dismissing my concern. She took one of the sandwiches from the plate, studying it. I chuckled at her skeptical expression. "Okay, Andrew made them. I took the plastic wrap off, though."

"They looked far too delicious to be yours."

I kicked up my feet on the coffee table and smirked. She was right.

"As for working too hard, you're one to talk, Rigid. You've hardly been home."

I held back my grin hearing her refer to the house as "home." I hadn't had to convince her to stay for another few days since a hole in the roof caused some flooding in her apartment, and Al was slow to get it fixed. The rain had stopped, and I knew she'd probably leave after the weekend, but I enjoyed having her *home*. It had been something she couldn't accuse me of orchestrating since even she admitted my control didn't reach "that far."

"How are the plans coming?" She looked at me over her sandwich.

I poured some coffee into the mug and handed it to her. "Great. Everyone's on board, and the architect has already impressed me. Maddox had met him a few months ago and liked his work. His ideas are almost as brilliant as yours."

"Right," she scoffed. "Brilliant."

"It's your idea. In fact, Maddox and Aiden want to make you part of the planning team—like an intern. Keep you in the loop. What do you think?"

"What would it entail? I'm so busy at school."

"Not much—especially right now. A few meetings. A couple of dinners. It'll be a while until it's all completed. I'd like you there with us when it opens." I hesitated. "It's a paid position."

"Oh, nice try."

"Honest, Emmy. Talk to Maddox. It was his idea. He wants to make sure you get some credit."

"I didn't do it to get credit. I did it to help you."

Leaning over, I stroked her soft cheek. "I know. And you did. Just talk to him, okay? I promise I'll stay out of it."

She rolled her eyes, mumbling about miracles having to happen, then tried to cover up a yawn.

"You're exhausted. Why is this test stressing you out so much? You know your stuff."

"It's worth a big part of my final grade. It's an entire business plan and proposal I'll be graded on. I have to present it to a panel and answer questions, plus there's a written test. I always tense up before tests. I freeze and have trouble remembering the answers. I do so much better when I'm given a project to do."

"What can I do to help?"

"Nothing. I'm meeting another classmate early tomorrow, and she is going to quiz me. She did hers last week, so she knows some of the things they are looking for and might ask me. Then I'll meet

Cami for coffee, and the presentation is at eleven, then the test."

"After, you can come home and have a nap."

"No. I can go to Al's and get more scones done."

I pursed my lips in vexation. "If you took on this project with BAM, you wouldn't have to work at Al's."

"It's part of my rent."

"The rent here is very reasonable. Free, in fact."

"Bentley—"

I held up my hands with a grin. "Think about it. I want you here, Emmy. I want to know you'll be here when I get home. That I get to sleep beside you every night." I indicated the room around us. "It feels like home when you're here. When you're not, it's just . . . space."

Her cheeks pinked. "Really?"

"Yes. Think how much easier life would be for you."

"What do you mean?"

"Frank would drive you to school and bring you home. You wouldn't have to bake so early in the mornings. You could work with Maddox on the project, which would be an excellent learning experience, concentrate on school, not have to worry about bills . . ." My voice trailed off at the frown on her face.

"If I decide to live with you, it won't be because of money."

"I know that. I was simply pointing out some good facts."

"I would have to pay my way." She lifted her chin. "Otherwise the discussion is closed."

I knew arguing with her was a waste of time. She was stubborn and proud, and scared to depend on anyone. I wanted her to depend on me, though. I wanted to prove to her she *could* depend on me and I wouldn't let her down.

"The house is paid for, and all the bills are done through my company." I fibbed a little. "Perhaps we could do an exchange. Like you have with Al."

"You want four dozen scones a day?"

I chuckled. "No, but I love your cooking and baking. It would give Andrew a break, as well. I've been thinking I needed to get him some help."

She pursed her lips. I lifted her hand to my mouth.

"Emmy, I don't want to take away your independence. I'm not going to stop you living your life. I only want to share it with you. Have you be part of mine. I admit, having you live with me would ease my mind. I want to take care of you. I've never felt that with another person. We can work out all the details, so we're both happy, but what I really want is to know you want it too."

She sighed, looking distraught.

"What are you thinking?"

"What if–what if my brother comes looking for me?"

Suddenly, I understood why she stayed in that tiny apartment. She was hoping one day he would come back and find her in the same place he had left her. That she would be important enough to him for him to return. Even after he walked away, she still held hope.

"Al will know where you went." I brushed my finger down her cheek. "If you want, Emmy, I can have Aiden get someone to look for your brother."

Her eyes widened. "You could?"

"If you want. You know, he could find you other ways aside from your address. You're on Facebook, Instagram—"

"I know. I don't think he's looking," she admitted. "That's what hurts the most."

"Then stop living your life waiting for someone who walked away from you to come back. I'm right here, and I want you. I want you with me every day. I hate it when you leave."

Tears spilled from her eyes, and I pulled her into my arms. I lay back on the sofa, letting her rest against my chest, her head tucked under my chin. "You've changed me, Emmy. I want your light and to see your beautiful face all the time. Please let me have it. Promise me you'll think about it."

She drew in a deep shuddering breath, but I felt her nod. I couldn't help the broad smile that stretched across my face.

"We'll talk and make some plans once this test is over, deal?"

"Deal."

CHAPTER 15

BENTLEY

I GLANCED AROUND the boardroom. I needed to pay attention to what was happening, except my mind was elsewhere. Greg's surly, judgmental mood, Emmy's stress over her presentation and test, her promise to consider living with me, and Aiden's insistence on security still being in place, all distracted me.

There wasn't much I could do about Greg. I had no idea why he was questioning my decisions so intensely. It wasn't as if I hadn't taken risks before, and it shouldn't matter to him. I paid him regardless if I made or lost money. Aiden's gut feeling was simply that—a feeling. I was certain he had been worried about the project for so long, he was jumping at shadows. They won the land battle, but thanks to Emmy's brilliant idea, I won the war. It was done. Over. We could move on to other things.

I planned to talk to Aiden once it all calmed down. He and Cami were great together, and he deserved a shot at happiness. In fact, I thought Maddox did as well, and he and Dee seemed well suited for each other, but I would pick my fights one at a time. Emmy would be okay after today was over. I knew Cami would have given her a pep talk this morning, and I would make sure to pamper her tonight. In the meantime, though, I could send her a funny text. She taught me how to use the emoji things so I would add them in. She loved those.

I reached for my phone just as Aiden lifted his to his ear. He listened for a moment, his face impassive, but the look he shot me made me instantly tense up. He stood, heading to the door, talking low, indicating Maddox should follow him. When he pulled open the door, Sandy stood there, holding a brown grocery bag. She looked upset, and my anxiety increased. My laptop pinged, and I glanced over, freezing as I looked at the small window that had appeared on the screen. The image was grainy and dark, but there was a girl in the frame, sitting on the floor of a dingy room.

A girl who looked exactly like Emmy.

Everything happened in slow motion.

I blinked, and the image on my screen disappeared.

Aiden clapped his hands. "Give us the room." His tone left no room for argument.

Sandy dropped the bag on the table. Aiden gripped my shoulder.

The boardroom door shut.

I looked up. "What the fuck did I just see?"

Aiden placed his phone on the table and pressed a button. A disjointed voice came on the line. "We have the girl. You want her back, wait for instructions at home. Involve the police, and she's dead."

I was on my feet without thought. "Is this a joke? Some sort of sick prank?"

Maddox opened the bag and dumped out the contents. Emmy's rucksack, the bane of my existence, fell onto the table.

"She never goes anywhere without that." I heard my voice say.

Aiden's hand felt heavy on my shoulder. "I know."

"She's at school," I insisted, as if by saying so it would make it true. "Frank drove her to school early this morning."

"She never made it."

Fear swamped me. *"What?"*

Maddox leaned forward. "Frank was found at the garage where the car is stored, knocked unconscious. Her bodyguard, Simon, got a text saying they would be late arriving at the school, but they never showed. He got worried, and started checking into the situation. The car was abandoned in an alley not far from the house. There were signs of a struggle." He sucked in a deep breath. "Some blood was on the seat. Whoever took Emmy must have picked her up."

"How much blood?" I needed to know.

"Not a lot, but there was some sort of altercation. Her messenger bag was in the back seat, and the contents dumped out."

I felt sick. I had watched her walk out the door to danger. My phone had rung, so she kissed me, and hurried outside, anxious to be on her way. I heard her call to Frank to stay in the car; she could open her own door. Except it hadn't been Frank. By the time I followed, wanting to tell her she would be brilliant today, they were gone, and I had no idea what I had allowed to happen.

I had let her walk right into their trap.

I shook my head, trying to clear it. "Frank—is he okay?"

"He has a bad concussion. They found him in the stairwell—he was knocked out before he ever reached the car. He didn't see who hit him."

The air in the room became too hot, too close. I tugged on my tie, struggling to drag in oxygen.

"Why?" I choked out.

"You know why."

"They got the land. They got what they wanted!" I swung around facing Aiden. "We did all of this as a precaution. Only a precaution! She has nothing to do with any of this!"

Maddox spoke up. "They thought they had won until you refused to give up the last piece. She has everything to do with you, Bentley. She's the one weak link in your armor. They want it all, and this is how they're going to make sure they get it."

I sat down, my legs no longer able to hold me up. "Are we sure? Was what I saw real?"

Aiden sat beside me and held out his phone. There was a screen capture of the same image I saw.

Emmy.

"Should we call the police?"

Aiden huffed out a big breath. "My gut is telling me no."

I glanced at the screen again. The huddled mass of her cowering, pushed into the corner of the room, angered me. She would be terrified and confused. Not understanding what was happening. I peered closer, trying to see, but the image was unclear. It looked as if her shirt was torn. Was she okay? Had they hurt her?

Images of my past, my dead parents, swam in front of me. The air in my lungs became constricted. I could hear my breathing coming faster, to the point I was panting. I clawed at my collar, desperate for air.

Maddox gripped my shoulders, meeting my eyes. "Calm down, Bent. We need you calm. *She* needs you calm. We'll get her back."

I dragged air into my lungs. "If they hurt her, I will kill them."

Aiden leaned in beside Maddox. "Not going to happen."

His gaze was tormented but steady.

I nodded. "Okay. What do we do?"

"We're going to the house. We wait."

"Cami!" I blurted, as a thought occurred to me.

Aiden frowned. "What?"

"She was meeting Cami. Do we know if she's okay?"

He grabbed his phone. "I'll handle it." He strode from the room, already talking.

Maddox sat beside me. "They're going to demand you sell them the last piece of land."

"I know."

He waited, his eyebrow lifted in a silent question.

I pulled a hand through my hair. "It's a fucking piece of real estate. She's my entire world. There is no question. It goes."

"Not until we make sure she is safe, Bent."

"I know. We have to find her."

"We will." He stood. "I'll get my things, and we'll head to the house. We'll take it one step at a time. Aiden and I are beside you, okay?"

"Okay."

I PACED AROUND my den, anxiety rolling off me. I stood in front of the concept model of what I had planned to be my legacy. It was nothing except buildings—brick and mortar. Businesses that would make money. Houses and condos other people would live in and create lives. Roads and sidewalks I would never use. There was nothing of me in it. It wasn't a legacy. It was a cash cow. Now someone else saw it for what it was and decided to take it. No matter what it cost.

The cost was too dear. They could have the land. I would give it to them, as long as they gave me back what really mattered.

Emmy.

Aiden came in, talking on his phone. "Good. See you soon."

I met his stare.

"Maddox has Cami and Dee. Cami got a text earlier from Emmy canceling coffee. She had no idea what was happening until I called her. He's bringing them here. Just as a precaution."

I snorted, gripping the back of my neck. "More precautions. I hope this one works better."

He held out his hands. "Bent. We all agreed they were focused on you. When they got the land, we thought it was done. She was being watched."

"Not everywhere."

He set down his phone and crossed his arms. "If you have something to say, spit it out."

"How did they get her, Aiden? Why wasn't there someone in the car with Frank? Why didn't we think of that? With everything else you insisted on, why didn't *you* think of that?"

He said nothing.

"You should have done more!"

"I know."

His simple words stopped me.

"What?"

"I thought we were covered. She left here in the safety of your car and driver. Joe or Simon picked her up at school and watched over her until she came back here later. It never occurred to me they were so desperate they would knock off your driver and take her! Jesus, we thought someone might approach her and try to talk to her *about* you, not kidnap her!" His voice rose to the point he was yelling. "And if you think I'm not already blaming myself, you're wrong!"

"You should be!" I yelled back. "I was depending on you to look after her!"

His voice became low. Angry. "It wouldn't have happened if you had walked her out to the car this morning, the way you usually do. That was always part of the daily routine. *You* could have stopped it."

His words brought me up short.

"Too busy working on another deal, Bentley? Or too exhausted from fucking her all night again? You let her walk out of here—right to them. Let me remind you, *you* told *me* to back off. So, I'm not the only one to blame here."

Rage set in. My eyes narrowed, hands curled into fists as I struggled for control. Maddox rushed in, glancing between us.

"What the hell is going on? I can hear the two of you from the front door."

Aiden stood, stiff and furious. "Nothing. Bentley is casting blame, the way he always does."

"Fuck you," I snarled.

He glared. "You usually do."

Maddox flung out his arms. "Knock it off! There is no blame here! Someone did this to get at Bentley—to get at us! Fighting is only going to make it worse." He turned to me. "You know this *isn't* Aiden's fault. We all agreed on how to handle watching her. None of us could have predicted they'd be so desperate they'd actually take her or how they would take her!"

Aiden and I stared at each other, neither of us giving an inch.

"The girls are here," Maddox informed us. "Can we try to be civil and concentrate on what is important? They're already upset enough."

My anger left me as fast as it had hit. Maddox was right. This wasn't the time to be fighting. We had to work together.

"You're right."

Aiden pushed off the desk with a huff. "Well, at least you agree with one of us."

"Aiden—"

He held up his hand. "You said enough, Bentley. I get it." Grabbing his phone, he walked out of the room, his shoulders stiff.

Maddox swung around. "What the fuck? You know this isn't his fault."

"I was angry." I yanked my hands through my hair. "I said shit I didn't mean."

"So, take it out on your punching bag. Swim a hundred lengths. Don't assign blame to someone you know is already heaping the blame on his own head." His voice softened. "You know he is, Bent. It's Aiden."

I dropped my head in my hands and rubbed my face hard. "I know. I'll apologize."

"Sooner rather than later," he advised, as he walked out of the den. "We've had enough shit today."

THE DAY DRAGGED, the house was filled with tension. Cami and Dee sat anxiously together on the sofa talking quietly. Often, one of them was in tears. Maddox and Aiden sat at the dining table with one of my other staff members, Reid Matthews, who was a whiz on the computer. I objected when Aiden hired him recently. Reid's honest disclosure of hacking skills, some run-ins with the law, and a brief stint in jail made me nervous, but Aiden insisted he was the right one for the job, and he had been correct. Loyal, hardworking, and currently, very handy. I should have been frightened by how good a hacker he was, but I was only grateful at this point. We needed anything that might get Emmy back.

The sound of the constant clicks of their keyboards drove me insane. At one point sandwiches appeared, Andrew firmly informing us all to eat. Maddox handed me a plate, and I ate without tasting, my mind constantly asking if Emmy was getting anything to eat.

All day they had been playing with us. Different images of Emmy would appear on one of our phones. In all of them, she was a huddled mass pressed into the corner. Some were close-ups where she looked at the camera, and her facial expression said it all. Pale, frightened, and alone in a darkened room. She was wearing the shirt she'd had on the second day I met her, but the tie was absent, and so was her constant extra layer of warmth. Had they taken them from her? Her shirt was torn in two places, and the knee on her pants ripped. Her hair was disheveled, and there were marks on her hands. She would be cold. It ate at me constantly, and slowly my icy anger turned hot and blistering.

None of Reid's traces turned up anything. The traffic cams he hacked into showed the car racing down my street and disappearing. He couldn't get a good angle to see the driver, but we were able to catch a glimpse of a second person in the back with Emmy.

How were they doing this? Why couldn't we find out? How dare they fucking take her and subject her to such cruelty? I vowed they would pay for this—whoever was behind it. If they wanted the land, they could have it. I would play their game, but it wasn't over—not by a long shot.

"Bentley."

I looked up, meeting Maddox's eyes. "Can you go do that somewhere else? You're freaking everyone out." He indicated my hands with the tilt of his chin. I glanced down, shocked to see the top rail of the chair I was gripping had splintered into pieces.

I loosened my grip, letting the chunks of wood fall to the floor. "Should I call Greg?"

"Are you going to sell?"

"Without question."

Cami spoke up; her voice saturated with emotion. She hadn't spoken directly to me all day. "Emmy told me you never let personal feelings influence your business decisions."

I sat beside her, laying my hand on her arm. "She isn't a feeling, Cami. She's my world. There is no question here. She matters more than any business decision."

"You promise me?"

"Yes."

A tear slid down her cheek. "Okay."

I glanced at Maddox. "Should I call Greg? Tell him I changed my mind?"

"Wait until we hear from them."

"When the fuck will that be?"

Aiden met my gaze. "When they decide to stop torturing you."

"Payback is going to be a bitch for them."

He nodded and went back to his keyboard.

I spun on my heels and hurried to the den. At least, on that matter, we were in complete agreement.

DARKNESS HAD FALLEN when my phone rang. I waited until Aiden gave me the sign, and I hit the speaker button.

"Ridge."

"We have a gift for you."

The screen on my laptop lit up, and there was a live feed of Emmy. The room was dark except for the camera light shining on her. They were close enough to her I could see the shivers racing through her body. There was blood caked on her knee.

"Look at the camera," someone instructed in a harsh tone.

Emmy raised her head, her expression fearful, but her eyes were furious. There was a bruise on her cheek and scrapes on her skin. They had tethered her to a pole, with a chain attached to a metal band around her wrist. Her hand also bore remnants of dried blood.

They had her chained up like a fucking animal. Fury built in my chest and my fingers gripped the edge of my armchair so hard the material began to tear.

"Don't you want to say hello?" The disjointed voice sneered.

I had to swallow before I could speak, so I didn't rage. I moved closer to the screen, even though I knew she couldn't see me, and I made my voice as steady as I could.

"I'm here, Emmy. Don't be frightened. It's going to be fine. I'll get you out of there as soon as I can."

"I'm counting on it." Her voice quivered, and she shivered, wrapping her arms tighter around her knees, making the chain rattle. She tossed her hair in defiance. "I prefer your place. The atmosphere here is *rank*."

I loved the flash of bravery. "I prefer you here, as well. You'll be home soon. I promise."

The camera zoomed out, and she dropped her head, her posture defeated.

Aiden rolled his hand indicating I should talk. "Why is she bruised?" I spat.

"She's a feisty thing. We had to convince her to cooperate."

"Touch her again, and you'll be sorry."

The snicker I heard made shivers run down my neck.

"What do you want?"

"You know what we want."

"A fucking piece of land? You're going to jail over a fucking piece of real estate?"

The voice scoffed. "No one is going to jail. You're going to give up the land, and you're going to drop the new development plan of yours. Move on and forget any of this ever happened."

"And if I don't?"

"You will. And you won't try to do anything once the transaction is complete. We got to her once, and we can do it again. We can get to everyone you care about."

His threat made my hands grip tighter, rending the material completely, and caused my anger to burn brighter. I wanted to reach through the screen and rip the head off the person with the disjointed voice. Another tremor raced through Emmy's body, and I snapped.

"*Get* her a blanket."

"You're not in a position to make demands. We're in control here—not you."

I leaned forward, my anger boiling over. "Listen, you fucker. You want the land? Then you're going to get a blanket and make sure she's warm. You fucking hurt her again, and I will hunt you down."

"I don't take kindly to threats. Do what you're told, or she'll feel real pain."

"It's not a threat. It's a promise." Suddenly, I was yelling. "Leave her alone and *get* her a *goddamn* blanket!"

"Bent!" Aiden hissed, moving closer.

"You mother fucking bastard!" I screamed. "Get. Her. A. Blanket!"

There was a commotion, the sound of Emmy gasping, then the screen went blank. I picked up the laptop, hurling it against the wall. The contents on my desk disappeared as I exploded in fury, sweeping it all on the floor. I pushed past Aiden, all my anger directed at the thing that started all of this. Mustering all my strength, I flipped the concept model over, watching as it crashed and broke into pieces.

Cami gasped, and Maddox grabbed my arm. "Bentley! Calm down!"

"I did this!" I roared. "My own fucking arrogance! I should have known they wouldn't just walk away. They were *never* just going to walk away. I thought I beat them—that Winston Bentley Ridge the third could do whatever the fuck he wanted and get away with it!"

I stopped as my throat thickened. "Now the woman I love is hurt, scared, cold, and alone. I can't help her, and it's all my fault." I looked at the destruction my anger caused. "I think I might have made it worse." I met Maddox's eyes. "She's cold, and hurt, Mad. Because of me—all of this is because of me. I can't stand it when she's cold." I shook my head, my shoulders bowing inward in despair. "She should have walked away when I told her. I should have left her alone."

He shook my arm. "No. Stop thinking like that. She loves you, and we will get her back. They'll get her a blanket. I'm sure she fought them, which is how she got the bruises. I'm certain they don't want to hurt her more, only scare you."

My voice broke. "It worked."

"I know. I understand. They'll call back." He pressed on my shoulder. "Bent, you need to stay calm. We'll get her back faster if you stay calm."

"I destroyed my machine."

"We'll fix it."

"I want to be alone."

"Okay. We'll be in the next room."

I nodded and turned away.

DEE CAME IN, carrying a mug of coffee. She set it down, taking a seat in front of my desk. She looked around the den.

"You made a mess."

"I'll clean it up."

"Blaming yourself or Aiden isn't going to help."

I sighed and let my head drop back. "I know."

She tapped her fingers on the desk. "Do you? Emmy was aware you were worried. She also thought you were overreacting. No one expected this to happen. She thought about your warnings. She talked to Cami and me about the differences in your lives and the worries you had. The worries she had about not being enough."

"She is more than enough. I'm the one not worthy of her." I scrubbed my face. "She should have walked away. She'd be at home right now or with you. Safe."

"She couldn't walk away, Bentley. She loves you. My goodness, she told you her history, and for Emmy, that says a lot." Dee pushed the coffee toward me. "Aside from this, I think you're the best thing that ever happened to her. I've never seen her so happy. I've never seen her trust anyone the way she trusts you."

"Her trust in me has put her in danger."

"I agree with Maddox. They're using her to get to you. I don't think they'll hurt her again," Her voice trembled. "I'm praying they don't."

I leaned my elbows on the desk, my words low. "She doesn't know that, Dee. She's alone. Scared. She's confused, and cold. It's fucking killing me."

"And we'll take care of her when you bring her home. *You'll* take care of her."

"Yes," I stated adamantly.

"You really love her."

"I do." I bent forward, wanting, *needing*, to talk to someone about Emmy. Someone who knew her well. "She has changed my life. I want to change hers. Make it easier. I asked her to come live with me."

"How did that go over?"

I frowned. "Not the way I hoped, to be honest. She was so hesitant. I know her past, and I know she struggles, but I'm not trying to take away her independence. I just want her with me. I want to share my life with her."

"If you know her past, then you know why she is hesitant." Dee shook her head sadly. "We tried to convince her to live with us, but it never happened. Her fear of depending on someone was too strong. She could never allow herself to love and trust anyone fully. And with you, she has much more at stake."

"I would never leave or abandon her."

"Bentley, you need to understand something. Even though she shows a different façade to the world, Emmy, in many ways, is more controlled than you are. People think she is carefree, humorous, and even flighty. She rarely shows her true feelings. She hides them under a smile or a laugh."

"I know. There is much more to her than one sees."

She tilted her head in agreement. "That's what she lets them see. She is intensely private, and she doesn't allow people in easily. The only way she survived being abandoned not once, but twice, was to take charge of her life. Be the one to make decisions about it. Where she lived, what she did, how much money she had. She has refused to depend on anyone for anything. Even Cami and myself." She shrugged ruefully. "She didn't expect you and the huge dilemma you present to her."

"I'm sorry—I'm a dilemma? I don't understand."

"You are her greatest desire—the one she would never admit to having—*and* her biggest fear. The one person she can be herself with, and depend on not to hurt her. The person she *can* entrust her heart to. You are the person she never believed could exist for her."

Her words hit me. I wanted to be that person for her. I wanted her to know she was everything to me and mattered above all else.

"I won't hurt her. I'll prove it to her."

She stood, indicating the destruction of the room. "I believe you have. Be patient with her. Bring her home, Bentley. I don't care what you have to give up to accomplish that."

"I will."

She walked out, and I sipped the coffee she had brought. I shut the door to the den and tried to straighten it up. The model was damaged, and I shoved it as far into the corner of the room as I could. That ambition was gone, and a new one in its place. I would get her back, find whoever did this and make sure they were punished. I went in search of a broom. Reid was tapping at his keyboard, Aiden beside him, staring at his screen. Maddox was stretched out on the sofa, his head resting on Dee's lap. She was stroking his hair absently, her eyes shut. He looked to be sleeping. It hit me I had never once seen him with a woman in a private moment. He never spoke of his personal life and had never had a long-term relationship. None of us had, until now.

I stopped and met Aiden's gaze. "You need some sleep."

"We have to keep going."

"I'll sit with Reid. You can get some rest, then come back." He started to protest, and I interrupted him.

"Aiden, I need you. I can't do this without you. Get some rest and come back fresh."

"What about you?"

The thought of going upstairs to my room, to the bed I shared with her, the sheets smelling of Emmy's soft fragrance, was too much to handle. "I'll grab a nap later."

He stood. "Okay."

A look passed between us. I knew I should apologize, tell him I regretted my words earlier, but he turned and walked away before I could speak.

I sat beside Reid. "Tell me what to do."

A HAND SHOOK my shoulder, and I looked up, disoriented and blinking in the early morning light. Aiden was beside me, frowning. I had fallen asleep at the table. Maddox was where Reid had been sitting, and he was frowning, as well.

How long had I been asleep?

A quick glance at my wrist told me it was only a couple of hours.

"What?" I asked, tension coursing through me.

"Greg is here." Aiden frowned.

I stood, confused. "What time is it? Why is he here?"

"It's seven. He says you texted him."

I shook my head as I picked up my phone. "I didn't."

Maddox spoke up. "I think it was done for you. They have made the next move."

"Where is he?"

"Downstairs in the vestibule. I haven't buzzed him up yet. I told him there was a problem with the door."

"You left him down there?"

"I wasn't sure how to handle the situation regarding him."

"Has there been any contact?"

Maddox turned his screen. "This."

It was a picture of Emmy, still in the same place, but now a tattered blanket draped over her shoulders. There were no new marks I could see. My stomach twisted looking at the picture. Not enough by far, but it was something.

"When did that come?"

"About thirty minutes ago. We were about to wake you when Greg showed up at the door."

I rolled my shoulders, feeling stiff and groggy. I had only been asleep for a short while, and I was exhausted.

"Andrew has coffee. Lots of coffee."

"Okay. Bring Greg in."

GREG SAT ACROSS from me, his expression blank. He took a sip of his coffee while studying me. He had appeared confused and snippy when Aiden brought him upstairs and into the den. His eyebrows rose looking at the destruction of the room, and he had sat down, accepting coffee and waiting for me to speak.

Maddox and Aiden stood behind me. I swallowed a mouthful of coffee to banish the dryness in my throat.

Greg set down his mug. "What the fuck is going on, Bentley? You look like hell."

I shook my head, dismissing his words. "I've changed my mind, Greg. I want to sell the land."

He gaped at me. "You changed your mind? After the lecture you gave me last time we met, you *changed* your mind?"

"Yes."

He glanced at the broken model. "Why?"

"It's not important. I need you to get in touch and accept their offer."

"All I have is an untraceable email address."

"That will work. They are waiting to hear from you."

He scowled. "I don't know what's going on. You text me at five a.m. I get an email with a new offer for less than you paid for the land—half of what their original offer was—and you want me to accept it?"

I heard Aiden's sharp intake of breath. They had made their move. We had wondered why they didn't demand I give them the land, instead of selling to them. Maddox surmised they wanted it legal and binding. Now, they dropped their offer. They would get the land, and financially, I would take a huge hit. I sucked in some much-needed air. I would also get Emmy back safe. The money was a renewable resource. She was not.

Before I could speak, my laptop screen lit up. There was a live feed of Emmy. The room was dim, and she was paler than ever, with dark circles under her eyes. She glared at the camera.

"Say it," a disjointed voice demanded off camera.

She raised her chin, defiant.

"You have the final offer. Accept it." She spat out the words, obviously angry, and not wanting to be their puppet.

Greg uttered a muffled curse, beginning to stand. Aiden held up his hand, stopping him from moving. I leaned forward.

"I'll accept it, Emmy. You'll be home soon."

Her eyes flashed, and she clutched the blanket closer. "I'm hungry, Bentley. Tell Maddox when I get home, I would kill for a curry."

The screen went blank. I swiveled in my chair looking at Maddox. "What the fuck did she mean?"

He shrugged, looking puzzled. "Damned if I know, Bent." He glanced away in thought, then snapped his fingers. "We were talking the other day about a new Indian place that opened up by my condo. I told her how good it was." He squeezed my shoulder. "Sorry, man. She's hungry and must have thought about our conversation. You know what it's like when you get a craving. You can't shake it."

I hated knowing she was hungry. It added to my anger. They were going to pay.

"We'll get her a whole whack of it when she comes home. Anything she wants." He stepped away, moving to the door. "I need some coffee."

I turned back to Greg.

"What's going on?" he asked.

"I can't tell you. I need you to accept the offer, and leave it alone."

His eyes narrowed. "You're being pressured."

"Leave it alone."

He started to say something, and I stopped him. "Do this, Greg. No questions, just do it. I need it done today. Do you understand?"

He stood, buttoning up his jacket. Even at this early hour he was groomed and unflappable. "I'm your lawyer, Bentley. Whatever you tell me would be held in the strictest of confidence. It's obvious they have some leverage over you." He indicated the laptop. "They've taken something of great value."

I remained silent. I wasn't risking her, and I didn't want Greg digging.

"If you won't confide in me, I'll do as you ask and we can handle it afterward." He huffed.

I stood, pounding my fist on the desk. I couldn't let anyone know I planned on pursuing the fuckers and get justice for what they had done. Not until I had Emmy back and safe. "*No.* I'm selling the land, and that is final. There will be nothing to handle or discuss afterward. It is done. We move onto the next project."

Aiden grabbed my shoulder. "Relax, Bent."

I shook off his hold, glaring at Greg. "*Nothing else.* Am I clear? *Leave it alone.*"

With a snarl, he grabbed his briefcase. "Fine. I'll send word when the offer is accepted."

"I need this done immediately."

He shook his head. "Yeah, that much I figured out on my own." He strode from the office.

I sat down heavily, rubbing my eyes.

Aiden hunched beside me.

"Bentley, it's almost over. She'll be home tomorrow."

"I want her home today."

"I'm trying. We're combing through every traffic cam, tracing down every piece of email, looking through every computer associated with you. Reid is using every skill he has to try to run down those numbered companies. Whoever is behind this doesn't want to be found." His voice was strained. "We're not going to stop, though."

I met his weary gaze. "I know, Aiden. And I know it wasn't your fault. I was out of line yesterday. I didn't mean what I said. I was angry, and upset, and I took it out on you. Please accept my apology for being an ass."

He blinked, stood, and held out his hand. "Forgiven and forgotten."

I ignored his hand and embraced him. His massive arms felt like vices around my shoulders.

"You and Maddox are my family. I need you."

He stepped back. "She's part of our family. So is *her* family." He jerked his thumb behind him to the room where I could hear Cami's and Dee's voices. "We're in this together, and we'll get her back."

I nodded. "Right."

"Go have a shower. Change. Andrew is making breakfast, and we'll keep digging."

"Okay."

⟳⟳⟳

I TOWEL DRIED my hair and slipped into fresh clothes after my shower. I felt more awake and anxious to get back downstairs. I had no idea how long it would be until Greg sent notice I had agreed to the offer, and they would allow Emmy to go free, but I wanted to know the instant it occurred. I prayed that was what would happen. That nothing would go wrong, and they wouldn't hurt her. I couldn't bear for that to happen.

I hurried downstairs, finding Cami and Dee at the table. Reid was gone from the sofa.

"Where are Aiden and Maddox?"

"They said they had to do something downstairs."

"Is Reid with them?"

"Yes."

Without another word, I turned and hurried downstairs. Something was up. I could feel it in every bone of my body. I burst through the door of the security room. Three heads looked up at once.

"What is it?"

"Shut the door."

I pushed it shut and moved closer. "What's going on?"

Maddox looked at me. "I lied."

"What?"

"There is no Indian food place. Emmy was giving us a clue."

I sat down, exasperated. "What? Why didn't you say something?"

He leaned forward, his voice dripping with fury. "Because she was telling us Greg is involved."

CHAPTER 16

BENTLEY

IT TOOK ME a minute to process his words.

"*Greg*? What the fuck does her wanting a curry have to do with Greg?"

"Has she ever said anything to you about him?" Maddox asked.

"No. She only met him once, briefly, here in the house. She didn't say much, except she found him cold and intimidating."

"She told me that, too. She also thought he was exceedingly intense. She said he reminded her of Tim Curry. We shared a good laugh over it because I had to agree with her." He let his words sink in. "She said she wanted '*a curry*' to tip us off. She knew I would remember." A smirk played on his lips. "She's clever."

"That's why she directed her comment to you."

"Yes."

My fists tightened, and hate tore through my body. "If you're right, I'm going to kill him. Right the fuck now."

Aiden's hand clamped heavy on my shoulder. "No, you're not. You're going to go upstairs and pretend this conversation never happened. When Greg calls you with information about the sale, you're going to do exactly what he tells you."

"Why would I do any of that?"

Aiden bent at the knees and met my eyes. "Because while he's busy celebrating his win, we're going to figure out where she is and get her."

"How?" I asked. "You haven't had any luck yet."

Reid answered. "We didn't know where to look. We've been looking for a needle in a haystack. Now we're focusing all our energy on *him*. His online presence, accounts, emails. He's been hiding using fake profiles, remote access terminals, and burner emails. I can hack into his life, and hope he's slipped up somewhere." He chuckled. "They always do. I'll find something. He can't hide from me anymore."

"Let's get at it."

Aiden shook his head. "I think somehow he's watching—or listening. Maddox is going upstairs with you. I need Reid's hacking skills, and this room is totally secure. Greg's never had access to it. In fact, he doesn't even know it exists. So, if he's watching your computer or listening in, all he is gonna see is the same gerbil wheel we've been on since we started, and all he is going to hear is failure."

"You really think you can find her?"

Reid and Aiden answered in unison, Reid never looking up from the computer. "Yes."

"Why would he do this to me?"

Maddox shrugged. "Who knows? Jealousy? Greed? I have no idea, but it's definitely him. He may not be alone, but he's part of it."

"He is going to pay."

Aiden laughed; a low rumbling sound in his chest that sounded like a snarl. "Big time. We are going to fucking nail him to the wall. I'm going to enjoy it, but first, we all need to act normal, and not make him suspicious."

"The girls?"

"They need to be kept in the dark. What we've discussed stays in this room. I'll keep you up to date."

"How do I explain where you are? Why you've suddenly disappeared? Won't that look suspicious?"

He grinned devilishly. "I think we're about to have another fight."

"BENTLEY! CALM DOWN!"

I shook off Maddox's "grip" and glared at him. Cami and Dee sat up straighter, staring at us.

"He's been up all night. Give him a break. Let him work out and have a nap. He'll be better able to concentrate. I'll work with you on trying to figure this out."

I threw up my hands and stormed into my den. "Whatever."

Maddox followed me. I sat at my desk, staring at the screen, wondering if I was being watched. He ambled around the room, seemingly not doing anything, but I knew he was looking for bugs. He stopped by the shelves in front of my desk and lifted a stone carving, arching his brow.

"When did you get this?"

"A few years ago. You like it?"

"Yes, I like it very much." He tapped the shelf. "I'll just put it back down, yeah?"

"Good idea. It's not yours, and it was expensive."

"Okay, then."

He set it down and took a seat.

"Comfy?"

"I am now."

"More?" I asked quietly, pressing the keys on my laptop.

"No idea."

"All right."

Maddox leaned back. "I was thinking about that piece of property on the East Side."

I looked at him, confused. We had dismissed it ages ago. A good price, but the costs associated with it made it unviable. There was too much work developing the area around it to make it a good decision.

His left eyebrow rose, and a smirk played on his lips. I caught on to his idea.

"You think we should go for it?"

"All the studies say it could be worth millions when done."

I sat back, hiding my grin. If the fucker was listening, we could help him lose some of the money he was stealing from us.

"Let's discuss. It will take my mind off things."

With a subtle wink, he started.

For over two hours, we bullshitted. He stood, yawned, and stretched. We had dropped over a half dozen red herrings. It had been a good idea on his part. It stopped me from going downstairs, and I enjoyed the crap stories we made up on pieces of land we had no interest in whatsoever.

"I should check on Aiden." He shot me a meaningful glance. "You should come with me and apologize. And mean it. It's not his fault he can't find anything."

"Yes."

We passed through the living area. The girls were gone, no doubt upstairs.

"You were pretty chummy with Dee last night."

"Shut it."

"Just an observation."

"She was being kind. I was tense and had a headache."

"Uh-huh."

"You want to razz someone?" Maddox huffed. "Ask Aiden where he and Cami disappeared to for over four hours. He looked rather rumpled when he reappeared."

I didn't have a chance to reply before we entered the security room to see Aiden and Reid bent over the same computer. Aiden was cursing.

"What?" I asked immediately.

"We hacked into Greg's personal and business computers."

"Find anything?"

"Lots, but the most important thing is that he, or one of *his* numbered companies, owns a warehouse not far from where the car was found. It's deserted. In fact, all of the buildings on the block are. No cameras, no people. What better place to keep someone you don't want to be found?"

Maddox whistled low. "We thought it looked like an empty warehouse."

"Let's go."

Aiden shook his head. "No. I have a plan, Bent. I need you to follow my instructions to the letter, though. No matter how much you hate it. Do you understand?"

"Will you bring her home?"

"Yes. When it's dark, and we're clear to move safely. We just need a few more hours."

"Then I'll do it."

EMMY

I PULLED MY knees tighter to my chest, desperately trying to get warm, even though I knew it was fruitless. I rubbed my hands on my legs trying to stimulate some heat. I grimaced at the dirt on my palms mixed in with some blood from the scratches on my skin. I was dirty, tired, hungry, scared, and angry. I wasn't sure which one was the most prevalent.

Darkness had descended again in the horrid little room where they were holding me captive. It was gross. The one little window was set so high, I had no hope of reaching it, and so much grime covered it, I hadn't realized it was a window until I saw a tiny sliver of sun through it in the early morning. The small room with the broken door across from me housed the disgusting toilet and filthy sink I refused to use.

I didn't eat the granola bar they tossed in, and I poured out the water a bit at a time. The seal had been broken, and I was certain someone had tampered with it.

The larger door on the far side of the room was shut, blackness showing under the bottom edge. Something was going on. They had removed the camera they'd set up, and it had been silent for the past while. I had tried to remove the thick band around my wrist, but had only succeeded in chafing the skin even more than it already had been. I strained to listen, but couldn't hear anything. Earlier in the day, I had heard voices somewhere down the hall, so I was sure I was now alone, but for how long I didn't know.

I wasn't sure what was worse. Alone with the four-legged rats I could hear scurrying in the walls, or worried about what the masked, two-legged variety might do when the door opened. I pretended to be asleep when they came in, so they didn't bother me. Usually, unless it was to make me say something on camera or take one of their stupid photos, they left me alone. The only time I had been hurt was when I tried to get away from them and fell in the struggle, landing on my face, and again on my knees when I tripped. Bentley had lost it when he saw the marks. His tirade about a blanket was frightening, and one of the men had knocked over the camera which stopped the recording.

Still, it had worked, and shortly after, one of them had tossed an old, dirty blanket at me. I unfolded it and sat on it as protection from the cold, stone floor, and pulled it over my shoulders to try to ward off the never-ending chill. I had buried my head in my hands and tried not to cry. It was a little later when I heard it: the sound of a new voice. The door had opened, and I didn't move, keeping my head down.

"She's constantly asleep," someone spoke. *"The drugs are keeping her quiet."*

"Good. Less trouble. Take a picture. It will satisfy him until we get what we want." Then he chuckled, the sound low and familiar. *"Until I get what I want."*

I had forced myself to stay still. I'd recognized that chuckle, and the voice, even if he did speak low and didn't think I could hear. It gave me chills, the same way it had the one time I met him.

It had been Bentley's lawyer, Greg. He was behind it all and betrayed Bentley's trust.

I fidgeted with the edge of the blanket. Did Maddox understand what I had been trying to tell them? Did they know?

A sound made me tense as footsteps and voices approached the door. They were back. I swallowed, not wanting to show my fear. I wanted Bentley. I wanted his arms around me, and his voice in my ear telling me I was safe. I wanted to curl up beside him and listen to him talk. I wanted to hear his laughter. He laughed more now than when I met him—he smiled more as well. Tears formed in my eyes thinking about him. He would be blaming himself and going crazy. I was trying to stay strong, but I was feeling weak from lack of food or water. My head ached, and I was so cold, but I was holding on to what he said. He would get me home. I had to trust him.

The footsteps seemed to be taking a long time. There were other noises—the sounds of doors opening and shutting and lots of quiet talking. A quake of anticipation went through me. Was it possible it wasn't Greg's men? Was it someone looking for me? Had Maddox figured it out?

I wanted to cry out, but I was worried. What if it were worse? Not the men who had taken me, and not Bentley's men, but someone else altogether? I drew in a shaky breath and stood, bracing myself against the wall. I had to try. I had to get out of there.

I opened my mouth and yelled. I was shocked how weak my voice sounded, but it was enough. Running feet headed in my direction, and there was the sound of the door being broken down. It flew open, smashing against the wall. Two men stood in the open doorway, their features hidden in the shadows with flashlights trained on me. I raised my hand, squinting.

"Help me, *please*."

A figure stepped forward. "Bentley sent us, Emmy."

Tears filled my eyes, and relief made me weak. "B-Bentley?"

He moved closer, a thick blanket in his hands. "He said he needed you home now, *Freddy.*"

With a sob, I collapsed.

BENTLEY

AIDEN PULLED HIS phone from his ear. "They have her."

Relief coursed through me, making my legs shake. I sat down, inhaling deep lungfuls of air.

"They'll have her here shortly."

"Are we covered?" I asked.

"This place is tighter than Fort Knox. I've verified the only bug was the one in your den. Greg is at home and hasn't gone anywhere since ten. I moved your car, so they'll pull in downstairs. No one will know."

I glanced at Maddox. "Did you get hold of Colin?" He was Sandy's grandson and an ER doctor.

"He'll be here."

I looked at Aiden. "Was it difficult to get to her?"

Aiden shook his head. "As I suspected earlier, he had pulled out. The only person in the building was Emmy. His men and the camera were long gone."

"He fucking left her chained and alone?"

"I think his plan was to send us the address and we would get her tomorrow."

"And risk us discovering it was his building?"

"Why would we, Bent? It's Greg. Your friend. Your lawyer. Someone we never suspected. He would offer to help trace the ownership, and all we'd find was another fucking numbered company. Another mystery. That bastard fooled us all. He even had the audacity to be here while they sent that last transmission. He arranged all of this shit—thought of everything. Even the phone call that stopped you from going outside with Emmy the other morning. He was watching Frank, and knew exactly when to grab her. How could we suspect a man who was with us while it was happening?"

He was right.

"Are you sure everything is in place?"

"It's all taken care of, Bentley. She'll be back soon, the land is still yours, and tomorrow we'll nail him."

"It's not the land I'm worried about."

"I know. I'm just pointing out all the positives."

I paced the room, feeling as if I wanted to jump out of my skin. "How long?"

"Not long. The ETA is ten minutes."

I hurried to the garage. I wasn't going to wait until they brought her to me. I was going to her. I was going to be the first one she saw when she arrived home.

I HAD HER in my arms as soon as the garage door slid closed. The lingering terror and the exhaustion on her face destroyed me. Her arms wrapped around my neck hard, and she buried her face in my chest, constant tremors running through her body. I headed to the waiting elevator, not saying a word to anyone. Maddox and Aiden could handle the crew.

In my room, I grabbed the heated blanket Andrew had thoughtfully provided. I wrapped it tightly around Emmy, knowing she needed the added warmth. Not a word passed between us as I held her, finally feeling her body begin to relax as she grew warmer. There was so much I had to say, but the relief I felt was so profound, I couldn't speak. My throat was thick, and my eyes burned with the intensity of the emotion I felt. All I could do was hold her, providing the one thing I could give her fully—the protection of my body.

She let out a long, shuddering breath, and leaned back, meeting my anxious gaze.

"I'm okay," she murmured, her voice raspy.

Clearing my throat, I reached for a bottle of water, lifting it to her chapped lips. "Slow, Emmy. Sip it slowly."

She sipped the liquid, her eyes fluttering shut as she drank. She drained the bottle with a small huff.

"More?" My eyes never left her face, hating the sight of the scrapes and dark bruise marring her skin.

She shook her head.

"What do you need?" I asked. "Tell me what to do."

She lifted her trembling hand, cupping my cheek. "You. I need you."

I covered her hand with mine, pressing it into my skin. Turning my face, I kissed the bruise forming on her wrist. "You have me." I inhaled. "Emmy, I'm so—"

A knock at the door interrupted me, and Maddox stepped into the room, Aiden behind him. Emmy dropped her hand, but kept it cradled inside of mine.

"Our guests are aware and anxious."

Emmy tensed in my arms. "Guests?"

"It's okay. Cami and Dee are here."

"Here?"

"I had to make sure they were safe."

For the first time since arriving, her eyes glistened.

"Thank you."

"Let them in."

Maddox opened the door, and the girls came in. They were dressed in nightclothes, rumpled, and already crying. I had to lean back as they hurried forward, wrapping Emmy in their embrace. I shared an amused glance with Aiden and Maddox, unable to move with all the girls piled on me. They drew back, their expressions relieved.

"Emmy—" Cami's voice caught. "We were so worried."

"I'm okay," Emmy insisted, her voice rough.

Dee stood and hurried from the room. I frowned at her sudden action, but neither Emmy nor Cami seemed surprised. I noticed

Maddox slip from the room to follow her.

Emmy whispered something to Cami, who nodded.

"What?" I asked. "What's wrong?"

Cami shook her head. "Emmy wants to have a shower. She asked me to help her."

"I can do that."

Emmy shook her head, not meeting my eyes. "Cami, please."

I ignored the fission of hurt at her rejection. If she was more comfortable with Cami, that was more important. She had been through a lot and needed her friend.

Aiden glanced at his phone. "Colin will be here in fifteen."

"Colin?" Emmy asked anxiously.

"He's Sandy's grandson. A doctor," I soothed.

"No," Emmy breathed out. "I don't need a doctor."

"Yes, you do. I want you checked out."

"I just need a hot shower, and I'll be fine."

I slipped my fingers under her chin. "Cut me some slack, Freddy. I'm certain you need more than a hot shower. After what you went through, the first order of business is let a doctor look at you."

Dee returned with Maddox right behind her. She carried a steaming cup and handed it to Emmy. "There's honey and lemon to soothe your throat. Bentley is right, Emmy, you need a doctor to examine you. Don't argue with him—it only makes sense."

"Sorry," Emmy mumbled, taking the mug. "It's my first kidnapping. I wasn't sure of the protocol."

I couldn't help the chuckle that escaped my lips. Maddox smirked, and even Aiden cracked a smile.

"I want a shower before I see this doctor. I feel so terrible."

Dee clapped her hands once. "We'll help you. Bentley, do you have something she can change into? Something loose and warm?"

"Yes."

"Good. You fetch it for me. We'll help her in the shower, the doctor can see her, and she needs to eat and rest." She pointed to Maddox and Aiden. "You can tell the doctor to wait a few minutes, so she is comfortable. Andrew is making coffee and sandwiches. He is going to get something light and warm for Emmy to eat. You should wait downstairs."

The three of us blinked, but we all knew we were going to do exactly as she ordered. I slid Emmy off my lap and kissed her head.

"Are you leaving?" Her voice was uneasy and the grip she had on my hand tight.

"No. I'll be here when you're ready." Despite what Dee said, downstairs was too far away. I wasn't planning to be far from where Emmy was for a long while.

She looked up at Maddox, holding out her hand. "Thank you for figuring out my message."

He came close, squeezed her fingers, and dropped a kiss on her head. "You were brilliant, Emmy."

Aiden studied her, standing back, his shoulders tense. "I'm sorry."

"No." She shook her head and reached out to him. "This wasn't because of you. Any of you."

He didn't move, and she waved her fingers. "I heard them in the van, Aiden. They said you've barely slept looking for me. *Please.* Let me say thank you."

He shrugged off her words. "None of us have."

"Please," she whispered, teary-eyed.

He moved forward, his expression tight. He bent over and whispered something to her, then hugged her fast and left the room. Emmy blinked away the tears.

Maddox cleared his throat. "I'll go and do, ah, yeah, I'll go do what I was told to do."

I went toward the closet. "Me, too."

After her shower, Colin checked her out, left some ointment for her bruises, and assured me she'd be fine once she got some liquids, food, and sleep. He gave me a couple of tablets, which would help her to sleep if she needed them, suggested Tylenol for the aches, said he would drop in the next day to check on her, and handed me a card.

"She may need to talk to someone. If so, I suggest this woman.

She's great with trauma victims, and Emmy might benefit from her experience in that field."

I shook his hand. "Thanks."

Returning to her, I kneeled by her side. She was in a heavy, knitted sweater and a pair of my sweatpants, both far too large for her, but warm. There was a large blanket draped over her shoulders and thick socks on her feet. The girls had blown her hair dry, and I pushed back the tresses, frowning at the bruise on her face.

"Andrew has something for you to eat. Do you want to stay up here or go downstairs with the others?"

"I feel shaky, but I'd like to go downstairs."

I stood, sliding my arms under her legs, picking her up. "I'll take you."

She trembled in my arms, her head falling to my shoulder. "Are you cold?"

"No. I'm . . . tired."

"You can eat, and we'll go to bed. We all will. Everyone needs to sleep."

"Can I stay with you?"

I hated hearing her sound vulnerable. She was always so strong. "Always."

We descended the stairs and joined our friends. I sat beside her, encouraging her to eat the scrambled eggs and toast Andrew had made. The rest of us ate the sandwiches. For the first time since everything started, I was hungry and wolfed down the food in front of me. I noticed it was the same for Maddox and Aiden. We cleared the enormous pile in minutes.

I tensed when Cami looked up and asked Emmy. "Did you fight?"

I started to object, but Emmy placed her hand on my arm. "I tried." She sighed. "When I realized what was going on, I prepared myself. I knew the car would stop and they would have to open the door. The driver had a gun, and after we rounded the corner, another man jumped in with one, too. When we stopped to change cars, I thought if I acted meek, it would take them by surprise, and I could run. They were strong, though, and prepared. I got one good punch in, and I tried to kick the shorter guy in the crotch, but I guess I missed the mark."

"Or his dick was too small to hit," Cami shot at her.

"There's that."

"We should take some self-defense courses."

Emmy pursed her lips. "Good idea. Next time, I'll be better prepared with my Ninja skills."

"There won't be a next time," I snapped, but she ignored me.

"Aiden, maybe you can teach me some of your karate skills. I bet I could take them if I tried. I don't know if there is, like, a kidnapper network, but if word got out I wasn't to be messed with, that would help keep them away."

I tamped down my anger. Remembering Dee's words about the way Emmy tried to diffuse her feelings, I stood. "I think we need to call it a night."

Everyone stood, and not giving her a choice, I picked up Emmy and carried her upstairs. I placed her on my bed.

She gazed at me warily. "Are you angry with me?"

"No. I'm not angry, but what happened is *not* a joke."

"I know."

"Then stop it."

"What?"

"I know what you're doing, Emmy. You don't have to make light of what happened and pretend you're okay. Not with your friends, and not with me. *Never* with me." I cupped her cheek, my thumb stroking the skin. "Let it out. Talk to me."

She was silent for a moment, then her shoulders slumped. She blew out a long, shaky breath and met my eyes. The tears she'd been holding in began to form. "I was so scared, Bentley. I didn't know what was happening, and I was so cold. I've never been that cold."

I lowered myself to the mattress beside her, wrapping my arm around her waist. "It killed me to see you chained up and shivering. Knowing you were hurt and cold because of me was overwhelming.

I've never felt such helplessness and rage all rolled into one."

"When I realized it was Greg, I was so mad, I wanted to scream at him, but I knew I had to fake it. I let them think I was drinking the water they gave me. It was drugged, and I pretended to sleep all the time."

"Thank God you're so clever."

"I didn't know what would happen if they figured out I knew it was him." Her voice caught. "I wasn't sure I'd ever see you again."

I pulled her into my arms, holding her tight. "You're home now, Freddy. You're safe, and you don't have to be scared. Greg will never get to you again. No one will."

"All I wanted was to come back to you. Home."

Her words made my chest ache. "You're here now."

Her arms tightened. "*You're* my home, Bentley. I want . . . I want to stay here."

I tilted her chin up, meeting her watery gaze. "You mean live here—with me?"

She nodded, tears coursing down her cheeks. "Wherever you are, as long as you want me."

"I want you always," I admitted. "I was afraid this would make you even more skittish about being with me."

"No. I won't let what happened change my mind." She hesitated, then cupped my cheek. "I love you. I trust you."

I reached over and picked up the small bag from beside my bed, placing her rucksack in her lap. "I kept this for you."

She ran her fingers over the worn handle, then pushed it back into my hands. "I want you to have it. You keep it for me."

"What?"

"You promised me one day when I was ready, you'd have a safe place I could keep it, and we'd both know I wouldn't leave again." The tears began to drip down her face. "I never want to be without you. I never want to leave." Her voice shook with the force of her emotion. "I'm not waiting for the past anymore, Bentley. I'm giving it to you for safekeeping. Just like my heart. I want my future to be with you."

I took the rucksack from her shaking hands and pulled her into my arms, knowing she was about to break.

"I've got you. Always."

She began to weep, deep sobs ripping through her chest as she shook in my arms. I kissed her head, keeping her tight to my chest.

"Let it out, baby."

I slid us under the covers, letting her cry, knowing she needed to do so, and grateful I was the one she allowed to see her true feelings.

I wanted to be that man for her—today, and always.

CHAPTER 17

BENTLEY

EMMY CRIED OUT, her hand flailing, pushing herself into me. I cupped the back of her head, whispering soothing words into her ear.

"It's okay, Freddy. I got you. You're safe."

She calmed, and gradually her body relaxed back into the sleep she so desperately needed. Despite the exhaustion she felt, and the pill she had taken, her mind wasn't letting her rest. I had hoped she would sleep, knowing she was safe, but nightmares had plagued her, no matter what I tried. I left the light on, I held her close, I murmured her name, but still, she only slept for short periods before the fear gripped her and she started crying.

Every time it did, my anger toward Greg grew a little more. When her hand reached out, and the bruise on her wrist caught my eye, the need for retribution became sharper. Still, I kept my voice soft and tried not to show my emotions when her eyes fluttered open, scared and anxious. I met her gaze; assuring her everything was okay and lulled her back into sleep.

At eight in the morning, my door opened, and Cami poked her head through the crack. I was sitting up against the headboard, Emmy's head in my lap. I stroked through her hair, the constant motion seeming to soothe her, and she was finally asleep.

"Can I come in?"

I nodded, watching as she approached the bed.

"We heard her all night."

"It was rough."

"It will get better. She needs some time."

"I know." I scrubbed my free hand over my face. "I have to go. Aiden and I are going to Greg's."

She grimaced. "Why don't you just get the police?"

"Aiden's arranged it, but I want to know why. I want to see his face when he realizes he failed. This is personal. He can be arrested after I am done with him."

"What will happen?"

I shrugged. "His career will be over. He'll probably go to jail. He'll be broke."

"And you'll be . . . ?"

"Sad someone I trusted did this to me for a piece of real estate." I looked down at Emmy. "Furious he did it to *her* of all people. Someone who did nothing wrong but get involved with me." I ran my hand over her head. "Grateful he won't be able to do it again."

"Do you feel anything for him at all?"

I was feeling so many things, but if I expressed them, Cami would be horrified. I had never experienced such dark thoughts. "Nothing positive."

She squared her shoulders. "Good." She stepped forward. "I'll stay with Emmy. You go and do what you have to do, then come home to her. I'll make sure she's okay until you come back."

Carefully, I slipped out of bed, and Cami took my place, curling up beside Emmy. I smiled at the sight of her protectiveness.

"You're a good friend. Thank you for being here for her. I wish you didn't have to be. I hate the fact she was hurt because of me, and is still so traumatized, she can't rest."

She shook her head. "Emmy is the best friend I ever had. I hate what happened too, but I know how she feels about you Bentley, and how you feel in return. I know this isn't your fault. This is on him, not you. Go and end it, so you can move on."

I patted her arm and headed to the closet to get ready. I wasn't looking forward to the confrontation, but it had to happen.

I SIGHED, LOOKING up at the building we were about to enter. Aiden and I drove alone. Frank was still recovering and wouldn't be able to drive for several weeks. The car ride over was tense, the air thick with anger. Maddox stayed at the house, all of us agreeing it would look odd to Greg if he accompanied us. He rarely did, since he had never been a big fan of Greg and kept their interactions to a minimum. They stuck to emails and phone calls when it involved finances.

Aiden exhaled; his shoulders slumped. "I'm ready for this to be done."

He'd been up all night. So had Reid and Maddox. Reid had proven himself to me; he'd gone above and beyond anything I could have ever hoped for, and now we had everything we needed to nail Greg. That kid had earned himself a place in my company for life, and he could write his own ticket. He knew it. I knew it. I was happy to give him whatever he wanted after all he had done for me. I had a feeling it involved a big office, lots of computers, and a hefty pay increase. All were his for the asking.

Aiden cast his eyes my way. "You ready?"

"Yes."

"Can you pull this off?"

"I only have to act as though I am upset over something other than his betrayal for a short time, so yes, I can handle it."

"Once he knows, it's bound to get ugly."

I snorted, the sound loud in the car. "Fucking right it is. It's going to get ugly on him."

"Okay, let's do this."

We were quiet as we went upstairs. I nodded at Mrs. Johnson, wondering what she would do once Greg no longer had a law practice. I hoped he'd been paying her well and she had a good retirement plan.

She was going to need it after today.

Aiden made his normal flirty remarks to her, making her chuckle. "He's waiting for you."

Aiden scoffed, the sound low in his throat. "I bet the asshole is," he muttered, following me into Greg's office.

Greg was at his desk, his usual self. Not a hair out of place, suit pressed, white shirt starched, and tie perfectly knotted. His face was clear, with no worry lines or frown. For the first time, I noticed his eyes. Emmy's brown eyes were warm and lit from within, whereas his were flat, dark, cold—void of expression. How had I not noticed that until now?

He wasn't even remotely concerned about the woman he thought was still chained up in a deserted warehouse. He'd lost no sleep over her welfare. All he cared about was the piece of land he was so desperate to get his hands on. I wanted to grab the tie and tighten it around his neck until he couldn't breathe, but Aiden's presence kept me calm.

"Ah, Bentley. You're later than I expected."

I sat across from him, and Aiden stood close.

I had to force the words out of my throat. "Rough night. Late start. I apologize."

He studied me. "I can see that. You look terrible."

I shrugged. I knew I had dark circles under my eyes from lack of sleep the past two nights.

"I wish you would tell me what's going on. Perhaps I can help."

My hands curled into fists beside me. He played his role well. The confused but helpful lawyer. Maybe that was part of his plan. He would get me to tell him, and he would by some stroke of brilliance, help me find her, sucking me further into his deception. I would never suspect the man who helped bring her back to me, would I?

My rage grew at his colossal gall.

"I said leave it. Do you have the offer?"

He ducked his head, sorting through some papers on his desk. I saw the glimmer of a smirk, though. The bastard thought he had won. "Here."

I pretended to glance over the documents. "I need a pen."

Greg handed me his expensive Mont Blanc. "Use mine."

I signed the papers, then handed them to Aiden. "You should make sure it's okay. I don't want to risk this deal, and I'm a bit distracted."

Aiden took the papers, turning his back as he looked at them as if needing privacy to concentrate. I knew he was covering up his grin at my 'signature'.

He turned back, flipping the top page down. "I'd say it's done."

I stood, taking the document, handing it to Greg. "I think so."

Greg set it down on his desk. "I'll take care of it from here, Bentley."

"I have no doubt you will."

"Whatever happened, whatever caused you to change your mind—"

I held up my hand to interrupt him, playing the part he wanted to see. "I said leave it. Do your job and leave it alone."

"As you wish."

I buttoned my jacket. "I have an important call I'm waiting for."

The smirk threatened again, and I couldn't take it another second. I wanted to watch that smug expression disappear from his face.

"You should make sure everything's in order before I go. I won't be returning."

He flipped up the page to give the document a cursory glance, his entire body freezing when his gaze saw my signature.

It read, *"Fuck You."*

He was on his feet in an instant. "What the hell is going on?"

I leaned on the glass desk, my hatred and rage so great I could barely spit out the words. "What's going on, you mother fucking piece of shit, is you lost."

"What?" He snarled through tight lips.

"I have her!" I roared. "Emmy is safe!"

He reared back, shock on his face, but he rapidly recovered, instantly falling into defensive mode. "Bentley, that is great news. I had a feeling something was going on with her. However, why you think *I* lost anything, I have no idea."

I flung my arms, pushing everything from his desk, scattering it to the floor. My voice became deadly calm. Anyone who knew me well knew that was a warning.

"I know, Greg. I know all of it. The numbered companies. The bug. The fact you were the one behind me losing on the bids. That you've been sneaking behind my back for months. Do you think you're the only one with connections? We were able to see my bids last night. The way you redid them—underbidding and making sure it was your own bid that came out on top!"

"Bentley, I would never—"

"Don't even *fucking* try to deny it. I know what you did!"

"This is all conjecture. Someone is filling your head with lies!"

Aiden and I laughed at his desperate attempt to convince me.

"No, counselor. We have it all. The paper trails. The forged documents. Your fingerprints on the bug. The trace back to your own computer at your house." I leaned closer, narrowing my eyes. "Something you should know about hackers, Greg. They know one another. They recognize each other's signature. Once we knew it was you, it was easy to find your hacker's signature on your computer. Easy to pay him more to tell us everything. He is already in custody and singing like a bird. The men you hired to take Emmy are, as well."

His face paled.

I drew in some much-needed oxygen. "What I want to know is *why*? Why the fuck would you do that to me? I've done nothing to you but help make you a very wealthy man!"

All pretense fell away. Greg stood in front of me with a sneer on his face. Hatred blazed from his eyes as he glared. *"Nothing* is the right word, Bentley. It's all been so easy for you, hasn't it?" he spat.

What the fuck was he talking about?

Greg continued, "Bentley Ridge, the successful 'touch of Midas boy' with all the real estate. Every project you work on turns to gold. Every woman wants you. Never any bad press. You and your fucking friends in your little clique. All so fucking high and mighty. All untouchable. You make me sick."

I shook my head. "What the hell?"

"I was never good enough to be part of your inner circle, was I Bentley? Good enough to do your grunt work, but never good enough to *belong*."

"I *asked* if you wanted a job in the company, Greg. You said no. You refused me, not the other way around."

"A job," he jeered. "I didn't want a fucking job. You gave that loser"—he indicated Aiden—"a piece of your precious company. An idiot who can't even read properly and memorizes everything. The same with that tight-assed control freak you call an accountant."

Aiden snarled from behind me. "I'm dyslexic, you arrogant asshole, not illiterate. I can read, just in a different way than you do. And shut your mouth about Maddox. He's a hundred times the man you are."

Greg stared at him, not even acknowledging his words.

"I would have given you everything, and made you even greater! But no, you give them part of the company and offer me a fucking *job*. As if I would ever answer to you—or to them," he shouted, his voice rising with every passing word.

"So, what . . . you decided to screw me over and teach me a lesson?"

"Yes."

"Because I insulted you—years ago—with an *offer* for a job."

"Because you needed to be knocked down a peg or two."

"So, "I began, my voice beginning to rise, "you kidnapped and frightened an innocent woman to teach me a lesson. You chained and locked her in a cold room, tried to drug her, and left her alone, helpless, and terrified, and risked her life because I needed to be knocked down a peg or two? Am I hearing you right?"

He waved his hand. "You're exaggerating." He scoffed. "She was never in any danger. She deserved it, too."

Aiden stepped closer. "What did she do to *deserve* it? You don't even fucking know her!"

Greg sneered, focusing his attention on me. "You never listened to me. You always put their opinions first. What Aiden thought, how Maddox felt. No matter how many times I showed you how valuable I was to you—I was just the fucking lawyer—the joke. I was so damn sick of it. It was fun to watch you squirm when you lost those pieces of land. I simply planned to sell them on to you and make a tidy profit. Seeing how indignant you were . . ." He laughed, the sound cruel. "I enjoyed it and decided to screw you over completely. I was going to buy the land and make you pay through the fucking nose for it. At least I'd get a piece of your company monetarily."

I stared at him, feeling ill. *How had I not seen what he was doing? The kind of man he really was under his expensive attire?*

He waved his hand in anger. "Then your stupid, precious Emmy, a woman you barely know, suggests an inane notion about some ridiculous building project, and instead of telling her to mind her own business, you actually listened to her. All of you!" He slammed his fist on his desk, bending so close we were almost nose-to-nose. "*Her!* Some dumb bitch you're *fucking,* over me! I give you advice, and you ignore it. My suggestions are discarded. You pick everyone over me; you listen to everyone but me. You did this, Bentley. This is all on you!" He was shouting by the time he finished his tirade, the last of his smooth veneer gone. His skin was mottled; spit flying from his mouth as he cursed me. "So, I decided to make you really pay and suffer. She was just the pawn, and I enjoyed making her pay since she was the cause—the interfering little bitch!"

My fist shot out, catching him square in the face, the sound of bone meeting bone loud in the room. He stumbled back, slamming into the wall, momentarily stunned.

Aiden lunged, dragging me back from going over the desk and continuing to pummel Greg. I wanted to beat him until he fell. Make him pay for what he did to Emmy in blood and pain.

"You bastard," I snarled, pushing Aiden back. "You self-righteous fuck! If you had any balls, you would have talked to me, but instead, you go after a defenseless woman. You hide behind numbered companies and computer hackers because you're feeling left out on the playground." I sneered. "As for that *stupid* woman? She is the one who let us know it was you, Greg. Right in front of your own men—with you listening! She *knew* it was you."

His eyes narrowed in disbelief.

"You should never discount the people you think are beneath you, Greg. The problem is you look without seeing. Emmy is more than you will ever know." I shook my head in disgust. "Now you will never have the chance because I am going to make it my mission to ruin you. What you have done is criminal. Inhumane. And unforgiveable."

He wiped at the blood trickling from his nose. "How exactly do you think you are going to accomplish that? You really think you can outsmart me?"

I laughed. "I've already done it. Copies of everything have gone to the press and the Law Society. You'll be disbarred, charged, and thrown in jail. Your life, *asshole*, is over."

He stared, stunned. "You wouldn't."

"The police are on their way," Aiden informed him.

"You bastard!" Greg seethed.

I shook my head in disbelief at his indignation. "What did you think?" I yelled. "That I was going to let you get away with all you've done? Shake hands and say thanks for making me see I was the bad person here? Offer you a place in my company to make it up to you? I paid you for your services—I paid you fucking well. There *is* no debt here, Greg—not to you."

I wiped my hand down my suit, feeling my knuckles swelling,

and the chaff of the torn skin.

"I hope they throw the fucking book at you." I spun on my heel. "Let's go. I'm sure Greg has things he needs to take care of before the cops get here."

Aiden muttered something to Greg, but I ignored it and headed to the door. I reached for the knob, but turned when Greg said my name, freezing at the sight of the gun he held in his hand. I had no idea where it came from. Aiden shouted, stepping in front of me, but Greg shook his head in disgust.

"He's safe, you idiot." He lifted the gun, pressing it to the skin under his chin. "I want him to see what he has done."

"No, Greg, you don't have to do this." I stepped from behind Aiden, not wanting this to happen. I wanted him to pay for what he had done, but not die.

His eyes were cold, his voice filled with hate. "This is *your* doing Bentley. Your fault. Live with it."

"No!" I shouted, lunging forward.

The room echoed with the gunshot, and I felt the spatter of blood hit me. Horrified, I watched as Greg's body slid down the wall, leaving a trail of blood and brain matter behind.

I stared at the man I had thought was my business associate and friend for years, lying dead on the floor in a pool of blood.

How had it come to that?

CHAPTER 18

BENTLEY

THERE WERE SO many voices around me. Police, paramedics, Aiden—all of them talking, gesturing, the movement constant. My head ached, my swollen hand throbbed, and I was still in shock from what happened. After Greg shot himself, his office door flew open, and it was the sound of Mrs. Johnson's screams that brought me back to reality. Aiden had taken charge of the situation, immediately calling 911 for an ambulance, pushing her out of the office, and returning to shove me out of the way and into a chair across the room.

Disoriented, I looked up at him, running a hand through my hair, then staring in confusion at the smear of blood I could see on my palm.

"Bent," he urged. "Look at me."

I met his gaze. "I need you to calm down. The police are on their way up, and there is going to be a lot of questions we are going to have to answer. I need you to relax."

It took me a minute to realize the odd noise I could hear was my gasps for air. Images swam through my head. Greg holding the gun. The sound. The look on his face before he pulled the trigger. The furious condemnation of his words.

My fault.

Aiden bent closer. "Breathe with me, Bent. Come on."

Slowly, my gasps stopped, and I could feel the numbness leave.

"I didn't want it to end that way."

"I know. The coward did this as a final fuck you."

I thought of his words as they wrapped the body and moved it to a gurney. A detective came over to me, introduced himself as the one in charge, and asked if I was up to giving a statement. I tore my eyes away from the scene in front of me and drew in a deep breath.

"Yes."

Hours later, Aiden and I walked into the front office, both of us still in shock, but our stories verified. Mrs. Johnson had informed the police Greg taped every meeting, and the whole thing was caught on camera. I had to avert my eyes as they played the scenario onscreen, showing the confrontation exactly as we stated.

"There will be other questions about his conduct, and illegal activities," Detective Armstrong informed me.

I frowned. "Why? The man is dead. Does his name have to be dragged through the mud?"

He cleared his throat. "There were some interesting files on his computer. I don't think you're the only person he was screwing with."

Aiden and I shared a glance, then thanked him for his help.

He shook our hands. "You're free to go. We'll be in touch."

In the elevator, Aiden spoke, "When we get to the house, you go upstairs and clean up. Don't let Emmy see you like this."

I caught sight of myself in the mirrored walls. I had flecks of blood on my face, jacket, and hair. I was unnaturally pale, and I looked like shit. I yanked off my suit jacket and used the lining to wipe at my face. I was never wearing it again.

"Have you spoken with Maddox?"

"Yes. He has everyone in the sunroom. You get cleaned up, and decide what you want to do."

My head fell back against the cold glass. "I can't even think right now."

"I know. Let's get home, and we'll talk there."

"Are you okay, Aiden?" He had witnessed it all too, and handled everything with his usual efficiency.

"I'm fine, Bent. It was awful, and I wish to hell it had never happened, but I'm fine."

I was too tired to question him further. I followed him out of the elevator and into the street.

"I guess no one is watching now."

His hand was heavy on my shoulder. "No."

⌒ჟ~

THE WATER WAS so hot it scalded my skin. I scrubbed away the blood, and let it disappear down the drain, wishing I could do the same thing to my memories. I toweled off and opened the door to find Emmy sitting on the edge of the bed.

Her face was drawn and wan, and in her hands, she clutched the pants and shirt she had given me.

"I thought you would want to be comfortable."

I crossed the room, and sank in front of her, wrapping her in my arms. Seeing her reminded me why I had gone to confront Greg. The bruises prompted me to recall my anger, and I held her tight, grateful she was safe.

She leaned down, pressing her lips to the back of my head. "I'm so sorry," she whispered.

I lifted my head. "It's not your fault. None of this is."

"It's not yours either."

"Greg felt it was."

"I don't think his judgment was very clear."

I pushed away, taking the clothes from her hands. I wasn't ready to talk about it yet. I needed to think it through. Dissect what happened, the same way I did when confronted with anything that confounded me.

"Do you want me to leave you alone?"

My head snapped up at her tone. I made sure to keep my voice gentle. "I have to talk to Maddox and Aiden. This is—" I exhaled. "There is going to be fallout, and we need to figure out what happens next."

She stood. "The girls are going to leave later. I'll go home with them."

"No! I want you here, Emmy. I just need a little time to talk to my partners. This affects them too." I cupped her cheek. "Your friends can stay as long as they like. No one has to go."

"Okay."

I brushed a kiss across her cheek. "Okay."

I dressed and went downstairs, once I made sure Emmy headed to the sunroom. Maddox and Aiden were waiting for me in my den, and I sat down with a sigh.

Maddox studied my face, looking concerned. "You okay, Bent?"

"As okay as I can be after watching a man shoot himself in front of me."

He frowned. "You know it wasn't your fault, right?"

I stroked my chin, thinking out loud. "I keep telling myself it isn't, but part of me says I am responsible. I should have seen it. Looked closer. Done more."

"What do you think you could have done?" Aiden questioned. "None of us saw Greg's true colors. He hid everything. His hatred for us. His distaste for everything we did. All of us—yet, none of us even suspected as much. He was simply looking for someone to blame, Bent. You ended up being his scapegoat."

I leaned forward, clasping my hands between my knees, hoping they wouldn't notice the slight tremor that had been there since it happened. A tick I couldn't seem to control. "Was he right? Did I ignore all the signs? Did I make him feel as though he wasn't good enough to be part of us—part of my team?"

Aiden snorted. "Even if you did, did that give him the right to betray your trust, go behind your back scheming and planning such an elaborate plot to get back at you? For kidnapping and terrorizing an innocent woman to get what he wanted?"

"No," I admitted. I bent my head, pulling on the tight neck muscles to try to relax them. "I don't understand. It was a land deal. Money. Just money. He had a lot of it."

Maddox shook his head. "Not as much as you."

I slammed my hand on the desk. "It wasn't a competition!"

"Not to you."

I sat back, unable to take it all in. "He must have hated me deeply to do all that. How could he even work with me if he hated me so much? Why would he subject himself to it?"

"Keep your friends close, and your enemies closer," Maddox quoted.

"I never thought of him as an enemy." I passed a weary hand over my eyes. "But I suppose I never treated him like a friend either." I turned to the window, staring out at the cloudy sky. "So I have to assume some of the responsibility."

Aiden leaned close. "If he felt that slighted he should have told you off and stopped being your lawyer. He played all of us. He came here, to your home, and planted that bug. That was how he knew about the plans. He heard us. He heard Emmy. He strung you along for months, ripping you off. He stole the deals from you and charged you while doing it! He manipulated all of us." He huffed out a long breath of air. "Then so he didn't have to face the consequences, like a coward, he killed himself."

His words all made sense. Yet, I couldn't escape the feeling of guilt.

"It's still on me."

"Bent—"

"I think I need to be alone for a while."

Aiden started to object, but Maddox stood and pulled him to his feet. "We'll go, but we're outside if you need us."

I nodded, my thoughts already far away.

DUSK WAS FALLING when I heard the quiet knock on the door. Emmy's face appeared around the edge, nervous and timid.

"May I come in?"

Another wave of guilt, one entirely different, washed over me. She was suffering, and I had ignored her all afternoon. I should have been with her, and instead, I sat by myself, my mind on a never-ending loop trying to piece everything together. I was stiff and tense as if all my nerves were on the outside of my body. I scrubbed my face hard, realizing I had never felt so exhausted in my life.

I held out my hand. "Of course."

She slipped in, shutting the door behind her. She held a file folder close to her chest. I indicated she should sit, and with a frown, she sat across from me. Immediately, I realized my mistake, and I held out my arms.

"Too far away, Freddy. Come here."

She slid onto my lap, curling into my body. I held her close, breathing her in, feeling more relaxed than I had all day. "I'm sorry," I murmured into her hair.

"It's fine," she responded. "*I'm* fine."

I pressed a kiss to her head in a silent apology.

"I spoke with my professor. He said Aiden had let him know what occurred. I get to take my test tomorrow. He's made special arrangements for me given the situation."

"Are you up to that?"

She nodded. "Yes. I can't let this affect me or my goals."

She was so brave and strong. "Okay."

I tugged on the manila folder. "Study notes?"

"No." She set it on the desk and turned to face me. Her expression was serious. "Aiden told me—told us—what happened this morning. He told us everything."

I didn't want that image in her head. "I wish he wouldn't have."

"No, he did the right thing. I'm sorry that happened, but Aiden is right. This isn't your fault. None of it."

"I'm having a tough time separating my guilt." I scrubbed a hand over my face. "He killed himself in front of me. Because of a stupid land deal and his greed, he ended his life. I can't get past that fact."

"I think there's more to it than what he said."

She rubbed her finger over the folder, hesitant and unsure. I was curious as to why she seemed so nervous.

"What's in the folder?"

"Maddox, Aiden, and Reid did some investigation work." She drew in a big breath. "I think if you look this over, you might think a little differently about your relationship with Greg." She paused. "Maddox wants to talk to you about it."

"Then why isn't he in here?"

She smiled, some of the mischievousness I associated with her showing through. "I think he thought he'd send me in to test the waters. Less chance you'd throw me out rather than him."

I felt myself smile despite how I was feeling. "He never feels this good on my lap. His ass is far too bony."

Her eyes grew round. "Are you saying I have a fat ass?"

I slid my hand under the curved perfection of her ass and squeezed. "No, I'm saying yours is my favorite ass in the world."

She kissed me softly and stood. "Can I send him in?"

"Give me a few minutes to go through the folder."

"We thought maybe we would order pizza and watch a movie later if you're up to it."

Pizza and a movie. So simple. Normal. She was trying so hard to reach out and bring me back from the edge. To remind me she was there, and she needed me to be there for her.

I nodded in agreement. "Sounds good."

With another kiss, she left the room. I pulled the file to me, curious what it contained. Inside were printouts of emails, copies of transactions, and I studied them all, perplexed.

What did Maddox want me to see?

"If you frown any harder, your face is going to stay that way. I doubt even Emmy is going to love you looking like a curmudgeon at thirty-two."

"What are you showing me here?"

He sat down, Aiden following him after shutting the door.

"Wow, he really messed with your head. Look at the emails, Bent. Look at the times you thanked him. The gifts you sent him."

"He deserved them. Especially after he stepped up on the Townsview building. It was his contacts that got us the 'in' we needed."

"For which you paid him handsomely, added in a bonus, and sent him on a cruise with his second wife. Now read the bottom line of that email."

"I offered him a spot in the company—again."

"You offered him a spot three times over the course of the past six years. You even offered him his own department. He had free rein."

"That's not what he wanted. He wanted a partnership."

Aiden barked out a laugh. "Bentley, how bad *is* your freaking memory? You have never simply *offered* a partnership—to anyone. You *hired* Maddox and me. You didn't make us a partner for over a year. You bloody well know you would have done the same with Greg. He turned down your offers. All of them."

Maddox added in his thoughts. "You did try, Bent. You invited him on several trips. The one he agreed to go on was a disaster, and he was the one who told you not to bother with another invite."

"The golfing weekend."

He nodded. "Our play wasn't up to his standard. Even yours. He ditched us to play with 'serious' golfers."

"He joined us for dinner the last night, so he could boast about the new clients he secured during the back nine," Aiden pointed out snidely.

I heaved a sigh, taking in their words of advice.

"Bent, you did try, but he didn't allow it. No matter what he said, he pushed back. I think it was part of the game to him. He wanted to hear you beg."

"Until I stopped offering."

"Yes. So, he twisted it, and it became personal." Maddox tapped the desk, bringing my attention to his serious gaze. "You're not perfect—none of us are. But don't let him fuck you up. Despite what happened today, you're at a great place in your life. Business is good. You found a girl who loves you." He grinned. "God knows why, but she does. She brings something out in you I've never seen until now. Don't let him take that away."

"I still can't wrap my head around it."

"And you never will. None of us will. He took all the answers with him. He played a dangerous game, one he arrogantly thought he would win, and instead of facing the consequences, he shot himself." Aiden shook his head. "Like I said earlier—it was his final *fuck you*."

I shut the folder. "Okay. I hear you. I just need time to come to terms with it all."

Maddox and Aiden stood.

"Don't dwell, Bentley. Let us help you. Let Emmy be there for you. You need to be there for her, as well."

I nodded. "I know."

THEY LEFT ME alone and I reread the folder. They were right. I had tried. Maybe I wasn't as clear as I should have been, but Greg, for some reason, had never opened the dialogue. Perhaps Maddox was right, and it was a game.

One that cost him everything in the end.

I stood, switching off the light and rubbing my eyes. I was drained. I needed a drink, and to talk to Emmy. She would listen, and I would do the same for her. She needed me, and I was an idiot trying to understand the thoughts of a dead man instead of concentrating on helping heal the woman I loved.

I pulled open the den door, surprised to find the living room empty. I glanced at my watch realizing it had been over two hours since Maddox and Aiden were in the den. No doubt everyone had given up on the pizza idea and gone to bed.

I headed to the kitchen to grab a cold drink, freezing when I pushed open the swinging door.

Maddox and Dee were alone in the kitchen. He had her crowded against the counter, his hands fisting her hair as he devoured her mouth. She was clutching the back of his shirt so tight, the seams were straining. The image of them was erotic and personal, and I carefully backed out of the room allowing them their privacy. I'd get a cold water upstairs.

My room was empty, and I went down the hall to find Emmy. Cami's door was closed, and I wondered if they were talking. I reached up to knock when I heard the unmistakable sound of a groan.

One filled with pleasure.

I heard Aiden's voice, a low murmur, as he coaxed his lover. "That's it, baby. Like that."

I stepped back, shaking my head. What the fuck was happening in my house? When had all that passion suddenly exploded? Despite the fatigue I was feeling, my need for Emmy was beginning to take hold. The thought of her skin on mine, the taste of her mouth, and the feel of her warmth made my cock kick up. I hurried up the stairs, taking them two at a time in my rush. I needed her closeness, much the same way Aiden and Maddox had sought out the women they needed. Now it was my turn.

Emmy was in the sunroom, on the sofa, laptop open, with all the lights on, but she was staring out the window toward the dark sky. I sat beside her, removing the laptop, and tugged her into my arms.

"Hey, Freddy."

Her head fell on my shoulder. "Hi."

"I thought you'd be in bed."

"No. I can't sleep. I thought I would study, but I can't concentrate."

"I'm sure we could get a doctor's note or something to postpone your test."

"No. I know the material, and I want to take it. They postponed my presentation until next week, so I could heal. I just . . ."

"Just?"

"I didn't want to be alone down there. I feel better up here. With the light and all the windows."

"I'm sorry, I didn't mean to leave you alone."

"Are you okay?" She caressed my face.

I shifted, pulling her onto my lap. "I will be. I'll never understand, but I have no choice. If I don't move forward, Greg will have won it all. I'll be stuck there in that room with him forever. Trying to figure out the impossible."

"Me too. He has me trapped in a different room."

I held her tight, momentarily silent, unpleasant thoughts rampant in my head. She could so easily have been taken from me forever. Left alone and chained in that room to die. If we hadn't figured it out, if something had happened, and Greg realized she knew. I shuddered when I realized if he were prepared to kill himself, killing an innocent woman wouldn't have been an issue either. He had hurt her, though, and she was suffering from the after-effects, much the same way I was.

"Tell me."

"I feel frightened. I'm too scared to be alone and in the dark. I'm terrified at the thought of going out tomorrow. I have never felt like this—even after Jack left."

"I think it's normal after what you went through." I pressed a kiss to her head. "I'm sorry he did that to you. Above all else, I hate him the most for doing that."

She nodded, not answering.

"Colin gave me the name of a therapist. Maybe it's something we need to explore." I huffed out a sigh. "I think perhaps I need some help, too. Aiden, as well."

"Okay."

"I'm sorry about today, Emmy. I've been absent since we got back. I know you're going through this alone. I promise I won't leave you again."

"Bentley," she whispered, aghast. "You watched a man die today. I understand your need to be alone and try to sort it out. I had the girls, and Maddox and Aiden stayed nearby. I was never alone."

"Still, I should have been the one comforting you."

"Well, you're here now."

"I am. I won't disappear again—I promise."

We sat, melded together, taking silent comfort from our embrace.

After a while, she leaned her head back, meeting my gaze. "I wonder if the others have gone to bed."

I chuckled. "In a manner of speaking."

She furrowed her brow. "What?"

"I sort of walked in on Dee and Maddox defiling my kitchen."

"Oh!" She giggled. "Which part?"

"Lord knows. They might use all of it. Maddox is an equal opportunity kind of guy."

"I hope they clean it up. Andrew will have their asses."

I smirked. "Cami and Aiden were, ah, having their own moment in her room."

"Oh, dear, your poor house. Debauchery everywhere." She kissed my cheek.

"What is it about you girls? You three weave your magic, and we're toast. You're impossible to resist."

She shifted on my lap. "Me, too?"

I slid my hand under the layers of thick cloth to the satin of her bare skin. I traced the delicate contours of her back with my fingers, enjoying the tremor from my touch.

"Especially you."

Her eyes glazed over as my other hand joined in, sliding higher, gliding over the sides of her full breasts. I pulled her closer, running my nose up her neck, nibbling on her ear. "I need you, Emmy. I need you to anchor me. Bring me back to you. To us."

"Yes," she breathed out. "I need you, too."

Our mouths fused as we fumbled and pulled on the clothes separating us. Her skin pressed against mine was silk on stone, her softness a soothing welcome to my tense body. I relaxed at her touch, losing myself in the taste and feel of her. Moments passed as we explored and caressed, our bodies relearning each other. We didn't need words, communicating it all with our lingering touches, and lips that teased and caressed. There, with the light to keep her safe, and my body to worship her, our worlds realigned as we moved and loved.

Cradled deep within her, I groaned. She was goodness and light. Strength and vulnerability. The one thing that truly mattered in our vast and crazy world.

She was my everything. She was my home.

She always would be.

CHAPTER 19

BENTLEY

GREG'S SUICIDE MADE the news, but faded quickly from the headlines. Little information was released regarding his underhanded business dealings, and for that I was grateful. Enough people had been hurt without the added sensationalism.

After several weeks, we had a visit from his lawyer, Hank Godwin, who was acting on behalf of Greg's sister, the executor of his will. He extended an offer for us to purchase the pieces of property Greg had bought from under us months prior to his death.

In addition, the final paperwork for the last piece hadn't been completed before he died, and we had been offered the opportunity to purchase the property by the city since we technically should have been the highest bidder. I was still thinking about the offer, unable to make a final decision on that parcel of land. It felt tainted.

The asking price surprised me. I looked at him over the documents and handed them to Aiden. Maddox sat on the sofa, watching us with interest.

"This is less than the current market value."

Removing his glasses, he polished them, took in a deep breath, and nodded. "The estate has some sizable debts against it. We are looking to liquefy the assets as efficiently as possible."

That surprised me. "I see."

"May I speak frankly, Mr. Ridge? I have my client's permission."

I waved my hand. "Of course. Whatever you say in this room remains between us."

"Mr. Tomlin—Greg—had developed a gambling problem over the past couple of years. He began placing larger wagers to try to make up what he lost, but as we all know, that rarely pays off."

"Gambling?" I glanced at Aiden and Maddox with raised eyebrows. It seemed so out of character for the person I had believed Greg to be. They looked surprised, as well.

"He liked cards. Poker, especially. He borrowed against his home and removed money from his company to the point there was really nothing left. We are trying to salvage what we can."

"Wow."

He continued with a nod. "Greg and Cindy weren't close. In fact, she hadn't seen him in five years. My client wants to sell the assets he had left, settle what debts she can, and move on. As you can imagine, this has been a trying time for her." He cleared his throat. "She was made aware of the, ah, lengths, he had gone to in his last few days, and she felt you should be given a chance to get back what should have been rightfully yours."

Maddox spoke up. "Will this sale cover his debts?"

"Almost. Once the rest of the estate is liquidated, it will be close."

Aiden and I shared a glance, and I looked toward Maddox. He dipped his chin, and I stood, extending my hand. "Let me talk with my partners. I'll be in touch before closing today."

Mr. Godwin shook my hand. "Cindy asked me to convey her sincere apologies for what occurred. She wants to believe Greg suffered some sort of breakdown due to the stress of his addiction."

"She owes me no apology. It was Greg's actions, not hers," I replied tersely. "I'll get back to you later today."

Aiden showed him out, and I sat, counting to ten in my head the way the therapist suggested. I flexed my hands and took a calming breath, repeating the exercise. Any time someone mentioned Greg, I had the same reaction, and listening to someone else apologize for his behavior was too much.

"Okay, Bent?"

I exhaled one last time and opened my eyes. "Yep."

Maddox looked over the documents. "What do you think?"

"I think I don't want any part of any of that land, given the blood that's been shed over it."

He pursed his lips thoughtfully. "Or . . ."

"Or what?"

"We buy it all, the way we originally intended. Then we do some good with it."

"I thought we were going ahead with the condo tower. We all agreed."

"Let's change it a little."

Aiden crossed his arms. "I'd like to hear what you're thinking, Maddox."

"Seven floors instead of ten. Across the street, on the new piece, make it higher, with more the usual type of condos on both sides of the building. The top floors get the view, the other side a city view. Make it more affordable than its neighbor across the way, but still special. Keep it ours."

"The other pieces?"

"Parks. We'll build them, then donate them to the community. Some good can come out of this mess."

I leaned my chin on my fingers, mulling over what he said. He and Aiden talked; their voices muted as I went through various scenarios. What they said made sense. Someone was going to buy the land and build. We could control it. Give something back.

Still, something felt off. I lifted the papers from Mr. Godwin and realized what had to happen.

"If we do this, I'll pay fair market value."

Maddox frowned in confusion. "Bentley?"

"I've been told that to move forward I have to forgive and let it go. To forgive means, I have to give him the benefit of the doubt. Maybe his sister is right—it all became too much, and he stopped thinking with the logic I know he was capable of. I don't know, and I can't pretend to understand. I can't believe the man I trusted all those years was some sort of psychopath. However, I know one thing—I won't compound this entire fucked up situation by getting a *deal* on the land that cost someone so much. I pay full market value, his sister can pay off his debts, and we move ahead."

Aiden and Maddox glanced at each other, then Aiden spoke up.

"Under that stuffed shirt, you're a good man, Bentley."

"Whatever."

Aiden grinned. "You're still an ass, but a good man."

I rolled my eyes at his teasing, and Maddox chuckled. "I'll make the call if you want."

"Yeah, do that. Stop slacking off and lounging on my sofa. Get me some numbers."

"How about the number for the local pizza place? I'm starving."

Aiden clapped his hands. "Excellent idea. I think I need an extra-large of my own."

"As usual." Maddox and I spoke up at the same time.

"Hey, I need to keep up my strength. I've got boxes to move later for your Emmy."

That made me smile. It was official. Tomorrow she was moving in permanently. I tapped my pocket, feeling the surprise I had for her. I hoped she liked it.

"Pizza, then after lunch maybe we can get some work done?"

Aiden saluted me, his middle finger prominent, then left, shouting for Sandy. Maddox grabbed his phone and called in the usual pizza order, the file tucked under his arm.

For the first time in weeks, things felt as if they were getting back to normal.

WE'D PILED EMMY'S boxes into one of the empty rooms on the top floor. I scowled as I looked at them. There weren't many—only six. It made my chest constrict, thinking of how little she had. I wanted to give her everything she could ever ask for—except she never asked.

She brought no furniture with her, insisting none of it would fit into the style of my house.

"It's yours as well now, Freddy," I reminded her.

She shook her head. "The few pieces I had were old when I got them and whoever moves in can have them. I brought my books and the things I loved the most. One day I'll figure out where to put them."

I took her hand. "I think I have a place." I led her down the hall to the room closest to her favorite part of the house. I opened the door with a flourish. "Your own space."

She went in ahead of me, her hand covering her mouth as she looked around. An old-fashioned, delicately carved desk sat in front of the windows, the view of the oak trees spread out before us. Shelves lined one wall for her books and anything else she wanted to put there. The laptop I bought for her was on the desk, and all the extra equipment I knew would make life easier for her was added and ready to use. I made sure to have a thick rug installed, and in the corner where the sunlight lay the longest daily, was a deep chair and ottoman in a bright blue, piled high with lacy pillows and a thick blanket to ward off the constant chill she felt. The walls were a dove gray, and the accents were all white. It was light, airy, and feminine.

She stepped forward, running her fingers along the satin of the wood on the desk.

"Do you like it?" I asked with a smile.

"It's beautiful."

"It was my mother's. I never had a place for it, but I want you to have it."

Her tear-filled eyes met mine, her dark gaze shimmering in the light.

"How?" she asked, astonished.

I grinned. "Aiden, Dee, and Cami. Apparently, he loves shopping as much as they do, and they put it all together for you. Andrew made sure it was all arranged and kept it a secret."

"I was okay in the sunroom. You didn't have to do this!"

"Emmy, you're going to want a space of your own. To study, chat with the girls, or escape when I piss you off. The sunroom—any room—is yours to use, but this space is just for you."

She flung her arms around my neck. "I love it! Thank you."

I lifted her easily off the floor, keeping her in my arms as I pressed a kiss to her neck. "Good."

"It feels like a dream."

I shook my head. "It's very real, I assure you."

I set her on her feet, dropping a fast kiss to her nose. "I have something else to show you."

"You've given me enough."

"No. I'm just starting, Freddy." I pointed to the shelf. "Recognize that?"

She peered up at it and gasped. "My picture! It's so clear!"

"Reid knew someone who enhanced and altered it. The original is safe." I bent and pressed on a hidden door at the bottom of the shelves. "Right here with your rucksack."

Once she had given it to me, she had never asked about it, showing me her trust about keeping it safe for her. A stifled sob escaped her mouth as she peered into the cupboard. "It's fireproof, and once you set the combo on the wall, lockable. You will never lose what is inside, Emmy. It's safe—like I promised."

"Thank you." Tears glimmered, and she wiped them away. "I-I have no other words."

I sat on the chair, and pulled her to my lap, feeling strangely nervous. "You entrusted something to me that was precious to you, and I want to do the same thing."

"You have, Bentley. You gave me your heart. Your home."

"No, I have something else." I pressed the flat box into her hand. "I want to entrust this to you."

Her hand shook as she opened the box. Her eyes grew round as she looked at the contents.

"Bentley," she breathed out. "These are . . ."

I lifted the delicate pendant from the box. The small chocolate diamond caught the light, glimmering the way her eyes did. It was nestled in a filigree of gold and set off with four polished accents. "The pearls. My mother's pearls."

"But you carry them with you everywhere!"

I slipped the chain around her neck. "And now you will. We've shared our past, and now it's time to start our future. I'll keep your rucksack safe; you hang on to my pearls. We'll safeguard each other's hearts. Deal?"

Her lips were soft against mine. "Deal."

THE OFFICE WAS quiet, the afternoon almost over. I looked out at the heavy clouds, wondering if we would get snow today. I tried to recall if Emmy had worn her new coat this morning, then shook my head in amusement. Of course, she would have. She'd sleep in it if I let her. Light, filled with down, she said it was the warmest thing she'd ever owned.

Her thanks had certainly warmed certain parts of me.

I shifted in my chair thinking of that night and adjusted myself. Maybe I should head home early, relax with her since she wasn't in the boardroom with Maddox and Aiden working on the expanded Bentley Ridge Estates. She was such a bonus to the project, bringing fresh ideas to the table. My partners enjoyed spending time with her, and they found her intelligent and diligent. I loved hearing her laughter throughout the office and listening to her creative ideas. She was amazing, and I hoped to persuade her to have an office of her own here once she graduated. She could run her business, and I would happily be her first client, even though I knew she had more to offer than graphic design. I could foresee a time when she was part of my team. In every aspect.

She had agreed to see the therapist Colin had recommended, and I went with her. I was surprised to find how much the sessions helped each of us in different ways. Chloe saw us separately, and on occasion, we went together, if she felt it was necessary. Emmy's nightmares had mostly ceased, and although she was still skittish in public at times, it was better. She no longer fought me on having Frank drive her places, since she felt safer, and it gave me peace of mind. She was glad, however, Aiden no longer felt bodyguards were necessary.

I was learning to deal with my anger in a positive way rather than yelling at those I cared for the most, and she was helping each of us come to terms with our pasts. I was incredibly proud of Emmy for not only her strength but also her resilience and determination to move forward. She inspired me to do the same.

Thinking about her made me miss her more than usual. I picked up my phone, sending her a text.

Hey, Freddy. What are you up to this afternoon?

Her reply was prompt.

Studying.

Are you at home?

No, I was feeling nostalgic and am at Al's with Cami.

I chuckled at her words, deciding not to say anything about wanting to see her.

Okay. See you at home.

She sent back a heart emoji along with my favorite words.

I love you.

Aiden strolled in, sitting on the sofa, kicking his feet up on the coffee table. He munched away on a huge pastry, throwing a grin my way. "What's up?"

"Your cholesterol. That's your third one today."

"Fourth. Not my fault Sandy brought in a box of them, and I can't resist. It was the last one left, and everyone has gone home. I can't let it go to waste."

"Of course not," I replied dryly. "You have no self-control."

He snorted. "You have enough for both of us"—he paused with a smirk—"*Rigid.*"

"Fuck you."

"No thanks, you're not my type."

It was my turn to smirk. "No, I suppose not. I don't have dark hair with green eyes and can put you in your place in about five seconds flat."

We glared at each other. As private as I was with my relationship with Emmy, I had no idea what was happening with Cami and Aiden. There was something, of that I had no doubt, but he refused to discuss it, and Emmy hadn't been able to get much from Cami. Obviously, he wasn't going to share today either. I had tried to talk him into counseling, but he refused to go, insisting he didn't need to talk to anyone about Greg or anything else. No matter how much I tried to convince him, he was adamant in his refusal. Maddox told me to ease off and allow him to work it out on his own.

"Forcing him to go is a waste. He's a grown-ass man, Bent. When he's ready, he can make the call. It has to be his decision."

I had backed off, not wanting to drive a wedge between us. In this case, however, I could give him a nudge in the right direction.

"Emmy and Cami are at Al's, studying. I thought I might surprise her and take her to an early dinner or something."

Aiden sat up a little straighter. "Oh, yeah? You want me to take you there?"

I shrugged, feigning nonchalance. "Frank can drive me."

"I should probably go with you, and you know, make sure

everything is okay."

Life had gone back to normal since Greg's passing. No more notes, only the random, odd letter demanding my money, as per usual. Aiden had finally relaxed and was no longer my constant shadow; although, he still came with me to every meeting. I needed him more for his incredible memory retention than security, and I hoped it stayed that way. I couldn't resist poking the bear though.

"I think I'm fine on my own. Unless something happened that I need security with me?"

"No," he admitted with a frown. "It's not a great area, though, and I should check with Al on those improvements we made. Plus his fritters are damn awesome."

He needed more food?

"His fritters . . . right."

"Bent—" he warned.

I shut down the laptop and stood. "Well, if you want to make sure everything's going okay there and get a *fritter*, you'd better come with me then."

He jumped to his feet. "Okay."

When we arrived at Al's, I went toward Emmy's spot. Cami glanced up and saw me coming, then spotted Aiden in the line waiting for his fritter. She said something to Emmy, who nodded, not even glancing up from her laptop. Cami went past me with a grin, laying her hand on my arm, brushing my cheek with her lips.

"She'll love that you came for her," she murmured. "She keeps looking at her phone."

I winked and waited for a moment, pulling out my phone and taking a picture of Emmy. My once empty camera roll was now filled with pictures—mostly of her, but of us, our friends, and our life. For the first time, I had good memories to capture and keep.

The light over the table caught her earrings and glinted off the rings on her fingers as she typed away. She wore the necklace I gave her, rarely ever removing it since I had clasped it around her neck. Her hair was up, her tattoo on display, and her new coat wrapped around her shoulders. I had discovered another favorite color on her. The brilliant red fabric looked lovely against her skin. I had bought her another shawl in the same color, silencing her objections with kisses as I draped it over her shoulders one night.

"I know you're there."

I dropped a kiss on her head and sat across from her.

"Stalking me again, Rigid?"

I leaned over and snagged a piece of her muffin. "Is it still stalking if we live together?"

She looked up with a grin. "No, it's obsessive, then."

"Guilty as charged. I am obsessed with you."

"Is that a fact?"

"Totally. You're on my mind more than anything else in my life."

She leaned back, staring, her eyes slowly traveling over me. She closed the lid of her laptop, not saying anything, but continued to stare. Her gaze was frank, open, and I felt my cock stir at her appraisal.

"See something you like?"

She leaned forward, her voice low. "I love what I see."

"Tell me."

"I see *you*. Bentley. The sexiest, sweetest, kindest—" she paused and licked her lips—"dirtiest man I know."

"Not how most people describe me."

"I love the fact the world sees you one way, and I get to see the real you."

"The real me needs to take you home now."

"I . . ."

I tapped the top of the scarred wooden table. "*Now.*"

She stood fast, almost toppling her chair. She grabbed her messenger bag, shoving the laptop inside.

She hesitated. "Uh . . . what about Cami?"

I glanced over to see her and Aiden deep in conversation. He looked up, and I tilted my head to the door. He grinned and went back to talking to Cami.

"I'll send Frank back for her and Aiden."

"Okay, that works."

I caught her in my arms, kissing her hard. It didn't matter we were in a public place; I didn't care who was watching anymore. I pulled away, smirking at the pink deepening her cheeks.

I tugged her behind me, stopping only long enough to clap Aiden on the shoulder.

"We're out."

"I can see that."

"Try it. You might like it."

He shook his head, escorting Cami back to the table we had deserted. I smiled at Emmy, thinking how much happiness she had brought to my life. I threw one last look back at my friend, wondering why he didn't see what I could. Cami could do the same for him.

He needed to figure it out.

Because, despite what he thought, he deserved it.

I opened the car door, letting Emmy slide in first, then sitting beside her.

"Home, sir?"

I glanced at Emmy, each of us feeling the same way. As long as we were together, we were already home.

I tucked her close and smiled.

"Yes, Frank. Take us home."

Turn the page for a sneak peek at *Aiden*—Vested Interest #2

Coming May 2018

PROLOGUE

IT STARTED THE way it always did. Voices, shouting, flashes of panic. Broken fragments of memories, images that blurred and blended into each other.

"You're like your father. Worthless."

"He can't read? What a surprise. He's always been so stupid."

"I'm not paying for anything extra for him. If he can't keep up, that's his problem."

I was running, frightened, and out of breath. I needed to hide, to get away. Rocks hit my legs, one cutting into my neck. I felt the wet of blood as it seeped down the back of my neck to my spine. I rounded the corner, ducking into the alley and behind the dumpster. I held my gasps of breath, trying to stay silent.

The running feet stopped; the voices angry.

"Where did he go?"

"Do you think he's in the alley?"

"No, the little bastard is scared of his own shadow; he'd never go there. Let's keep looking."

Like a miracle, they moved on, but I stayed huddled, knowing they could be back. Knowing that even if I avoided them today, tomorrow they would find me.

My body shook as it recalled the number of beatings I took at school. In the playground. At home. I could hear my gasps of air, the panic setting in. It wasn't real, but I was useless to stop the barrage of fear coursing through me.

Slap.

"You worthless piece of shit! All you do is cause me disappointment!"

"Please, Momma, no, not the belt . . ." My voice sobbed.

"You'll get that and more, you ingrate! I wish you'd never been born!"

The pain from her strike was so vivid, it almost felt real, and I felt my body jerk in reflex. I heard my own shout. Still, I couldn't break through the grip keeping me trapped in the past.

The room was bright, the décor familiar. I realized I was in Greg's office on that fateful day, staring at him holding a gun to his chin. Except, this time, he wasn't holding the gun. It was me. I had the gun pressed to my throat, staring at Bentley. He shook his head.

"You're such a coward."

"I don't want to do this, Bent," I begged. "Please. Help me."

"I'll be glad when you're gone. You've been nothing but a pain in my ass. I've put up with you long enough."

"No—we're friends! You said so!"

He shrugged his shoulder dismissively. "No, you were useful, but I'm done. You might as well rid the world of the waste of space you are."

He turned, walking away, ignoring my pleas.

The room felt cold, the air making me shiver. I looked around. I was alone, abandoned by one of the few people I thought I could trust. I shut my eyes, pressing the cold steel to my skin.

"Stop."

My eyes flew open at the sound of her voice. Cami stood in front of me.

"Don't do this, Aiden."

"I have no choice."

"You do." She extended her hand. "Come with me."

"No. I'm not what you need. I'm not what anyone needs."

"If you pull that trigger, you'll never find out."

I shook my head, pressing the gun closer.

I felt her leave. The darkness surrounded me.

I squeezed the trigger.

With a loud gasp, I bolted upright in bed. I drew in much-needed oxygen, trying frantically to tamp down my panic. Swinging my legs over the edge of the bed, I fumbled with the light, snapping it on, staring around the room. Still terrified, I ran my hands over my torso and head, feeling for the blood, the hole left by the gun. There was nothing but a sheen of sweat that covered my entire body.

Desperately thirsty, I reached for the water bottle on the nightstand and drained it, then tossed the bottle to the side. I hung my head as my breathing gradually returned to normal, and my heart rate slowed down.

It was a nightmare. Not the first, and certainly not the last I would have.

However, this one was different. More intense than ever, and vivid with the last part of Greg. I knew his death was still on my mind. It lingered on the edges, drilling itself deep into my psyche, and coming out when I tried to sleep.

The last time I'd had a bad dream, I woke up beside Cami. She had soothed me. Held me close, and comforted me until I fell asleep again. Wrapped in her embrace, the nightmare hadn't returned.

Tonight, I was alone, and I knew, without a doubt, it would keep coming back until I dragged myself from my bed and started the day.

It was how it had to be. Because, nightmare or not, the message of the dream was correct, and always would be.

I *was* worthless, and she wouldn't be beside me again. She deserved so much more than I could ever be for her.

I rose and grabbed a pair of sweatpants. I'd work out, then head to the office. At least there, I could be something other than what my dreams told me.

I could be Aiden, loyal friend to Bentley and Maddox. Part of a successful company. Respected by many, admired by some. Wealthy, humorous, and without a care in the world.

It was a great cover. No one ever looked past it to my real self.

The one I kept hidden.

A NOTE FROM THE AUTHOR

Depression, anxiety, and other thoughts can make someone feel isolated.

Know that you are not alone. If you are struggling, reach out to a mental health professional.

Someone is ready to listen.

Call:

1–800–273-TALK (8255)

Visit:

www.suicidepreventionlifeline.org
www.afsp.org
https://letstalk.bell.ca/en

A WORD OF THANKS

THERE ARE ALWAYS so many people behind the scenes when writing a book. They inspire, suggest, encourage, and often lift you up when the words don't come.

Eli, thanks for your help and friendship. You rock. Sws to you!

Denise, for your input and encouragement, I thank you. You are an inspiration to me in so many ways, and I am so honored to be part of the journey you are on.

Caroline, thank you—your keen eyes and support mean so much.

Deb, your skills and suggestions make my books better. You smooth out the rough edges, and make my words work. Thank you for everything.

To Beth, Shelly, Janett, Darlene, Carrie, Sue, Jeanne, Claudia—I cannot even begin to thank you. All your encouragement and the love you have shown to me and my work is beyond words. The friendships we have formed enrich my life.

To Jess at Inkslinger PR, thank you for all your help and guidance. Cookies are coming.

Flavia, thank you for your support and belief in my work. You rock it for me.

Karen, my wonderful PA, and friend. You make my author life easier, and my real life brighter. I love our hour-long daily phone calls, your snarky orders, and the care and attention to detail you show to whatever task you set your mind to. The compassion and love you heap on me is so amazing. I am beyond grateful for you in both worlds.

Love you loads, my friend.

To all the bloggers, readers, and especially my new review team. Thank you for everything you do. Shouting your love of books, posting, sharing—your recommendations keep my TBR list full, and the support you have shown me is so appreciated.

To my fellow authors who have shown me such kindness, thank you. I will follow your example and pay it forward.

To Christine—thank you for making my words look pretty!

My reader group, Melanie's Minions—love you all.

Finally—Matthew. I can't begin to list or thank you for all the countless ways you make my life better. How can a heart expand every day to love someone more? I can't answer that question, except to know it is true. Love you to infinity and beyond.

BOOKS BY
MELANIE MORELAND

ABOUT THE AUTHOR

NEW YORK TIMES/USA Today bestselling author Melanie Moreland, lives a happy and content life in a quiet area of Ontario with her beloved husband of twenty-eight-plus years and their rescue cat, Amber. Nothing means more to her than her friends and family, and she cherishes every moment spent with them.

While seriously addicted to coffee, and highly challenged with all things computer-related and technical, she relishes baking, cooking, and trying new recipes for people to sample. She loves to throw dinner parties, and enjoys travelling, here and abroad, but finds coming home is always the best part of any trip.

Melanie loves stories, especially paired with a good wine, and enjoys skydiving (free falling over a fleck of dust) extreme snowboarding (falling down stairs) and piloting her own helicopter (tripping over her own feet.) She's learned happily ever afters, even bumpy ones, are all in how you tell the story.

www.melaniemoreland.com

Made in the USA
Monee, IL
20 May 2021